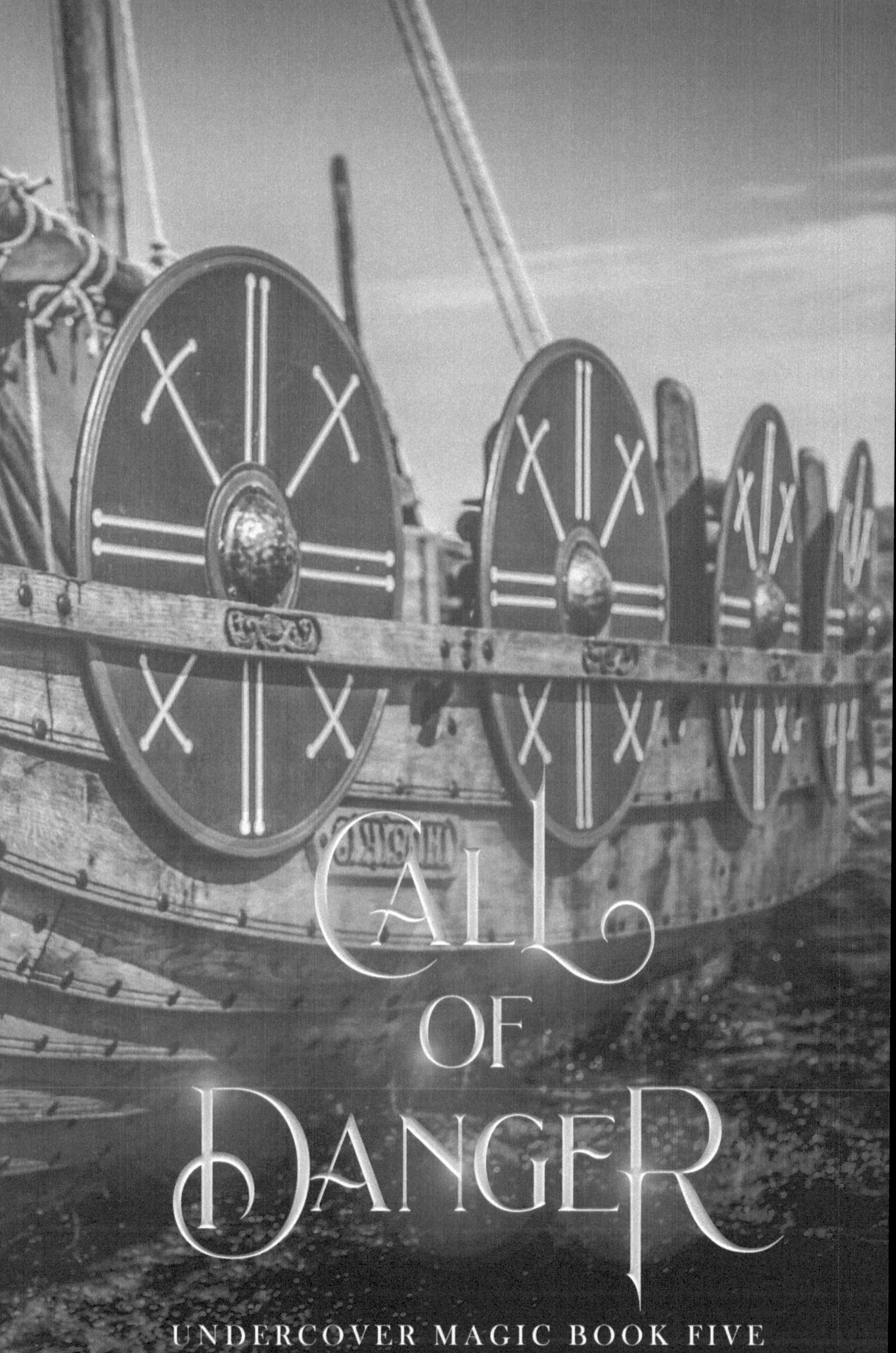

CALL OF DANGER
UNDERCOVER MAGIC BOOK FIVE

ISBN 978-1-951738-32-7 (Paperback Edition)

Cover Design by CReya-tive Book Design

Edited by Mo Sytsma of Comma Sutra Editorial

Proofread by Suzi of Royal Reads and Dominique Laura

"The course of true love never did run smooth."

- William Shakespeare
A Midsummer Night's Dream
Act 1, Scene 1

CALL
OF
DANGER

CHAPTER 1
CROMBIE

Cold sweat broke out over his ravaged body as a bloodcurdling howl shattered his illusion of safety. He'd long ago lost count of how many times he'd heard the same unearthly wail, heralding a fresh cycle of torment and torture. No matter how many times he'd run or how many different routes he'd taken, there was no escape. Once they caught your scent, they'd always find you.

They.

The Wild Hunt.

A notorious band of Faerie's most depraved, vile beings. Beings so notorious, in fact, word of their exploits has transcended the veil and spread throughout the mortal world. Cruel, utterly without mercy, and fueled entirely by their prey's deepest fears. The Hunt was the Night Court's most ingenious creation, and by far its most terrifying.

These were the beings that gave the Nightmare its name. The original Nightmare, that is. The place that inspired mortals to use the word when referring to the unspeakable things that sent them gasping awake in the middle of the night. Things which were a pale imitation of their namesake.

The Court was often referred to as the Land of Twilight and Dreams, but no one who'd stepped foot beneath its star-filled sky ever forgot the truth. For all its beauty, the Night Court had given rise to something every bit as sinister and deadly as it was breathtaking. The Nightmare was the heart of Faerie's Night Court, the very realm he'd been born to rule.

The very realm which now held him prisoner.

An agonized moan tore from his lips as the once-prince pushed to his knees, eyes already scanning the shadowed horizon for what horrors it might reveal. Or more specifically, a hint as to which form they'd take this time.

He stumbled as his feet sank into the damp earth, his body trembling with fatigue and unrelenting pain. Given the state he was in, he stood little chance of evading his tormentors for long. The muscles in his left leg were still little more than ribbons from the last round of twisted hide and seek, and the rest of him was one endless ache. Though that was nothing new. Pain was his constant—and only—companion in this labyrinth of horrors.

Any solace he might have hoped to find in his homeland was peeled away as easily as his flesh. Everything he'd sacrificed to return and clear his name had proven fruitless. There was nothing left for him here. Not anymore.

Maybe there never had been.

Maybe all of this was little more than a fool's dream, and he the biggest fool of all.

He sagged against a nearby tree, attempting to catch his breath and summon his strength as the lone howl became a chorus. They were close.

Too close.

Chills skittered down his spine, and he lurched forward in an instinctive attempt to flee. But his mutilated leg couldn't handle the strain. It gave out, sending him toppling back to the ground.

He'd never make it.

No.

He *had* to make it.

Winning was only a matter of outlasting his tormentors. He just had to want to live more than they wanted him to die.

Squeezing his eyes shut, he fought hard to reach the quiet, emotionless place within, where things like fear and pain couldn't reach him. That arrogant, fae part of himself that refused to bow or quit no matter how impossible the odds of survival. In the wake of his constant failure, it took longer to find each time. He feared the day he went searching for that indomitable safe haven—the very core of who he used to be—only to find it wasn't there.

With a roar of sheer desperation, he attempted to stand once more. When his body refused to obey, he crawled instead. Digging his fingers into the earth, he pulled himself forward, slithering on his belly like the pathetic creature he'd become.

He moved deeper into the maze, knowing as he did the overgrown hedges would never protect him. The beasts chasing him weren't the only fiends here; they were simply the most dangerous.

With each labored breath, he inched forward. The howls growing louder until he felt warm, fetid puffs of breath on the back of his neck. He refused to look back, not wanting to know which face the monster had selected. The smell of rotting flowers and the sick twisting in his stomach told him he already knew.

Evalina.

Her visage was a favorite of theirs.

He'd often wondered what she might think if she ever discovered she'd become the instrument of his destruction. Would she revel in the knowledge? Or would she pity him his fate?

Claws sharper than any dagger raked down his back, sending a torrent of fresh blood dripping into the earth. Where the drops splashed on the ground, little buds shot up, growing in the blink of an eye. He was soon surrounded by garnet-colored leaves and velvety petals the precise shade of midnight.

He grunted through the explosion of pain, trying to scramble on, but an unassailable grip on his ankle held him captive. Knowing there was nothing for it, he focused on the bed of flowers, noting how the sanguinina lilies were rather beautiful for something with such a macabre lineage. The buds only grew where fae blood had been violently spilled.

The creature behind him crawled forward, pressing its full weight into the seeping wounds on his back and causing him to hiss in pain.

A familiar voice—hers, though deeper and more guttural than he'd ever heard her employ on the mortal plane—stirred the strands of hair not currently stuck to his skin by blood or sweat.

"Betrayer. Deceiver. Defiler of purity and light."

Each word was punctuated by a heavy rattle of breath and another slide of those wicked claws over his skin.

A part of him knew it wasn't really her, that those words of condemnation were not hers. But he ignored the truth because they may as well have been. Lady knows he'd earned them. This was the reason the monsters preferred her countenance over all others. His guilt and regret, more than the brute on his back or his ruined body, anchored him to the spot. Lina was the one person he would not—could not—run away from.

Not after what he'd done.

"The debt you owe cannot be repaid by word or deed. You will pay in blood."

The creature leaned forward, sinking its teeth into the side of his neck and biting down until fang scraped bone.

The once-prince cried out, his pain so acute it momentarily blinded him.

"And when that runs dry, you will pay with your life."

His screams continued to ring out as the creature made good on its promise, filling the night sky with the sound of his misery and defeat. It paused only long enough to tip its face to the sky and shriek in triumph. Celebratory howls soon joined in from every direction, layering with his own screams and producing a ghastly symphony that would haunt him for the rest of his miserable life—however long it may be. If mercy still existed for one such as him, perhaps it wouldn't be much longer at all.

He writhed as the creature continued to tear into him, too lost to the pain to fully register something had changed. While he still felt what was happening, there was now a weightless, ephemeral quality to his body. As if his physical form was no longer fully present. The realization immediately preceded an explosion of lavender light. It all happened so fast; he wasn't sure what transpired until he opened his eyes and saw the maze had been replaced by mortal living quarters.

This is new.

In all the depraved machinations he'd endured at the hands of The Hunt, he'd yet to be transported out of the labyrinth. Instead of calming him, the knowledge sent him spiraling further into the depths of his fear. If they were trying a new tactic, they must have decided their usual methods of torture were no longer effective. That his pain, while absolute, was not enough.

They wanted to break him.

No, not break. *Shatter.*

Destroy him so completely no one could ever put him back together.

"C-Crombie?"

That name. *His* name. How long had it been since anyone, even he, had thought of him as Davis Crombie, owner of the most exclusive and tantalizing nightclub on Earth? Lady above, they really had changed tactics. Not once since entering Faerie had anyone referred to him as anything other than The Betrayer.

Perhaps even more concerning, while still her voice, it was no longer laced with terrible, unending violence. She sounded worried. Genuinely worried . . . for him.

His blood ran cold, and his head snapped up.

No. Oh no.

Just as he feared. It was Lina, but her face wasn't twisted with rage. Her eyes no longer two burning coals or her mouth stretched eerily wide and filled with row upon row of jagged teeth.

Instead, she looked upon him in shock and something scarily akin to sympathy.

Crombie started to shake. Her hatred he could handle, but not her compassion. It cut far deeper than any weapon, if only because it drove home just how little he deserved it. If The Hunt had sought the means to finally annihilate him, they'd just succeeded. His inner defenses were no match for this.

He couldn't take it.

Never, not once, had he begged them for anything, but he was begging now. "No! No more! Please, no more."

She frowned, crouching down to reach for him, and he scuttled backward, desperate to get away. If she touched him with anything resembling kindness, he'd fall apart entirely. He couldn't let them see what her forgiveness meant to him. It was the one key to the single lock that kept him intact. If he handed it over to them, he'd be finished.

"Crombie. Crombie, it's me. It's Lina."

He froze at her use of the name. For all they plucked from his mind, The Hunt only had access to the images stored there. Not names. And he'd been careful, so careful, never to utter it.

The feeling that surged to life in his chest was so foreign he struggled to place it. But once he did, the revelation rocked him.

Hope.

His fractured brain couldn't process the sheer impossibility of this moment, of everything it meant. All he could do was feel, and Lady, did it hurt.

There was nothing more painful than hope.

"Is it really you?"

Her eyes flashed with an emotion he was unable to place, and her expression softened further. "Yes, Crombie. It's really me."

He wasn't aware of crying. The world was going black at the

edges. It was a struggle to remain upright, let alone focus on anything other than her face peering down at him without a single ounce of anger. For several agonizing heartbeats, the best he managed was to stare at her and try to draw air into his overworked lungs.

Once he'd caught his breath, words were torn from deep within him. They poured out without conscious thought because even in his current state, he needed her to know the truth. In case this was his only chance, in case none of this was real, in case it was . . .

"I'm sorry. I'm so fucking sorry."

He might have said more, but he couldn't be sure because everything went suddenly and blissfully dark.

CHAPTER 2
NORD

"Is he . . . dead?"

Lina's stricken expression set Nord in motion. While the sight of Crombie's limp form was darkly satisfying and he secretly wished he'd been the one to inflict those wounds, he couldn't stand idly by in the face of such obvious suffering. Even if he was having trouble summoning an appropriate level of sympathy for the man who'd undermined and toyed with them at every turn.

Recalling Alistair's notation, Nord uttered the word to drop the magical barrier—the one required to let Crombie out but also to allow Nord *in*. There was a slight sizzle and the wafting smell of ozone as the invisible barricade dissipated. That done, he crouched beside Lina and called on his power as he placed his hand on the other man's head.

Nord didn't hide his wince as he used his magic to investigate the extent of the damage. Crombie was in even worse shape than he looked, which was saying something given how he currently appeared to have caught a mild case of death.

"How is he?" Finley asked, joining them.

"Alive, but only just."

Lina let out a relieved sigh. "Well, that's something."

Nord frowned, noticing something strange. "Fin, take a look at this."

"What is it?" Lina asked.

"Not sure yet," he said, his attention drawn to the first of a series of foreign objects peppered throughout the fae's body.

Lodged in the muscle as it was, Nord's first assumption was that it was a bullet or projectile of some kind. But the object was too large and misshapen for the theory to hold weight. It would have done far more damage as it tore through the skin and sinew, so the fragment must have been implanted some other way.

Using his magic, he carefully brushed against the object and confirmed what he'd suspected. Iron. The only substance known to render fae completely powerless. It took very little contact with the metal to cause extreme pain, which was amplified when a fae attempted to use their magic.

Nord couldn't help but be impressed. The sheer amount of iron currently housed throughout Crombie's body should have killed him. It was a testament to his strength and will to live that he hadn't succumbed long ago.

It also explained why Crombie hadn't been able to defend himself. The pain from the contact alone would have been excruciating, but even that would feel like a feather's gentle caress compared to the absolute agony he must have experienced when trying to draw on his power. Nord supposed there was a karmic sort of justice in that. He'd stolen Lina's magic only to find himself robbed of his own when he'd most needed it.

"Bloody hell," Finley breathed. "How is he still breathing?"

"What's wrong?" Lina asked.

"Iron. A lot of it," Finley answered.

"Iron?" she repeated, her brow furrowing. "Where?"

"Everywhere," Nord replied.

"Jesus."

Nord shifted his focus to the largest metallic mass located in the center of his chest. Easily five times the size of the other pieces, the iron here was so deformed it took him a second to realize it caged Crombie's heart, engulfing the vital organ in deadly barbs. Even more sinister, with every beat it pressed against several jagged spikes which shot out in all directions.

An involuntary shudder ran through him. Nord was no stranger to torture or the need to get creative when attempting to extract information, but the level of depravity employed here went far beyond his own comfort levels. This was the work of a true sadist.

"Whoever did this to him wanted him to suffer," Nord said, his voice grim.

"Looks like they succeeded," Finley murmured, while Lina asked, "Can you save him?"

Nord nodded by way of answering them both, already at work repairing the broken fae. Removing the iron fragments was going to be tricky, especially the piece around Crombie's heart. If they weren't careful, they would only cause more damage. If they simply vanished the iron without first repairing the flesh it was embedded in, he'd bleed out. In his current state, Crombie wouldn't survive.

The Guardian blew out a heavy breath, giving voice to what Nord had already discovered. "Some of this damage is months old. The injuries have already healed, causing new tissue to grow around these shards."

"Months?" Lina asked. "But he was only gone a couple of days."

"Time functions differently across the realms, remember?" Fin reminded her gently.

"So, what you're really saying is that whoever did this to him tortured him for *months*?"

There was no point in either of them confirming it. The injuries, along with the other changes to his appearance, such as his emaciated form and longer hair, spoke for themselves.

"Poor Crombie," she said belatedly.

"Let's not get carried away feeling sorry for him," Finley said. "What he did to you aside, the man has always had more enemies than friends, and that doesn't happen without good reason."

Lina bit down on her bottom lip, looking conflicted, but ultimately nodding her agreement. "I know, it's just—" She blew out a breath. "Did you see how afraid he was? No matter how mad I am at him, or how badly he fucked us over, I never wanted whatever put that haunted expression on his face. I mean, he's Crombie. He's supposed to be one of the biggest, baddest faeries out there. He should be the one causing that look in people's eyes, not the other way around, you know?"

Nord understood exactly what she was trying to say. Crombie was an arrogant, unaffected ass and—at least until now—seemingly untouchable. Witnessing him brought so low was jarring, to say the least. It was disturbing to learn something you believed to be intrinsically true was, in fact, patently false. Such paradigm shifts were always uncomfortable. They tended to make you question other things you believed, and that was the worst sort of spiral. Because if you'd been mistaken about something that fundamental, what else were you wrong about?

"This is going to take a while," Nord said. "We should move him somewhere we can all be more comfortable."

"And maybe give him some clothes," Lina added.

Finley grinned. "My specialty. But we'll worry about the healing first. Don't want to bloody up my hard work."

Lina snorted and shook her head. "We definitely wouldn't want that." She turned to Nord, offering, "You can use my room. At the rate we've been going we should probably just convert it into an infirmary anyway. It's not like I really use it anymore."

He squeezed her shoulder in silent thanks and then stood, scooping up the unconscious fae as he did and making his way to Lina's bedroom.

"If you'd have told me a week ago we'd be willingly helping the fae bastard, I'd have laughed in your face," Finley muttered.

"As would I," Nord agreed.

This was unfamiliar territory for him, coming to the aid of someone he viewed as an enemy. The berserker side of his nature wasn't sure how to feel about the situation. Enemies were for killing, not saving.

Nord didn't *want* to help Crombie, but he had to. Because there was also the other part of him. The half who'd been raised to value honor and loyalty above all else. He told himself he was saving Crombie only to force him to remove the necklace around Lina's neck and restore her access to her magic. But while that was certainly true, it wasn't the only reason.

Begrudgingly or not, Crombie had come to his rescue. Now was Nord's chance to return the favor and finally settle the debt. His honor demanded it.

"Who do you think did this to him?" Lina asked in a quiet voice as Nord laid Crombie carefully down on her bed.

"You can ask him yourself as soon as he wakes up."

Even as he said it, Nord knew it might not be as simple as that. Once he regained consciousness, it would still be Crombie they were dealing with. He was rarely forthcoming, and there was no way of knowing what kind of mood he'd be in. Men such as him rarely responded well to finding themselves in vulnerable positions. Especially when surrounded by those they didn't fully trust.

Lina slipped her hand into his. "I wish there was something I could do to help. I hate feeling useless."

Nord leaned down and brushed his lips against hers. "You are helping."

She blinked at him. "How?"

"By being here."

Lina rolled her eyes, but he felt the flutter of pleasure his words caused. Giving her hand a final squeeze, he let go and concentrated on Crombie.

"Ready?" he asked Finley.

The Guardian nodded, his eyes blazing silver.

As anticipated, it was an arduous process. Easily the most complicated healing Nord had ever attempted. Even with the two of them working together, it was painstakingly slow extracting the metal fragments while simultaneously reforming almost the entirety of Crombie's internal structure.

When the last trace of iron had finally been removed, and they were certain he was stable, Nord dropped his power and stepped back. It was a shock returning to himself. Not only had night fully fallen while they'd been working, but he'd drained far more of his power than he realized, leaving his body considerably weakened. If not for Lina, he'd have collapsed to the ground. But she was right there, her arm wrapped tightly around his waist while she supported the bulk of his weight.

"My thanks, Kærasta," he murmured, lifting an arm to wipe the sweat off his brow.

She gave him an impish grin. "Just doing my part."

He returned her smile with an exhausted one of his own.

"There. That's better," Finley said, drawing their attention to him as his eyes flickered from silver back to their natural hazel.

Lina's body quaked with laughter, though the only sound she managed was a series of wheezing snorts. Nord could only offer an amused smile, but he had to admit, Finley had outdone himself.

Still out cold and lying on his back, Crombie was now attired head-to-toe in a child's fairy costume. No detail had been overlooked. From the lime-green sequined leotard to the slightly darker tutu with its flashing LED lights, all the way down to the little velveteen slippers with glittery white pompoms on the toes. Finley had even gone so far as to add shimmering green make-up and styled the fae's hair in an elaborate topknot and tiara. He'd also made sure to include gossamer wings that stretched out on the bed and were attached to Crombie's back with some kind of elastic straps. But without question, Nord's favorite touch was the light-up star-tipped wand that was somehow clutched in one of Crombie's softly fisted hands.

"Fin, you're a freaking genius," Lina said, wiping away tears as she tried to catch her breath.

Finley gave her a slight bow. "I live to serve."

"Seriously, you've outdone yourself. I was going to suggest a fuzzy pink bathrobe and some unicorn slippers. Maybe throw a couple of curlers in his hair."

"That can always be arranged."

"No, no. This is perfect. Quick, someone take a picture. We'll need it for an emergency pick-me-up if nothing else."

"Or blackmail," Nord said, warming to the idea as he imagined plastering the photos throughout The District with some outlandish headline.

"You'd mock a man on his deathbed?" Crombie croaked, his eyes still closed.

"Relax. You're not dying," Finley said. "And a little dress-up is the least of what you deserve."

Crombie cracked open his eyes, his steely gaze falling on a smirking Finley before sliding over to where Nord and Lina stood. Then he glanced down and saw what he was wearing. "Consider us even," he said with a grimace as he lifted his eyes back up to Lina.

Her eyebrows flew up. "Even? How do you figure?"

"I recall promising to wear whatever you wanted once you obtained my heirlooms." He gestured weakly to his torso with the hand not holding the wand. "I think this more than counts."

Lina bit her lip, her eyes still shining with laughter. "I suppose that's fair. Even if I wasn't the one to select the outfit."

"Enjoy it while it lasts, sweetheart. This is a one-time deal."

"Oh, I intend to," Lina said, just as a soft electronic click sounded.

Crombie scowled at Finley, who was holding up his phone.

"Say cheese," he crooned, immediately snapping another picture.

Crombie pushed himself up and flung the toy wand across the room with a low growl. "If you three hadn't just saved my life, there's absolutely no way I'd endure this. But even I know it's poor form to repay such altruism with murder."

Nord laughed as the little wings fluttered delicately behind Crombie as he attempted to make himself more comfortable.

"Oh, for fuck's sake," he snarled, tearing off one of the wings and sending it flying in the same direction as the wand.

Lina doubled over as Crombie's temper tantrum sent a cloud of glitter raining down from his hair. Meanwhile, the remaining wing inched down Crombie's other arm as if attempting to escape before meeting the same end as its twin.

All in all, Crombie's humiliation painted a glorious picture.

"You know, this look really works for you," Finley said, canting his head to the side.

Crombie glowered at Finley, but the menacing expression was undermined completely by his fairy costume. He looked more like a sulking child than a pissed-off prince.

"No joke," Lina said, still cackling. "You should consider wearing silver eyeliner more often. It does incredible things for your eyes."

"I hate all of you."

"The feeling is entirely mutual," Nord assured him.

Crombie held his gaze and sighed. "Regardless of that, I do suppose thanks are in order."

"I'd really rather you didn't," Nord said.

"Oh?" Crombie raised a brow. "Why's that?"

"Because then I'd feel bad about doing this," Nord said, cocking his arm back and sending his fist flying into Crombie's nose.

There was a satisfying crack and then a muffled shout as blood went flying.

Lina gasped while Finley's voice sounded approvingly in his mind.

"Nice one."

"What the hell was that for?" Crombie demanded, his voice muffled, and his eyes narrowed in outrage.

Finley reached out and undid Nord's handiwork before Crombie could say anything further.

"Just be thankful I'm willing to stop at one," Nord said, crossing his arms and giving Crombie a pointed look.

The urge to keep going had been strong, but considering how he'd just spent the better part of the evening putting the man back together, he didn't want to waste all that effort. Besides, it wouldn't be long before Crombie's actions earned him another punch in the face. Nord could wait.

The fae held his stare, something dark and threatening burning in the back of his eyes before guttering out as he sighed once more. "You mean for now," Crombie said, obviously following the berserker's train of thought.

Nord smiled darkly. "Glad to know we finally seem to understand one another."

"You do realize I'm still here by choice, don't you?"

"Only because I removed the scraps of iron littering your body."

At the reminder, the mood in the room sank faster than a lead balloon.

All fight left Crombie as a shudder rolled through him. "Does this mean we've finally arrived at the storytelling portion of the evening's festivities?"

"I think we've earned some answers," Lina said softly, taking a seat facing him at the other end of the bed.

Crombie's eyes dropped to the pendant hanging just below the hollow of her throat. "Yes," he drawled, looking pained, "I suppose you have."

The fae was usually more careful about what he let his expression reveal. His naked distress, combined with his overall lack of pretense and guile, told Nord more than anything else he could have said or done. While his body may be repaired, his mental and emotional shields were down. The realization helped soften some of his months-long anger and resentment toward the other man. Not completely, but enough to sate his berserker's need for revenge.

Whatever happened to Crombie in Faerie appeared to be more than enough of a punishment.

Lina seemed to agree because instead of immediately demanding he remove the necklace and restore her magic, she asked the question they'd all been wondering.

"Crombie, what the hell happened to you?"

CHAPTER 3
LINA

"I assume you're referring to my being ripped apart by a faerie wearing your face and not the part where you saved my life?" Crombie asked with a mocking tilt of his head.

Shock tore through her, and Lina's eyes flared wide. Perhaps it shouldn't have been such a surprise to hear him say it aloud, but she'd just assumed someone else had gotten their hands on him. Everything she knew about the fae indicated that their culture was steeped in tradition, and their royals revered and above reproach—at least until they were overthrown. She'd never suspected Crombie had been brutalized at the hands of his own people. Let alone one who'd impersonated her while torturing him.

She wasn't sure what to do with that little nugget just yet, or how to feel about it, so she focused instead on the other part of what he'd just revealed.

"The fae did this to you? But aren't you their—"

"Future king?" Crombie supplied with a dark laugh. "Not if they have anything to say about it."

"It's been a while since I've had personal dealings with the monarchy, but I doubt things have changed so much that it's now akin to a democracy. Since when do the people of Faerie get to choose their rulers?" Finley asked, his voice surprisingly bitter.

"You might be surprised to learn what a rumor wielded by the right set of wagging tongues can do to a man. Even one of royal blood."

"No," Finley said, his voice flat. "I wouldn't."

The detached way he said it, combined with the odd sharpness of his gaze, bespoke of a long-familiar pain. As if he had to carry himself just so in order to avoid damaging himself further. Lina was familiar with that kind of trauma. The wound might be old and long scabbed over, but poke at it enough and it still had the power to cut. She made a mental note to ask Finley about his life prior to the Brotherhood—once they weren't in the middle of an all-out war, that is. This wasn't the first time her charming friend said something to indicate his own past was fraught with betrayal. She couldn't help but wonder how long it had taken him to cultivate his rakish, unaffected persona. Or what secrets it helped him hide.

Crombie raised a curious brow. "Well, then it should be no surprise to learn I am a victim of the same."

"Rumors caused this?" Lina asked, finding it hard to believe that alone would be enough to fuel the amount of hatred required to achieve the level of savagery he'd been subjected to. She'd experienced the power of gossip firsthand, but after seeing what the fae had done to him, this felt different. Not the act of an angry mob, but more personal. Like it was retaliation for the vilest possible insult.

"Rumor and greed," Crombie confirmed.

"Add in jealousy, and you've got yourself the unholy trifecta," Finley said.

Crombie's mouth quirked up. "That goes without saying. Not that I blame them. I mean, look at me."

Lina snorted. Still sporting his mostly intact fairy costume, he looked like he belonged in a parade. Or at a tea party. Five-and-six-year-old girls everywhere would most definitely be jealous of him and his tiara.

His smug expression fell at her reaction, and he groaned as his gaze dropped back to his lap. "How long are you going to make me wear this?"

"Until it stops being funny," Finley answered.

"Forget the why for now," Nord said, interrupting their tangent and returning to the original conversation. "I'm still having trouble understanding how any of this was possible. Aren't members of the royal fae bloodlines supposed to be incredibly powerful? And even if that wasn't a factor, didn't you have the aid of Lina's stolen magic to supplement your own?"

"I take it what you're really asking is how anyone managed to overpower me?"

Nord nodded.

"Was the iron you found lining my insides not enough of a clue?"

"That only explains how they kept you from fighting back, not how they caught you in the first place."

Crombie clasped his hands in his lap and looked down. Lina followed his gaze, her eyes zeroing in on, and finally registering, his naked fingers.

"Where's the ring?" Lina blurted, her voice unnaturally high pitched. If he didn't have it, who did? She loathed the idea of Crombie siphoning off and playing with her power, but she enjoyed the idea of a stranger running around with it far less. On the heels of that thought came a far more troubling one. Could he even remove the necklace if he wasn't in possession of its counterpart?

"Oh, that," Crombie said. "Well, coincidentally, both your questions have essentially the same answer."

"Which is?" Nord pressed, impatience seeping into his tone.

"Fucking Faerie."

"Care to be more specific?" Finley asked.

"Ever heard of The Hunt?"

"Answering a question with another question doesn't constitute an explanation," Lina snapped, frustration and panic making her lightheaded. She tried to breathe deeply but only managed to achieve short, shallow pants.

Nord reacted immediately. He shifted until his body pressed firmly against her side, anchoring her while one of his hands curled around her neck so his thumb could brush up and down her nape. His touch brought immediate relief, each of his slow, intentional strokes sloughing away a layer of her anxiety until she felt steady once more.

Lina leaned into him, welcoming his strength as well as the healing nature of their Transference-forged connection.

"Sure it does," Crombie said. "The name alone tells you everything you need to know. Assuming, of course, you're familiar with it."

"Assume I'm not," Lina said, holding the fae's stormy gaze.

He waited a beat before saying anything, as if seeking out the answer to some unknown riddle in her eyes or perhaps simply buying himself a few more seconds to figure out where to start.

Once he began, Lina wasn't sure she wanted to hear his story. After seeing how it ended, learning what contributed to his downfall didn't seem very appealing.

"As soon as I arrived in Faerie, I was hunted. Had I known The Hunt—"

"You're referring to The Wild Hunt, I assume?" Finley interjected.

"See? Someone knew what I was talking about," Crombie said, tipping his head toward Finley with a quirk of his lips.

"The Wild Hunt?" Lina repeated, Finley's use of their full title stirring up vague memories. "Like from fairytales?"

Crombie's smile stretched, taking on a mocking edge. "I am a faerie, darling."

Surprised laughter bubbled up until she could hardly breathe. His cocky statement, when paired with his outfit, was absolutely absurd. And yet all the more perfect because of it.

He winked, letting her know he'd said that wholly for her benefit as he picked back up with his recounting. "Had I known The Hunt had been offered my contract, I do not think I would have risked a return. No," he said, correcting himself after a brief pause, "I probably still would have risked it. Even knowing how it would end." Crombie blew out a breath, lost to his memories for a long stretch of time. "Sorry, where was I?"

"Not much farther along than you were five minutes ago," Nord grumbled.

"The Hunt had your contract," Lina said, still not entirely sure what the words meant.

"Right. Well, as all things are in Faerie, the contract is magical. It provides all members of The Hunt with not only my scent, but the ability to do with me what they will until the terms of the sentence have been met."

"And your contract's terms?" Nord asked.

"Life," Crombie answered with a bitter smile. "As a member of the Night Court's royal family, the fact that my parents ever allowed the contract to happen is pretty indicative of what kind of people they and the rest of the Court are. The fae have long memories. I should have known better than to try to change their minds. Anyway, there's no hiding from The Hunt once they've caught your scent. They were on me in a matter of hours. And since I didn't know they were after me to begin with, I made no attempt to cover my tracks. It wouldn't have mattered in the end, them being who they are and all, but perhaps it might have bought me enough time to at least attempt what I'd set out to do."

"Which was?"

Crombie scowled at Nord. "Are you going to let me tell my story or not?"

"Just get on with it."

"I'm trying to, but as always, you three love interrupting me." Crombie's eyes narrowed. "Say, where is your merry weaver? She's not usually one to willingly pass up such an opportunity."

Lina nervously bit her lip, wondering the same. Quinn had told them she'd be back before whatever they'd attempt that evening. It wasn't like her not to keep her word. Lina just hoped whatever she was up to, she was safe.

"She's on her way," Finley answered evasively. "Now stop stalling."

Crombie sat back against the headboard with a shrug. "Well, this part is rather depressing, if I'm being honest, so I'm sure you'll love it."

"Just as I'm sure honesty's a stretch for you," Nord bit back.

"Guys, come on," Lina said, though her attempt at putting an end to their machismo back-talk was half-hearted at best. She actually enjoyed the amusing way they took shots at one another, but they had other things to do, so they needed to set all that aside and focus. "This is going to take forever if you don't just let him get through it."

Crombie seemed caught off guard that she'd taken his side, at least on the face of things. He gave the other two men a self-satisfied smirk which caused Finley to roll his eyes and Nord to . . . well, Nord's expression didn't really change. He just maintained his usual I-can-rip-your-spine-out-with-my-hands stare.

"The long and the short of it is they caught me in a traditional hunter's snare. By the time I even knew they were there, I was already hanging upside down, suspended in a net of barbed iron threads, and nearly blinded by the pain. Now, usually, this is where normal jailors would bind their prisoner in chains, if not slit their throat outright. But it's no fun to hunt something when it can't provide you with a proper chase.

"So, like the sadists they are, The Hunt set about stripping me and claiming all of my possessions for themselves. This included Nocturna's ring, though I doubt they ever realized what they had. Once that was accomplished, it's my personal belief they intended to graft the thrice-damned metal to my skeleton. But thankfully—or not, given how things turned out—it hurts them to play with iron as much as me. Instead, they settled for impaling me with it in an attempt to maximize the effectiveness of their game while limiting their own contact with the iron."

"Which is how you ended up with the barbed cage around your heart," Nord murmured.

Lina blanched. "The what?"

"Who's interrupting now?" Crombie asked.

"I'm sorry, it's just . . . wow."

Crombie glanced up at Nord. "You didn't tell her?"

"Some things are best kept buried. She saw what happened to you. She didn't need to be scarred by further detail."

"Oops," Crombie said, pressing a hand to his mouth.

"Oh, shut up," Lina said, only just now starting to fully comprehend exactly what Crombie had been up against. And how thoroughly those brutes had done their job. The worst part was they didn't even realize it. When they robbed Crombie and took the ring, not only had they started down the path of destroying him, but they'd managed to drag Lina right alongside him.

Nausea crawled up her throat, and even with the continued aid of Nord's soothing touch, she had to take a few breaths through her mouth before she felt well enough to ask, "What happened then?"

Crombie stared at a fixed point on the wall somewhere to her right and gave her an insolent one-shoulder shrug. "The same thing that happens to all fae when they encounter iron. Pain. Pain. And, oh yes, more pain."

His lips twisted in a grimace Lina suspected was supposed to be a derisive smile that fell far too short.

Still not meeting her gaze, he continued, "There was no end to it. I couldn't make use of my magic without serious, excruciating side effects. Side effects I was no match for within a few hours, let alone after the months they'd held me captive. That didn't mean I didn't try, but my attempts were clumsy at best. For all that I'm a would-be king, in their clutches I was little better than a mortal. It's not arrogance but a simple statement of fact when I say there are very few, even in Faerie, whose power is anywhere near a match to mine. Diminished as I was, however, I could hardly face off against a fly, let alone a single member of The Hunt. I think the lack of fight disappointed them. I couldn't make it very exciting for them without my magic, could I? Well, except by refusing to die. They didn't like that. Not one bit."

Crombie's eyes flashed silver with barely restrained fury, but the smile he shot her way was tight and emotionless.

Lina shivered, goosebumps breaking out all along her arms and the back of her neck. Here was the man she'd met that first night. The monster lurking behind a façade of human beauty and grace. One made even more dangerous because you'd never see him coming. He'd been scary before, but Lina sensed now he might be more than a little unhinged. The combination was mildly terrifying. Like finding out a beloved pet was rabid and that any bonds which might have once existed between you were no longer enough to keep you safe.

Nord shifted restlessly behind her, likely reacting to the prickling echoes of her fear. She tilted her head so that she could brush her cheek against his forearm, knowing he'd recognize the gesture as the reassurance she intended it to be.

"That's when they got creative. The Hunt was no longer interested, or should I say solely interested, in destroying my body." Crombie let out a low, dark chuckle that echoed around the room like a distant rumble of thunder. "No, they wanted my soul, as well."

He fell silent then, and it felt almost as if he had to reel himself back from the brink of whatever depths he'd been peering into. His eyes were wild, his pupils fully dilated until they found Lina's. The sight of her seemed to do what he could not and snapped him back into the present. Crombie shuddered and rapidly blinked.

Lina reached out a hand, but he started speaking again as if nothing had happened.

"Contrary to popular belief, I was never banished from Faerie. I left. I'd been accused of stealing something that belongs to me by right. And though I could never prove my innocence, the insult of the accusation—and knowing there was only one person who could be responsible for its spread—was enough for me to turn my back on the place that should have been my kingdom. For years, I chased down every lead regarding that which I was said to have stolen—"

"The jewelry in the vault," Lina said unnecessarily, finally understanding just how important the heirlooms had been for him to reclaim.

"Just so," Crombie agreed. "And the irony of me using you to help steal them back isn't lost on me. I'm fully aware that by doing so, I've essentially committed the very crime for which I'd originally been accused. But, in order to clear my name, I needed to return to my homeland, using the items I'd been said to have taken in the first place."

"Why?" Lina asked. "Wouldn't showing up after all this time with them in your possession just prove your accusers right?"

"Perhaps, had it not been for you."

"Me?"

"You were the boon I never could have hoped for even in my most desperate imaginings. With your power, I would finally have the ability to change reality in any way necessary to prove my case. And so I had a plan. I'd return to Faerie with Nocturna's treasure and incriminate my accuser. Obviously, he was responsible for the original theft, and it was well past time to prove it. Then, assuming all went according to plan and my name was clear, I'd come back here and return your power to you."

His expression was painfully earnest as his gaze bore into hers. Lina could feel how badly he needed her to believe him.

"I'd only ever intended to borrow your power, you see, never keep it."

"And you couldn't just ask for my help?"

"Would you have helped me? Would you have willingly handed over your powers for an indeterminate amount of time, no questions asked?"

"Of course not—"

"Well, there's your answer."

"That doesn't justify you taking what doesn't belong to you. I might not have just handed it over, but I probably would have gone with you. Isn't stealing the exact thing that got you into this mess in the first place?"

"I didn't steal; I borrowed."

She shot him a narrowed-eyed glare.

"Without asking," he amended.

"Which is the definition of stealing," Lina pointed out.

"Trust me, I know now I never should have bothered. But the one thing I never counted on was The fucking Hunt."

"So they were the ones that had you the entire time? You never managed to speak to your family or the person who betrayed you?" Lina asked.

Crombie shook his head. "I don't even know if they ever realized I was there. I belonged to The Hunt the second I set foot in Faerie."

"Do you know how long you were with them?" Nord asked.

"It's hard to say. I was in a realm of endless night and lost track of time rather quickly. Even if I hadn't, there's no way to know how much time has passed on the mortal plane once you've left. It's not a strict month-to-day equivalent. Time passes faster or slower depending on the season or where in Faerie you end up. I have to assume I was there at least a year, maybe more."

Lina let out an involuntary gasp. She shook her head, wordlessly trying to deny it. He'd been tortured for over a *year*? It was bad enough when she'd thought it had been months. But a year?

She couldn't begin to make sense of the tangled mess her emotions had twisted into at his news. There was her anger and hurt at his betrayal—and her berserker's need to avenge it. Dismay and fear that she may not reclaim her power in time to deal with Mikel. But more than anything, there was a vast sense of empathy for the soul sitting across from her.

Eyes prickling with unshed tears, all Lina knew for sure was she felt an overwhelming urge to hug him. She'd never seen him look so vulnerable as he did when his gaze finally returned to hers.

Nord let out a warning rumble as Crombie's hand snaked out,

but he didn't interfere when Crombie's fingers clutched hers. Lina interpreted it as a warning for Crombie to behave, but you only had to look at the angst darkening the fae's eyes to see there was no threat here.

"However long it was, it was certainly long enough to know that I never should have attempted what I did without asking for your permission. Long enough to know that I made a grievous mistake. It was never my intention to do something that would cause you harm. All I ever wanted was to clear my name so that I could return home free from disgrace. But that was selfish of me, and I certainly paid the price for my hubris. More than that, I owe you a life debt."

"Crombie—"

He shook his head, speaking over her. "Whether you intended to or not, what you did by bringing me here was save my life. You saw the state I was in. I wouldn't have lasted much longer. I don't know about your kind, but where I come from, that sort of thing demands repayment. And so, I vow to you, Evalina Cuska, Ascended Heir of the Mobius Council, Warrior of Odin, and Champion of the Animagi, if ever you find yourself in mortal peril, I will be notified and summoned to your side. No matter where you are."

His magic took over then, completing his vow. Their clasped hands sizzled with electric energy that raced up her arm and shot into her chest.

"What, no blood?" she asked with a wobbly smile as the tingling settled to a pleasant warmth.

He returned it with a wry one of his own. "You sound disappointed."

"You once told me fae only deal in blood."

"I think there's been enough of my blood shed recently, don't you?"

"Uh, yeah. I think that's probably a fair assessment."

His expression softened, and she could feel the twist of something that tasted oddly like grief as he let go of her hand.

"Crombie, there's just one more thing."

He raised his brows, signaling for her to continue.

"If you no longer possess the ring, are you still able to release me?" Lina hooked a finger under the chain settled snugly around her throat, drawing his attention to the dangling pendant.

Crombie blanched, as if he couldn't believe he'd forgotten her magic was still bound. "Of course, forgive me. Why didn't you say something sooner?"

"There's been a lot going on," she said with a laugh as he leaned forward and grasped the delicate chain in each of his hands. There was a burst of magic, sort of like the warm fall of water cascading over her shoulders and down her back. By the time the sensation faded, the necklace was cradled in his palm.

Lina lifted her hand, rubbing away the pins-and-needles webbing across her neck. Her relief to see the pendant in his hand instead of resting against her chest made her giddy, and she let out a breathless laugh.

"Did it work?" Nord asked.

She gave him a confused look before realizing he was asking if her magic had returned, not whether Crombie had been able to remove the necklace. Lina reached down into the abyss that had replaced her source of power, more laughter bubbling up when her magic rose eagerly to her call.

Giving Crombie a playful look, she tilted her head to the side. "Let's see about putting you in something more comfortable, shall we?"

"Lina," he said warningly, holding up his hands and causing the two halves of the necklace's chain to swing wildly. "Don't you dare."

Finley, picking up on her game, projected an image straight into her mind. It was the first time he'd ever used his Guardian abilities to do something like that, and she stiffened in surprise before her grin stretched wide.

Holding onto his image, she used her magic to will it into being. Nord and Finley's deep barks of laughter soon filled the room.

"Oh, fuck you," Crombie softly snarled as her new outfit replaced the fairy costume.

"What?" she asked, her attempt at innocence failing miserably as she started to snicker. "I thought you liked the Apocalyptic Unicorns."

Crombie plucked at the purple crop top bearing the band's logo and then down to the miniscule silver-sequined hot pants. "Not this much. I don't like *anything* this much."

"But you look so good."

The words were shockingly true. Crombie—even glowering and visibly incensed—looked smokin' hot. To be fair, his broody, bad boy attitude probably had a lot to do with why he pulled it off so damn well. But his body certainly didn't hurt. His lean, sculpted form filled out the tight shirt and booty shorts in the absolute best way while providing a tantalizing look at well-defined muscles and an impressive bulge. Not that she was intentionally checking it out, but it was sort of staring at her and daring her to look. And well, once you noticed, how were you supposed to un-notice?

She cleared her throat with an embarrassed chuckle, lifting her gaze to find Crombie glaring at her, all his earlier vulnerability and emotion walled away once more.

"Are you quite done?"

"Would you rather I change it back?"

"I'd rather—"

Whatever he'd been about to say was lost to the bang of the front door slamming open.

"Lina?"

Quinn's panicked shout had all of them on their feet and spinning toward the sound of her hurried footsteps.

"We're in here!"

Lina had just barely beaten Finley and Nord to the door as Quinn came barreling into view, skidding to a halt in front of them. Her hair was disheveled, her skin ashen, and her eyes wide with terror.

"We've got to go. Now!"

CHAPTER 4
LINA

"Go? Go where? Quinn, what are you talking about?"

"No time to explain. Fin, can you—"

Her question was cut short by an unexpected sway of the building. Lina lurched, her body unprepared for the shift in gravity. Nord caught her easily, holding her steady with an arm around her waist.

"Thanks," she murmured while Finley demanded, "What the hell was that?"

"Um, an earthquake?" Lina guessed as the floor pitched again.

"We don't have earthquakes in Bell Falls."

"Fuck. He already knows I'm here," Quinn said, biting down into her bottom lip and squinting back down the hallway. "Mom?" she called.

"We're here, just moving slow," came Cora's breathless reply. "Your Aunt Sylvia is having a little trouble."

"Yeah, a sledgehammer to the kneecap tends to do that," Quinn growled darkly.

Lina placed a hand on each of Quinn's shoulders. "Quinn, darling, what the fuck is going on?"

"Mikel," she said, blowing out a heavy breath.

"H-here?" Lina stuttered. It shouldn't have come as a surprise, but she'd naively assumed they'd have more time. The sound of drawers opening drew Lina's attention. She glanced back to find Crombie rummaging through her clothes. "I don't think you're going to find anything that fits you in there."

He pulled out a spare pair of Nord's sweats and one of the T-shirts Lina had borrowed and conveniently forgotten to return. "You were saying?" he drawled.

Lina knew things must be really bad when Quinn didn't bother to make a crack about Crombie's crop top. Instead, she gave him a slow head-to-toe and then turned her attention back down the hall toward her mother and aunts, who were still just out of Lina's view.

"Way to be resourceful," Lina told Crombie, though her eyes were trained on Quinn's pinched expression. "Probably easier to fight in something less restrictive."

"Oh, I'm not staying," Crombie said with a laugh. "I mean, I could. But I've had my fill of fighting for my life as of late. And even if that wasn't the case, I hate all of you, remember?"

"But what about the life debt?" Lina asked, blinking at him in surprise.

"Well, if things take a turn, I'll end up right back here, won't I?"

"That's comforting."

"Yes, I suppose it would be," Crombie said with a nod, completely ignoring her sarcasm. "Anyway, do try to stay alive for me. I could really use some me time."

Crombie was gone as soon as the words left his lips, leaving Lina to sputter in the direction he'd been standing.

"What an ass!"

"You're surprised by this?" Finley asked.

Lina waved a hand. "Not even ten minutes ago, the guy was in tears, apologizing to me and swearing to save my life. And then the instant the opportunity arises, he poofs away."

"Again I ask, are you surprised?"

"No," she said after a moment, "I guess not. Maybe a little disappointed, though."

"We don't need him," Nord assured her as the building rocked a second time.

"You sure about that?" she asked him.

Nord's lack of response was more troubling than the quaking ground. He seemed lost to thought. She knew him well enough by now to know he was busy working through a series of potential scenarios to determine the best way to keep everybody alive.

"But we should still be safe here, right?" Lina asked, her eyes darting between a frowning Nord and a sober-looking Finley.

Fin opened his mouth to respond, but Quinn vehemently shook her head. "I already told you we can't stay here."

"But Mikel can't breach the wards." A sick feeling twisted Lina's gut. "Can he?" she asked, her horror at the thought causing the question to come out in a whispered croak.

"I never thought anyone would be able to breach the wards," Finley said. "But it's happened at least half a dozen times in the last few months alone. At this point, it's probably safest to assume that he can, and he will."

"Some security system," she muttered darkly. That's when Cora, Sheridan, and Sylvia limped into view. "Holy fuck," Lina breathed, bile clogging her throat.

This time Cora seemed mostly unharmed—thank God—though the amount of blood splashed across her white silk blouse was beyond concerning. Sheridan and Sylvia were in far worse shape, the twins having each sustained serious injuries. Though none more gruesome than the bloated, misshapen mess that had once been Sylvia's left knee. At least, not that Lina could currently see.

She staggered forward, intent on doing what she could to heal the three women. Quinn stopped her with a hand around her bicep, her long nails digging into the tender flesh of Lina's underarm.

"We don't have time."

"Quinn, she can barely walk," Lina gritted out, her free arm slashing toward Sylvia.

"You think I don't know that? We've spent the last hour and a half trying to get back here. One of the guys can carry her. We need to get the fuck out of here. What about that aren't you understanding?"

Quinn didn't lose her shit often, but the near-hysterical waver in her voice was unmistakable. She was barely hanging on right now. Lina couldn't begin to imagine what the Satori women had been through. Nor would she blame them for prioritizing sanctuary above anything else.

With that thought in mind, Lina checked the impulse to demand information and shifted her focus to escape. While Mikel could potentially breach the wards, they were still intact for the time being, which meant they'd prevent Finley from summoning a portal within the penthouse.

"We need to get out into the entryway so Fin can portal us."

"Where are we going?" he asked, turning to her.

"Hope Street?" she suggested, thinking Alistair's hideout would be big enough for all seven of them.

"No," Nord said, seeming to come alive as he stepped out of the bedroom and into the hall. "They'll find us there. We'll return to Novasgard."

Without a way for Mikel or other Animagi to follow behind them, it really was the safest—not to mention only—choice. Even knowing that, Lina still had to ask, "Are you sure?" As she worried about what they might be bringing to the Novasgardians' doorstep, anxiety caused her palms to sweat and her heart to beat a little faster.

Nord gave her a tight nod. His next words proved he'd picked up on her unvoiced concern. "Astrid always knew this was a possibility. She and the others are more than capable of defending their home if necessary."

"All right," she said, reaching out and linking her hand with his. "Viking-town it is. Let's go."

They turned as one, already heading for the propped-open door when a distant chime signaled the elevator's arrival.

"Motherfucker," Lina growled, feeling a surge of adrenaline that always preceded a fight, along with the answering tidal wave of divine fury as her berserker rose to the surface.

It took less than a split-second glance to ascertain their current circumstances were far from ideal. Positioned as they were, their fighters were in the back while the three wounded Satori were caught in between them and whoever was on the other side of the elevator door, leaving them completely vulnerable to attack. The others realized this as well because all of them surged forward. The Satori in the hopes of obtaining cover, and the rest of them trying to get into a defensive formation.

Needless to say, seven people attempting to push past each other in a hallway was a recipe for failure.

The elevator doors slid open, revealing Nico, Mikel, and two Drakes Lina only recognized because they'd been at her trial.

"Oh look, a welcoming party," Nico drawled.

"Oh look, a piece of shit," Lina snapped back.

Nico smirked, ignoring her as he turned to Mikel. "And they're even in a nice little cluster for you."

"How considerate," Mikel replied, his lips twisting in amusement that never reached his eyes. Eyes that bled yellow while the pupils lengthened into two vertical slits.

Lina blinked, not trusting what she was seeing as Mikel's mouth stretched to an impossible size.

"What the hell is he doing?" Finley asked, the stunned disbelief in his voice a perfect match to what Lina was feeling.

"Duck!" Nord roared, clearly several mental steps ahead of them as he summoned a shield that shimmered into being between their party and the open door.

Lina realized what he had not even a second later as red and golden flames gathered in Mikel's gaping maw.

Fire. Mikel could *breathe* fire.

What the actual fuck?

That was as far down the rabbit hole as Lina would allow her panicked thoughts to fall.

Acting on pure instinct, Lina gathered her magic. As she twisted and shaped it, not so much into a specific object as an idea, a spout of flames poured from Mikel's mouth, aimed straight at Nord's shield, which melted as soon as the fire made contact.

And he didn't stop there. As fire continued to spew out of his mouth, Mikel shifted his head from side to side, spraying everything in sight.

There wasn't time for Lina to do more. She unleashed her magic in a torrent of icy water which poured from the entryway's ceiling, flooding the room and smothering any rogue flames. The hallway filled with smoke and steam, momentarily obscuring Mikel and the other Animagi assholes from view.

Lina did what she could to clear out the smoke as the others all started to cough and choke.

"Go! Get back!" Nord shouted.

"Mom, come on," Quinn urged, covering her nose and mouth with the elbow of one arm while reaching out with the other to grasp her mother's hand in her own.

Cora looked over her shoulder at her two struggling sisters.

"Go, it's fine. We're right behind you," Sheridan insisted, her arm tucked tightly around her limping twin.

As the four Satori squeezed past them toward the back of the penthouse, Finley's voice sounded in Lina's mind.

"With the entryway overrun, the only way I'll be able to portal us out of here is to disable the wards. I need you guys to buy me some time."

"Go," Nord answered, which was when Lina realized Finley had been speaking to both of them.

"I'll meet you in the living room once I'm finished."

Without another word, Finley took off running toward his office.

Lina spared Nord a glance, her attention still mostly focused on the wall of smoke in front of her. "Since when can he do that telepathic stuff on non-Guardians?" she asked in a low voice.

"Since always," he replied, his attention in the same direction as her own. "It's only courtesy and a desire to conserve his power that prevents him from using it more often."

"Good to know," she said under her breath as the shadowed forms of the four Animagi came into view.

"We only need to hold them off until Finley is done," Nord said, his expression fierce as his eyes changed from ice to endless black. "Use everything at your disposal to keep them busy. Hold nothing back, do you understand me?"

Lina nodded.

Nord wove one of his hands in her hair and tugged her head back as his lips crashed into hers.

"No matter what happens, Kærasta. You and I are going through that portal together. So do. Not. Die."

"No way, Viking. You and I have an aisle to walk down, remember? I wouldn't miss it for anything."

"Then let's shed some blood so we can get on with it." The grin he gave her was savage, his berserker fully in control.

Lina felt an answering pull as she allowed her bloodlust to do the same. "I'd be happy to."

As the last word left her lips, Mikel's dark, rolling laughter reached her.

"What's so funny?" she snarled as he stepped through the smoke.

"That you actually think you have any hope of besting me."

Just then, the sound of shattering glass and several high-pitched screams pierced through the penthouse.

Fuck.

CHAPTER 5
NORD

At the sound of shattered glass, Nord didn't waste any time. Drawing on his magic, he sent dozens of razor-sharp knives hurtling in the direction of Mikel and the others.

Looking unimpressed, Nico threw up a hand and transformed his lethal blades into a bunch of feathers. As they floated harmlessly to the floor, Nico raised a single taunting brow.

"Lina, go," Nord said.

"Not without you."

Nord let out a growl of frustration but understood exactly where she was coming from. Even knowing she was more than capable of taking care of herself, his berserker couldn't bear to leave her on her own either.

"Together," he said.

Lina gave a tight nod, her focus zeroed in on her cousin. He was hardly the true threat, but any magic they attempted to use against the other Animagi, he would continue to negate.

Calling on her power, Lina bound Nico's arms and mouth, dressing him in a tightly laced straitjacket and even tighter gag. It wouldn't last long since neither words nor hand motions were necessary for an Animagus to use their power. But it didn't matter because their goal right now was not to eliminate. It was to delay. Anything either of them managed to do to prolong the inevitable showdown would buy Finley the time he needed.

It also provided Nord with an opening. With the focus on Nico and Lina, he began to quietly draw on his immense reservoir of power.

Meanwhile, Nico's face turned an angry, mottled red as drool began dripping down his chin. He let out a series of garbled words.

Lina held a hand up to her ear. "Sorry, what's that? I'm having a little trouble understanding you."

"'Itch!'" he shouted.

She tsked, looking disappointed as Nico managed to make the jacket and gag disappear. "No, cousin. We've already talked about this—at length. But since you seem to have already forgotten, I'll remind you. *You* are the bitch."

Nord laughed while Nico fumed.

Mikel rolled his eyes. "Stop fucking around, Nico. I don't care what you do to him, but I need her alive."

One of the two Animagi guards cracked his knuckles, while the other openly smirked as if they relished the thought of facing off with Nord. The berserker begged for release, eager to rise to the challenge, but Nord pushed him back down.

Not yet, but soon.

There was a flicker of annoyed acceptance as the beast settled back down while Nord continued to draw on his magic, feeling an intense buzz vibrating beneath his skin as he held onto the crackling energy.

"But—" Nico protested, which made Lina laugh.

"Please, cousin. Don't embarrass yourself further by pretending you could actually take me out. No one here believes it." She tipped her head to the side to indicate Mikel. "Not even your sugar daddy."

Confident he'd drawn enough power, Nord slowly began to release it. The effect was not instantaneous, as it usually was, since he was funneling a great deal of energy but wanted to contain and limit the blast. Such nuanced work required greater effort and concentration.

The ground beneath their feet trembled, though this time, the rumbling was restricted to a one-foot area directly beneath each of the four Animagi's feet.

Mikel sneered. "Is that the best you've got?"

"For your sake, you'd better hope it is," Nord said with a dark laugh of his own. He wasn't interested in conversation, but it did make one hell of a distraction.

Mikel's mouth was open, ready to aim whatever uninspired insult he'd just come up with their way, when Nord's next burst of magic took hold, catching him completely off guard.

Four pillars punched up from the floor, sending Mikel, Nico, and the two other men straight for the ceiling. One man lost his balance, falling backward off the pillar.

Nord and Lina didn't stick around to see the fates of the Animagi.

"Do you think that was long enough?" Lina asked as they sprinted toward the living room and the sound of the Satori women's screams.

"It's going to have to be."

Lina skidded to a stop at the end of the hallway, her expression laced with shock and surprise as men and women clad head-to-toe in black swarmed through the windows via a series of ropes and ladders.

Quinn stood in the center of the room, trying to protectively shield her mother and aunts with her body while they huddled behind her. In a loud, clear voice, Quinn looked at the man nearest to her and said, "You'll die to protect us."

The man's mud-colored eyes clouded over, and his steps faltered. Spinning around, he flung the ball of swirling snow and ice he'd intended for the Satori back in the direction he'd just come. Animagi dove out of the way as his orb turned into an ice storm, sending shards of ice and hail flying out in a cone of shrapnel.

Seeing that Quinn had at least half of the room taken care of, Nord raced toward the other side with Lina right behind him.

Now.

The berserker rushed to the surface, breaking free with a savage cry as Nord began to swing, not even bothering to summon a weapon as he set about taking out the intruders. Too reliant on their magic and most lacking physical skill, the Animagi were no match for him and Lina.

He experienced a moment of unimaginable joy at seeing Lina fighting at his side, effortlessly executing the moves he'd taught her. She was his equal in every possible way. Her eyes shining, hands bloodied, and her mouth pulled back in a feral snarl. He couldn't have asked for a more perfect mate.

Perhaps others might find it odd that he'd experience such pure bliss in the midst of battle. But then, a berserker was happiest when he was coated in the blood of his enemies. Nord simply recognized the moment as the gift it was, smiling his most bloodthirsty smile and raining down unholy hell on those who'd dared try to harm what was his.

CHAPTER 6
QUINN

Quinn tugged on her mom's arm, causing her to stumble as they raced toward the back of the penthouse.

Fuck. Fuck. Fuck.

If ever there was a time she regretted turning down Nord and Finley's offers of crazy ninja training, this was so it. Why, in the name of all that's good and holy, was it up to her to protect her family? Who thought that was a good idea? Did they know her? She was the one who used the spear like a bat and got knocked out almost instantly during her last couple of battles. Was this one really supposed to end any differently?

Mild panic attack aside, the realization that she was with three people who were even more useless in a fistfight than her did help steady her nerves. Because if anything happened before the others joined them, it was up to Quinn to keep them alive.

Cora was scrappy and creative enough to hold her own, but Sheridan and Sylvia were no fighters. Nor had they ever been in a situation where they'd needed to be.

Sylvia was in rough shape. As soon as she and her twin made it safely to the cleared space in the middle of the living room, she collapsed on the floor, no longer able to support her weight.

Quinn swallowed to ease the constriction in her throat and refused to look past her aunt's pained grimace. The images from her mother's recent brush with Mikel were still far too fresh in her mind. She didn't need any other memories of her family's brutal injuries to join them.

"Quinn, I need you to listen to me," Cora said, drawing her gaze. "If the time comes and you need to make a tough call, don't worry about us. You just do what you have to do to stay alive."

"You know there's no way I'm leaving you guys."

"Mon coeur, listen to me. The most important thing right now is that you get out. She needs you. They all do. The rest of us—"

"Mom, you know how much I love you, but if you finish that sentence, I'm going to punch you in the throat."

Cora gave a humorless laugh. "Fair enough, though I have a feeling no matter what I said, that would never happen."

"No," Quinn agreed with a sigh. "But it sounded threatening enough to convince you anyway."

Cora gave her daughter's arm a squeeze. "It did. Just like I taught you."

They shared a look filled with the ghosts of many such conversations. There was a lot Cora had taught her over the years. Outside of the obligatory birds and bees talk, and perhaps the 'don't drink and operate heavy machinery' one, Quinn was sure the conversations she'd had with her mother were nothing like the ones most kids had with their parents. And, even during those obligatory chats, she was confident the caveats her mom made during them didn't come up for other kids either.

She was still haunted by her mother's mantras. Such as:

'It might take two to tango, but ultimately you're the only one you can depend on to keep yourself safe. Let me show you how to properly put on a condom.'

And her personal favorite:

'Never fake an orgasm. It only reinforces bad habits. If your partner can't properly stimulate you, they don't deserve the beauty of your climax. And if they give you shit for wanting to take matters into your own hands, dump 'em and don't look back. There's nothing more tragic than a selfish lover.'

Don't get her wrong, the advice was solid, and she'd absolutely taken it to heart. But teenagers—especially one with an eidetic memory—deserved the dignity of being able to forget the humiliation of such conversations, not to mention the associated mental images. No one in their right mind wanted to remember those kinds of moments in full, blazing detail.

Gift, my ass.

The thought was interrupted by the flash of something dark in her periphery.

Quinn snapped her head in the direction of the floor-to-ceiling windows just in time to see three men Tarzan-swinging toward them on ropes. There wasn't time for anything other than open-mouthed shock as their feet hit the glass in unison, shattering it and allowing them to swing unimpeded into the living room as shards of glass rained down around them.

Her aunts screamed, snapping her out of her stunned stupor. An all-too-familiar panic began to tear at her as more black-clad bodies began repelling down the ropes and into the room.

Oh God. Oh God. There's so many of them. What the hell am I supposed to do?

She really wished she had the foresight to ask for a weapon. Not that there'd been time for that, but then she'd at least have something to wildly hurl at these intruders.

The first of the three lunged toward her, and the time for thinking—strategic or otherwise—was over.

With no other options before her, Quinn did what she did best and buried her feelings as far down as they would go. Once she could breathe without a hint of that suffocating fear, she donned her most convincing mask, the one that oozed sex and confidence, the one she'd shamelessly used to lure so many unsuspecting men to nights they'd never remember.

Maintaining the man's gaze, she searched for any sign of recognition, but with his face covered in a mask, his brown eyes may have belonged to anyone. Her best guess was he was one of the Alinari, since they were the 'warriors' among the Animagi. Though, after seeing what Nord and the Novasgardians could do, she used that term loosely. She'd never really seen the Alinari do more than stand guard and perform surveillance duties.

When one of the other men began to summon a ball of swirling ice, Quinn jerked her head in surprise. Alinari didn't have any elemental magic to speak of. So maybe these were Thortons, then? It was hard to know, and there wasn't enough time for her to find out. Whoever these intruders were, they might be Animagi, but they were not her allies.

Calling on her gift, Quinn reached out and latched onto the first man's mind, implanting her suggestion deep within as she drew within hearing distance when she repeated it out loud.

"You're going to take that dagger and shove it straight into your fucking heart."

He blinked, his brown eyes clouding over as her suggestion took hold and he did exactly what she said. With a soft gasp and tiny bubbles of blood dribbling down his chin, he dropped to his knees and collapsed at her feet.

The sound of pounding footsteps came from behind, but Quinn couldn't afford to shift her attention while she was this deep into her power. If it was Mikel, they were as good as dead, so she may as well take out as many of his men as she could. If it was Nord and Lina, they'd jump straight in.

Eyes already on the man with the ball of snow and ice, Quinn reached for his mind, ordering him to protect her and take the orb and hurl it back toward the others who'd come in after him. Just like his friend, he was compelled to obey.

As did the next. And the next. In a matter of minutes, Quinn had more than half the room fighting each other, if not outright turning their own weapons on themselves. With each man and woman she successfully manipulated, she felt stronger and more sure of herself and her gift. She might not be a badass berserker, but she was far from defenseless. She could do this. She would protect her family.

Fate chose that exact moment to prove her wrong.

Sylvia cried out, the sound she made distinct and foreign all at once. Not quite as shrill as a scream, but so much more than a gasp and conveying a unique mix of shock, pain, and perhaps worst of all, relief. It was the last of these which filled Quinn with dread.

She spun, but not in time to save her aunt from the javelin one of the intruders had conjured and thrown straight into Sylvia's chest. As horrific a sight as it was, Quinn knew the hunk of wood jutting out of her aunt's torso wasn't the real danger. The black, bubbly ichor oozing out of the wound and her mouth was. The fucker had tipped their weapon in poison.

Clutching her twin in her arms, Sheridan tried to pull the spear free, but it was too late. The poison had taken hold. Sylvia's already pale skin was ashen, and her eyes clouded over as they rolled back in her head. Her lungs let out a final hoarse rattle, and then she fell utterly still.

Grief twisted sharply inside of Quinn. She'd always known they weren't going to get through this war with Mikel without casualties, but she'd naively hoped her family might be spared. She should have known better. Mikel always found a way to rob her of the people she loved.

With a furious cry, Quinn turned to the last of the Animagi still standing and ordered them to show no mercy until the living room was free of the threat. Certain no one else was coming in through the broken windows, she rushed back to the center of the room and sank to her knees beside her mom.

Cora slipped an arm around Quinn's shoulders, squeezing tight and easing her pain in the way only a mother could. The support was enough to stave off Quinn's tears, if not the entirety of her pain. It also gave her the strength to meet the grief-stricken gaze of her last remaining aunt.

"I'll make him pay for this, Sher. I swear it."

Sheridan swallowed, her eyes red-rimmed but dry as she reached out and took Quinn's hand in hers. "I know you will, sweetheart. You're a Satori."

CHAPTER 7
FINLEY

Bits of ceiling rained down as Finley cradled his bloodied palm against his chest. As a large piece of debris crashed to the floor, he did his best to ignore the damage and focus instead on his task. He was so close to being able to get everyone safely away from here. Just one more sigil to go, and then he'd be able to open the portal to Novasgard. He'd worry about whether there'd be a penthouse—or priceless automobile collection—for him to return to later.

The arcane symbols, which activated the penthouse's main wards, were placed in areas throughout the house that corresponded with the four main elements. Having already dealt with Earth and Air, he mentally crossed Water off his list as he sprinted through the gym and out of his personal oasis. With only the Fire sigil remaining, he raced toward the living room as if the hounds of hell were nipping at his heels. Since he was pretty sure Mikel was as close to a real-life devil as he'd ever come, the comparison was an apt one.

Finley was more grateful than ever he'd had the foresight to develop emergency evacuation protocols. He just never expected to need to put them into action. He'd assumed, perhaps like an arrogant jackass, that the wards would continue to protect him as they always had. But then, that was before he'd gone and met a new breed of magic users who blew that belief right the fuck up. He hadn't known to ward against them because he hadn't known they existed. And even if he had, what good were magical barriers against reality shapers who were able to create or undo whatever they damn well pleased?

He still wasn't one hundred percent sure how he managed it, but Finley would bet everything he owned that Nico was responsible for today's breach. Not necessarily the plan itself, but the fact that it was even possible. However he'd done it, Finley knew the earthquake was only the beginning. If given the chance, far worse things would be coming their way—which is why he could not let that happen.

Thankfully, Quinn had given them the heads-up, so they weren't caught completely unaware. Now it was up to him to ensure that advantage didn't go to waste. The reminder spurred him on faster.

As he surged into the hallway, he made note of the sheer destruction of the place that had been his home and sanctuary for the last seven decades. The entire stretch between him and what had once been the foyer was smoking and in complete shambles. He winced, hoping his friends were in better shape.

Turning the other way, he spotted Mikel and Nico just ahead of him, looking a little worse for wear. The two buffoons they'd shown up with were nowhere to be found.

Good.

Spotting Nord on the opposite side of the two Animagi who'd yet to realize he was right there—and not wanting to give himself away—Finley sent the berserker a telepathic request for assistance.

"A little help, mate."

Nord's head swung around, his gaze landing first on Finley and then narrowing as he took in the Animagi sandwiched between them.

Blocked by the two men as he was, Finley couldn't quite make out what happened next, but from the look of it, Nord quickly dispatched the person he'd been fighting with a well-aimed blow to the face. Then, turning his full attention on Mikel and Nico, he let out a menacing snarl.

"Brute strength will only get you so far," Mikel said.

"Says the man who clearly lacks any," Nord replied as a phantom hand the size of a coffee table shimmered into existence directly above Mikel.

Before the Animagi even noticed it, Nord sent the hand straight down, slamming them both to the ground. The hand dissipated, leaving the hallway wide open for Finley, minus the two people-shaped speed bumps groaning on the floor. Knowing he had mere seconds before the men were back on their feet, he took off, hurdling over them and landing easily on the other side.

"Thanks," he panted at Nord, still in a dead run aimed straight toward the hearth. Though he faltered slightly when he saw the number of bodies on the floor and the dozen or so people still fighting around the living room.

"Anytime," Nord called after him, his attention still wholly trained on the men who'd already pushed themselves upright.

"Your parlor tricks will not save you," Nico spat.

"They seem to be working well enough," Nord said, sounding amused.

Finley glanced over his shoulder in time to see how much Nico didn't appreciate that. The younger man sneered, drawing on his own power to conjure a blade aimed straight at Nord's back.

"Behind you!" Finley shouted.

Without missing a beat, Nord dropped low, tackling Nico, who'd positioned himself protectively in front of a dour-looking Mikel. Without its target, the blade flew harmlessly through the air.

Looking back to find Finley still staring at them, Nord frowned. "Damn it, Fin. Don't worry about me. Get us the fuck out of here."

"I'm working on it!"

As he turned back toward the mantle, he saw Lina out of the corner of his eye, her blonde hair streaming behind her as she ran to join Nord. He spared only a second more to ascertain Quinn and her family were safe. When he realized the few intruders still standing were fighting each other instead of her, he allowed himself a small, proud smile. He should have known she'd have things well in hand.

Checking to make sure the wound on his hand hadn't closed, Finley dipped his fingers in the small pool of blood, then used his elbow to send the items lovingly displayed there crashing to the floor. He winced as a set of mother-of-pearl inlaid dueling pistols gifted to him by his grandfather clattered against the black marble. He forced himself not to look at the other items, not wanting to know what fate the irreplaceable heirlooms had met.

Top of the mantle now clear, Finley smeared the fingers dipped in blood across its surface, watching the once-invisible sigil flare an angry red before sizzling to a dull, ashy gray. As soon as the sigil snuffed out, electricity hung heavy in the room, reminding him of the way it feels just before a storm. One by one, the wards fell.

There were shouts behind him, along with the sounds of fighting, but Finley ignored all of it as he focused on his task. He knew he'd succeeded when that oppressive, electric air was sucked out of the room.

"No, you fool!" Mikel screamed. "We need her alive. Do what you want with the rest of them, but she's leaving here with us."

Finley didn't need to see what was going on behind him to know their time was up. The world around him transformed into a sea of hundreds of glittering threads as he dove deep into the well of his power. Creating portals was second nature to him, so it wasn't difficult to spot the thread he needed hidden within countless others. Gathering the mainstay, the name for threads that tethered specific locations—such as the penthouse—to their realm of origin, he used his magic to anchor it to Novasgard instead. And voilà, just like that, a portal came flickering to life beside him.

"To me!" Finley shouted, his eyes finding Quinn crouched over her aunt's still form in the center of the room. His heart twisted in his chest at the sight of her stricken expression.

At the sound of his voice, she wrapped her arm around her mother's waist as they both stood to obey. Her aunt Sheridan was slower to move, clearly loathing to leave her dead sister behind.

Quinn reached down and placed a hand on her aunt's shoulder, urging her up. With a final look, Sheridan brushed her fingers across Sylvia's face and then joined Quinn and Cora in their race toward Finley and the portal.

Before they reached him, Cora stopped, breaking free from Quinn's hold. Quinn turned to protest, but Cora waved her and Sheridan on. Curious as to why she stopped, Finley watched as Cora zoomed toward the discarded Codex, which had been lying forgotten on one of the sofas he'd pushed out of the way for their earlier summoning ritual.

Bloody hell.

If Mikel had any clue at all what had been sitting right in front of him, this whole thing might have gone far differently. Thank God for Cora.

Gathering it in her arms, she started running back, slowing only once more to swoop down and pick up Alistair's cane, which had fallen from its resting place against the chair Alistair had always preferred to use when visiting.

Both items in hand, Cora joined the other Satori, who were hovering anxiously at his side. Without a word, Cora jumped straight through the portal. Sheridan followed right on her heels. Quinn was next, giving him a fleeting look filled with meaning he didn't have time to decipher as she stepped through the shimmering veil.

"No!" Mikel shouted again. His face twisting with fury as he realized they were going to escape.

Nord and Lina had already started making their way toward the portal, using a combination of their magic to keep Nico and Mikel busy while the others snuck through.

Mikel's outrage seemed to revive a couple of Drakes, who had labored back to their feet. As one, they drew the wind in from the broken windows, using it to create huge gusts that threatened to knock Nord and Lina over as they struggled to move the rest of the way to the portal. With a mighty battle cry, Nord grabbed Lina's hand and leapt, pulling her with him through the air and straight through the portal.

As soon as they were clear, Finley pivoted, diving in after them. The sound of Mikel's angry roar was uncomfortably close as it chased him. Not waiting until he landed on the other side, Finley smudged out the thread linking the two realms, thereby closing the portal before Mikel could follow.

While the move was near seamless, it wasn't quite fast enough. Mikel might not have made it, but one of his huge fireballs did. Finley gritted his teeth, attempting to swallow his bellow of pain as the smoldering orb collided with his backside, the flames burning through his clothes and searing the skin beneath.

The shock of being hit caused him to stumble, and he arrived on the other side of the portal on his hands and knees while the others stood around him and gaped.

Hands on her hips and eyebrows raised in surprise, Astrid stared down at him. "Welcome back."

CHAPTER 8
NORD

"This is more embarrassing than getting shot," Finley groaned as Lina lightly pressed her hands to his burnt flesh.

"Stop being a baby and let me fix it," Lina gently chided.

"Easy for you to say, love. It's not your bare arse exposed for your future in-laws to see."

Despite the grief still heavy in her eyes, Cora pressed her lips together to hide her amusement.

Quinn raised a brow. "Now, now, you know as well as I do Astrid isn't your future in-law. Your bromance with the berserker may be legendary, but he's off the market. And last I checked, it was Lina wearing Nord's pretty ring, not you."

Finley glowered up at her, a hiss of pain escaping as Lina shifted, causing her to bump his charred skin.

"Sorry," she said, hands starting to glow as she got to work healing his burn.

"Be a good boy, Batman, or I won't kiss it and make it better."

Nord smothered a smile as Finley shot a grumpy look Quinn's way.

"Why should I believe you? You're always making promises you fail to keep."

Cora laughed outright at this, causing both Quinn and Sheridan to glance at her. Sheridan looked confused, but Quinn shook her head. "Don't listen to him, Mama. He's delirious with pain." Then she crouched down beside Finley, lowering her voice as she pressed her lips against his ear and whispered something that made his jaw go lax. Quinn leaned back and studied his expression with a smirk.

"There you go, Lady B. He should be a picture-perfect patient for you now."

Lina smiled distractedly but continued to focus on her healing.

Astrid nudged Nord with her elbow, keeping her voice low as she asked, "Are they always like this?"

"Always."

She straightened. "Well, this has been highly entertaining, as usual. But what was she saying about a ring? Though, perhaps it would be best if you started by explaining why your friend just took a fireball to the ass."

Nord glanced at his cousin. "A lot has transpired since we were here last."

"I see that. Come. Let's go for a walk, and you can fill me in."

Nord hesitated, not quite ready to let Lina and the others out of his sight just yet.

Astrid placed a hand on his forearm, easily guessing the source of his discomfort. "They'll be fine. I've already called for Søren and Strega. They'll get everyone settled and make sure they're well looked after until we return."

He knew then it wasn't so much an invitation as an order. One he couldn't refuse, at that. Which, fair enough. He'd damn near brought a battle straight into the heart of her peaceful realm. The least he could do was bring her up to speed.

Lina looked back at him, likely in response to the twinge of his emotions reverberating through her. "Go. I've got this handled."

He took a few steps forward, leaning down to feather a kiss to the crown of her head. "You always do, Kærasta."

She blushed. "Well, I don't know about that. But healing, at least, comes naturally. And this is far from the worst thing we've had to fix recently."

"Says the woman with the unmarred buttocks," Finley grumbled.

Lina pinched him. "Hush, you. Yours has already been restored to its previous, superhero-worthy status."

Finley craned his neck around to glare at her. "Well, you could have said something. You just left me here with my dignity flapping in the breeze."

"Come off it, Fin," Quinn said, crossing her arms and giving him a thoroughly put-out look. "Everybody knows you don't have any."

"Have any what?"

"Dignity."

"Are you really going to allow her to speak to me this way after what I just endured saving our lives?" Finley asked Lina.

Lina tipped her head. "*She* is a grown woman and can speak to you however she wants. Furthermore, she just lost her aunt while also saving our lives, and taking shots at you is her favorite coping method. So yeah, I'm definitely going to allow it because anything that makes her feel better right now is A-okay with me."

Quinn blew Lina a kiss, but she was still in the midst of a full-blown rant and didn't notice.

"But if *you* have a problem with it, maybe you should man up and do something about it your damn self. Same with your pants. You keep claiming to be the master outfitter, so have at it, Mr. McQueen." She gave him a light tap on the ass and stood, turning to face Nord. "See, handled. We're all set."

He cast his eyes over their group, cataloging expressions that ranged from stunned silence to outright awe.

"Impressive," he said with a laugh. "You've rendered them speechless."

"I have a lifetime of experience putting men in their place."

"It shows." He ran his knuckles down her cheek and gave her a quick kiss, reluctantly pulling back and telegraphing with his eyes everything he couldn't say in front of the others. "I'll be back soon."

"Good, or I might have to find myself another handsome Viking to keep me company in your absence," she teased as the ever-broody Søren and his familiar came into view.

Nord gave her hair a light tug, making her eyes deepen to a brilliant cerulean. "Careful, Lina. Don't forget whose ring you're wearing."

She shivered at the primal growl that ran beneath his warning. Licking her lips, she said, "You have nothing to worry about. I'm not even his type."

"Tease me all you like, Kærasta. But you and I both know what would happen to any man who dared try to take what belongs to me, even in jest. Berserkers aren't known for their cool heads or their senses of humor."

Her eyes turned hazy with desire, and her cheeks flushed a rosy pink. "No, they are not." With a cheeky grin and a lift of her brows, she added, "Praise Odin."

Nord shook his head but gave her another soft smile before turning and following his cousin out of her house and away from his friends' bickering. From the outside, you'd never guess they'd just been balls-deep in battle a handful of minutes prior. But since that also seemed to be a regular occurrence these days, he understood why moments of levity were essential. They needed the reminder that there was more to life than war. More importantly, they needed to remember who and what they were fighting for.

As he and Astrid walked deeper into her garden overlooking the bay, and consequently further from Lina, his good humor plummeted. Those moments of light-hearted fun were easier to hold on to when he had her at his side. But without her sunny presence to bolster him, reality had an insidious way of sneaking back up.

"Were there casualties?" Astrid asked once they were well away, her voice gentle despite the probing nature of the question.

"One."

"My condolences, cousin."

"Thank you. I didn't know Sylvia well, but every loss cuts deep in battles such as these. Especially when your numbers are few to begin with."

"How well I know it. Has the impending war you spoke of last time finally found you?"

Nord nodded. "We've managed to deal with two of our enemies, but this last one is proving a more challenging foe than we initially anticipated."

She shot him a curious look. "How so?"

He blew out a breath. It was a loaded question, and one he wasn't entirely sure he had an exact answer for.

"Mikel Drake is . . ."

There were far too many ends to that sentence. Clever, manipulative, diabolical, to name a few.

The uncomfortable truth was Mikel outplayed them at almost every turn. Sure, they'd escaped today. But if Quinn hadn't reached them first, they may not have had the opportunity to do so. And he'd proven time and time again with Lina's trial, Nord's capture, and Cora's punishment, that he was always one, if not several, steps ahead of them. Even when he'd seemingly lost, he had plans in place to reestablish his control of the situation. As if the outcome had been a foregone conclusion, and they were all merely walking down a predetermined path he'd laid out for them.

He'd had too long, and far too many allies, to aid his scheming. They needed to start thinking like Mikel and planning their attack on a larger, more unpredictable scale. Otherwise, there was no hope of ever truly defeating him.

"Yes?" Astrid prompted when he still hadn't finished his sentence.

Still unsure how best to express the full extent of the problem they faced. Nord tried a different tactic.

"Do you know the stories of the Halfdan?"

She gave him a startled, stricken look, though she was quick to suppress it. Nord couldn't fault her for her shock. It was well known that he never, not once, uttered the name of the man who'd slaughtered his family. To bring him up now, in conjunction with an enemy they were currently facing, expressed more than Nord could ever adequately verbalize. A fact Astrid clearly picked up on.

"Of course I know the stories surrounding that madman's reign of terror. Why do you ask?"

"Halfdan is a mewling babe compared to Mikel Drake. I've come across my fair share of power-crazed, ruthless men, but he's something else. A creature with the ability to incite fear as easily as trust and a heart so black I doubt there's any act too depraved to commit if it would ensure his victory. To speak plainly, I don't think I've ever met his like, and it troubles me because it means I cannot predict his next move."

Astrid was silent for a long time, her gaze trained on the glittering horizon before finally asking, "Can you beat him?"

Nord's hands clenched uselessly at his sides. It pained him to admit the truth, but any fight with Mikel would not be one-on-one. While incredibly powerful in his own right, he enjoyed hiding behind his minions far too much to ever risk a solo battle. And they simply did not have the numbers to deal with his army.

"Not alone."

"Which is why you are here."

There was no judgment in her observation. It was a mere statement of fact, and yet Nord still felt guilty for putting her in the position of having to decide whether she would place the citizens of Novasgard in harm's way.

"In part," he said with a heavy sigh. "We were in a precarious situation, and our sole means of retreat led us here. Without a way to portal or any knowledge of this realm, Mikel has no way of following us, making Novasgard the only safe option. Tonight's attack also emphasized just how much we've underestimated the power he wields. We should have been safe at the penthouse, but he shattered that illusion easily enough." Nord let out a bitter laugh. "I'm willing to bet he barely scratched the surface of his power in dealing with us. Mikel is the kind of man who only dirties his hands to send a message. He relies on others for matters he considers beneath his personal attention."

"And yet, he made a point to personally participate today. Given your assessment, that suggests he considers you and your party a great risk indeed."

"True. Though he'd be a fool not to after seeing what Lina can do. I think he considers it a grievous insult that there might be someone in existence more powerful than him."

"She's a threat to his reign."

Nord nodded. "And she's openly defied him."

"For that alone, he'll not stop until he's destroyed her."

"I know," Nord said, his low, angry voice betraying his simmering rage. Astrid had only given voice to what he'd always known, and yet hearing the words aloud had his berserker desperate to break free.

Astrid was quiet for so long Nord grew restless beside her. He could not beat Mikel without her and the aid of the rest of Novasgard, but he would not beg. It had to be her choice. Too many innocent lives were at stake. He forced himself to take a deep breath.

"I understand if you are unwilling to risk your people's lives to fight at our side," he said, already resolved to find another way.

It would not be easy, but they had other allies. None as well-versed in warfare as the Novasgardians, true, but allies nonetheless. Even if Astrid refused them, he would not give up. Not until Mikel was nothing more than a pile of smoldering ash carried away by the breeze.

He was so certain she'd refuse him, he didn't dare believe he'd heard her correctly when she said, "Novasgard stands with you."

"Come again?" he said, his head snapping around to look at her.

Astrid's expression was stoic as always, her shoulders straight and proud, her hands clasped behind her back. She looked so much like his grandmother he couldn't help but stare, even with her hair cropped short instead of hanging down her back in braids. Her eyes were the same color as the water below when she finally met his gaze.

"A monster such as you described should not be left alive, no matter which realm they walk."

Hope made his chest painfully tight. "But last time you said—"

Astrid lifted a hand. "I know what I said. And I spoke the truth. I will not put my people's lives at risk for someone who was not clan." Her fierce expression softened as she took in the arrested expression on his face. "Yes, Gunnar Bloodaxe, although you no longer use that name, you are still clan. You defeated the wyvern and were presented with its spoils at our feast where we toasted your homecoming, so why does this come as a surprise to you?" she asked, tilting her head.

Throat thick with emotion, Nord admitted, "It's just been a long time since anyone from my homeland referred to me as such. I had not thought to ever hear it again. Or how much it would mean when I did."

Astrid's lips quirked up, and she rested her hand lightly on his arm as she said, "You are the Allfather's chosen, and already one of us by blood. It is a little matter to rejoin us by choice. Say the word, and it is done."

It was tempting, but he didn't want her to help out of a sense of familial obligation. He had to be sure she knew what she was signing up for.

"And if I told you Mikel was Lina's enemy, and not mine?"

Astrid gave him a shrewd look. "She wears your ring."

"She does."

"Then any enemy of hers is yours as well."

That had been the case long before he asked Lina to be his wife, but it did not change the truth of Astrid's statement.

"I'll tell you what," she said, linking her arm in his.

Nord had been around Lina and Quinn far too long to not recognize that overly agreeable tone. Astrid was up to something.

"If you're that worried about us willingly fighting alongside you, let me put your mind at ease. No one will set foot on a battlefield unless it is by their choice. And to reassure them that they fight for clan, you and Lina will indulge me and speak your wedding vows here, honoring the old ways."

"You think they'll agree to go to war if they see us get married?" he asked, disbelief heavy in his voice.

Astrid raised a brow. "Why not? What better way to show the people you and Lina are clan in more than just name? Besides, all battles deserve to be preceded by glorious celebration."

"Is that really the only reason?"

She shrugged. "Well, we need time to prepare for war anyway. And it will be at least three days before everyone can return to town to attend an official war council. So, what better way to pass the time? Besides, who knows what fate we'll meet in the days to come. This might be your last chance."

The woman made a hell of a point.

"Why?" she asked, peering up at him. "Do you have cold feet?"

"No," Nord said, a genuine smile stretching across his face. "No two people could belong to each other more completely than Lina and me, marriage vows or no. It's just when I'd asked her to be my wife, I told her I wanted to make my promises in front of the people who mattered most to us. You unknowingly made my wish come true with your offer."

It seemed that, for once, things were falling perfectly into place. The realist in him questioned it. Experience had warned him not to fall for anything too good to be true, but Astrid was right. They were heading into war. If these were to be their final days of safety and freedom, what better way to spend them than surrounded by family and friends? For once, he was simply going to allow himself to sit back and enjoy what fortune had so kindly offered.

Astrid beamed at him, giving his hand a little nudge with hers. "Well, that settles it. We cannot deny a union clearly blessed by the gods. I'll take care of everything."

"Should I be afraid?"

"Probably. But I promise you, Lina will love it."

"That's all that matters."

"Smart man. I see she's trained you well." Astrid laughed, giving Nord's arm an affectionate squeeze before pulling him along and resuming their walk around her garden. "Now, tell me what else I missed since I saw you last, cousin-mine."

CHAPTER 9
LINA

"How's Sheridan holding up?" Lina asked, looking up from the Codex lying open in her lap as Cora breezed through the front door.

She sighed, crossing the room to sit down beside her daughter on the sofa. "As well as can be expected. Sher's still a little confused about where we are exactly, but also not really in a state of mind to care so long as we are safe for the time being."

Lina didn't blame her. Safety was a novel concept lately. Personally, she'd have been happy anywhere that provided an actual reprieve from Mikel and his twisted games. Finding sanctuary in a picturesque city by the sea, while surrounded by nothing but friendly faces, was like winning the jackpot.

And winning anything right now felt pretty damn good. So good, in fact, Lina had nearly burst into tears when Strega had arrived to escort them to their lodgings.

"Did you miss me that much?" she'd laughed, giving Lina an awkward pat on the back in response to her overly enthusiastic bear hug.

"It's just really good to see you again. Allies are a rare commodity these days."

"So I gathered."

After taking one look at the rather haggard appearance of their unexpected guests, Strega had sent Søren off to round up something for them to eat while she ushered them into their rooms so they could clean themselves up and rest before dinner. They were staying in the same building as before, though this time they'd been given two rooms across the hall from each other due to their larger party size. The Satori women were rooming together, while Nord, Lina, and Fin were in their original suite.

In news that surprised no one, the Guardian was beside himself at having not only a bed, but an entire bedroom to himself. "Things are finally coming up, Finley," he'd said before sauntering off to take a shower and 'mourn the loss of his beautiful babies in private.'

Lina had tried to reassure him that they didn't know what state the lower half of the building would be in once they returned home, but Finley wasn't holding out much hope it would still be standing, let alone filled with his priceless automobiles. Side note, if you ever want to see a grown man cry, try pointing out to an avid, dare she say obsessive, collector that he could always start over. Lina was still cringing from the memory of the aghast, somewhat nauseated look her comment had brought to Finley's face.

At least she still had her promise to make good on. Maybe he'd feel differently once things calmed down and she finally found the time to present him with a few of the items on his wish list.

"And how about you? Feeling any better?" Quinn asked her mother, bringing Lina back to the present and the women sitting across from her in the chic living room.

Cora let out a humorless laugh. "Even though I'd warned my sisters what to expect, it still came as a shock. No matter how old I get, I never get used to losing someone I love. But my little sister wasn't one for wallowing. She'd absolutely detest the idea of us sitting around crying over her passing. I'm doing my best to honor her memory by conducting myself in a manner she'd appreciate." A wan smile ghosted Cora's lips as she smoothed down her pristine dove-gray pencil skirt. Since her clothes had been notably bloodstained the last time Lina saw her, she could only assume Cora had made good use of the Novasgardians' hospitality via their magically stocked closet. "Though truth be told, it feels like the only thing holding me together right now is sheer force of will."

Lina's heart gave a sympathetic squeeze. She knew exactly what Cora meant. She didn't think she'd ever truly get over the loss of her uncle. "No one would guess it, looking at you," she said, giving Cora a reassuring smile. "You appear as stunningly put together as always.

"Never underestimate the restorative powers of a hot bath and a new outfit," Cora said, demurely patting her elegant chignon. Then she winked and added with patented Satori sass, "Or a fifth of whisky."

"Mom," Quinn said, huffing out a laugh. "You're incorrigible."

"Don't act like you aren't, mon coeur. I raised you, remember?"

"Yes, and I've barely recovered."

The three women laughed, and more of the tension from the day's events ebbed away. Mikel's attack and Sylvia's loss still hung over them, but in this moment, it was more of a light haze than an oppressive fog. There was no forgetting what had happened, but they were shielded from him here, and that protective shroud went a long way warding against any lingering fear.

As their laughter subsided, the soft pad of footsteps announced Finley's approach. He stepped into the suite's main room dressed only in a pair of low-slung sweatpants with a towel draped across his shoulders.

Lina couldn't help a small, knowing smile at the sight of him. Unless he was working out, he never dressed so casually. To do so now was a definite statement. And the appearance of sheer, unadul-terated lust currently suspended on Quinn's face was absolutely the reason why. Lina had to give it to him; the man knew what he was doing. Looks like the gloves were finally coming off.

It's about fucking time.

Idly, she wondered who would be the first to surrender in this little sexual standoff of theirs. Usually, she'd never bet against the unfailingly bull-headed Quinn, but the cracks in her bestie's armor were starting to show. Stubborn or not, she might not have the strength to resist what she so clearly wanted for much longer.

Cora not so discreetly nudged her daughter with an elbow and then exchanged an amused glance with Lina as Quinn cleared her throat and tried to look anywhere but the still dripping Fin. Taking pity on her, Lina drew the others' attention back her way.

"Thanks again for grabbing these," she said, lightly drumming the fingers of one hand over the Codex while resting her other one on top of her uncle's cane. "I don't know what I would have done if I lost either of them."

"Of course. When I saw the doorway of light and shadow, I had a feeling you'd be needing them."

Lina went still at the reference to Cora's warning from the day before. "But I thought the doorway referred to the one we needed to summon Crombie back from Faerie? I mean, that's how I found the spell in the first place."

Cora lifted a shoulder. "Sometimes my 'feelings' refer to multiple things. If you can be happy or sad for more than one reason, why shouldn't my feelings be attributed to multiple sources?"

"But they always seem so specific."

"They certainly can be," she agreed, "but not always. In matters of destiny, things are rarely cut and dry. So many possible futures hang in the balance, little more than wisps of potential until our choices determine which ones solidify and which ones fade away. Who's to say the doorway in question couldn't have been something else entirely had you not chosen to search the Codex for your answers? We can never know for sure."

"But . . . I . . ." Lina ultimately closed her mouth and shook her head. "Sometimes talking with you and your daughter makes my brain feel like a pretzel."

"Welcome to my world," Finley muttered, sitting on the arm of Lina's chair and rubbing the end of his towel over his damp hair. "Speaking of the puzzling ways of the Satori," he said, leveling his gaze on Quinn, "now would be an excellent time for you to tell us what the hell happened after you left this morning."

She bit down on her bottom lip, looking guilty.

Lina knew Quinn far too well to ever doubt her or her intentions, but she'd be lying if she said her friend's obvious reluctance didn't put her on edge.

Cora patted her daughter's knee. "There's no need to beat yourself up. They'll understand once you explain. And Lina especially has a right to know. She's at the heart of it, after all."

Well, that was nothing new, but Lina's palms slickened with sweat and her stomach started doing barrel rolls anyway.

"I know," Quinn said with a heavy sigh as she turned her wine-colored gaze Lina's way. "I wasn't completely honest with you."

"What do you mean? When?"

"I may have, sort of, definitely glossed over what Mikel asked of me. Well, that's putting it lightly; you know how he is—"

"Quinn," Lina huffed in exasperation.

"Calm your tits. I'm getting to it. Basically, Mikel gave me an assignment, and I didn't let you in on what my intentions were regarding it, knowing you weren't going to like anything about my plan."

Lina set the Codex on the table in front of her so she could rest her elbows on her knees. "Since when do we go off making plans without clueing each other in?"

"I know, I know, but you can spare me the lecture. I didn't have a choice. There wasn't time to breathe, let alone phone a friend. And I couldn't show any sign of hesitation, or he would have been onto me. So when Mikel demanded I bring him your Codex, I agreed."

"But you clearly didn't give it to him, so what exactly did you do?" Lina asked.

"I wanted to make him believe I obeyed and buy us time."

Lina nodded. It was the exact sort of thing she would have done had their positions been reversed.

"And it was working . . . for a while. Things fell apart when Mikel realized I'd played him. Not only did I hand over a false Codex, I didn't wipe your memories either. Or do anything else he'd ordered me to, for that matter."

"How'd he figure it out?"

"Well, it wasn't like I stuck around to get a front-row seat. I handed over my fake and got the fuck out of there. But suffice it to say, he was beyond pissed I'd managed to dupe him at all. I mean, you saw what he did to Sylvia when he got his hands on her. Those aren't the actions of a sane, rational fellow."

"Okay, fair enough. But your plan hinged on your ability to undermine and lie to him. How did you think things were going to end?"

"Well, my plan was a bit more sophisticated than that, and I only did it to buy us time not to permanently deceive him, but okay, I see where you're going."

"And, to be fair, it wasn't just Quinn who lied to him. It was all of us."

Lina and Finley's heads snapped to Cora.

"What do you mean?" he demanded.

Quinn sighed. "In order to make Mikel successfully believe I obeyed, I needed access to memories."

"I don't understand," Finley said.

"Me either," said Lina. "What do memories have to do with the Codex?"

"See, he didn't just want the book. He wanted me to hand over all your memories regarding it. Everything Alistair had taught you. Any notes you had in your possession regarding its secrets. All the things I was supposed to have taken from you when I wiped your memory.

He basically wanted me to provide him with a cheat sheet of all things Codex so he'd get a head start cracking it."

"Which is where Sylvia and Sheridan came in—and why he was so irate with them," Cora added.

"Poor Sylvia. She didn't deserve to die like that."

Cora reached out and rested her hand over her daughter's. "No, she didn't. But we knew what we were up against when we started down this road. The weight of her death does not belong on your shoulders."

Quinn took a shuddering breath, visibly pulling herself back together. "No, that honor is all his. And I'm *so* looking forward to reminding him of it when I turn his brain into my personal playground."

A savage smile lifted the corners of Quinn's lips, and Lina found herself mirroring it with one of her own. Nord's berserker ways were really starting to rub off on them. He'd be ecstatic when she told him.

Surprised Finley had nothing to say about it, Lina glanced up at him. His brows were furrowed, and his eyes were trained on Cora but not really looking *at* her. He seemed deep in thought, as if trying to work out a puzzle.

"You okay?" she asked, pitching her voice low so as not to startle him.

He blinked. "Hmm? Oh, yeah. Fine. Just trying to recall if I'd ever learned what the twin's gifts were so I could understand how they fit into all of this."

"They can record and preserve memories, allowing them to be viewed by others," Lina explained.

"And with Quinn's ability to modify, as well as remove or implant them, my sisters were able to produce an entire library of false memories for her to hand over to Mikel," Cora added.

"Well, that was the plan," Quinn said.

"It didn't work?" Finley asked.

"Oh, we were able to falsify them, and it wasn't all that hard to come up with something to stand in as the Codex."

"So what went wrong?" Lina asked.

"I don't know," Quinn said, looking truly lost. "It should have worked. I have no idea how he could tell the memories were counterfeit. And if he's never seen a Codex, he shouldn't have been able to tell it was bogus either." She blew out a frustrated breath. "At least not that fast."

"It's okay. It's not your fault. Everybody knows about the Drakes and their luck. His gift must have tipped him off," Lina said.

"Or someone else's did."

Lina looked up at Finley. "What do you mean?"

"You guys have mentioned the Drakes have uncanny luck. Is it possible someone in Mikel's inner circle can detect duplicity or sense residual magic?"

"Like a lie detector?" she asked.

"Yes, or like how Guardians can use their power to find magical traces and see through illusions," Finley said.

Lina glanced at Cora. As the one who'd worked alongside Mikel on the Council, she'd be the one who would know.

"It's possible, but it wouldn't be a Drake ability," Cora said slowly, her eyes far-off as her mind worked overtime trying to figure out who might have such a gift. "But it sounds like something that belongs to the Alinari. Their line has always been known for their incredible senses. We've always just assumed they were our fighters because they were physically stronger than most of us, but it seems plausible someone among them could see magic or detect lies. I mean, we've used them as our interrogators and guards for centuries, and a gift such as that would be invaluable to them."

"Do you think it might be one of Emerson's gifts?" Quinn asked.

Finley straightened. "Isn't that the Alinari heir?"

Quinn nodded. "I mean, it makes sense, right? All the heirs in our ascendency have inherited rare and powerful Animagi gifts that haven't been seen in ages. If such an ability did appear, it makes sense he'd be the one to possess it."

"Yes, but isn't Emerson still in hiding?" Lina asked.

Cora shrugged. "I'd assumed so. But maybe that's what Mikel and Kristoff wanted us to think."

"Seems like a dangerous person to keep around with all the lies Mikel's spewing," Quinn said, crossing her arms. "Perhaps he's not in hiding so much as locked away to keep him from accidentally blabbing about what he knows."

The comment was offhanded, a throwaway, but something about it gnawed at Lina. As a possibility took root, her blood turned to ice. "Maybe that's the real reason Kristoff is so far up Mikel's ass. He's not loyal because he agrees with him. He's protecting his son."

"You're saying the father toes the line in the hope that his son, though imprisoned, remains unharmed," Finley said with a slow nod.

"And the son does the same, knowing if he acts out, it's his father who will pay the price," Lina continued.

"Mikel does love to use our relationships against us," Quinn said bitterly.

A vein throbbed in Cora's temple, her eyes flashing with remembered pain. "Emotional blackmail has always been his favorite. What better strings for a puppeteer to pull than those of the heart?"

"What a fucking monster," Quinn spat, her lip curling in disgust. "He needs to die, Lina. I mean it." She gripped her mother's hand, both of their knuckles turning white as they clung to one another. Then, in a voice trembling with emotion, she continued, "We cannot let this psychopath destroy any more families."

"We won't," Lina assured her, though she still didn't have the foggiest clue how. But she'd figure it out. She had to.

The alternative was a world with Mikel at the helm, and that wouldn't be any world worth living in. It'd be hell on fucking earth.

Mikel Drake was the true harbinger of the apocalypse. Screw the four horsemen and their mighty steeds. Unless they found a way to stop him, Armageddon would be ushered in by a dragon.

And by the time he was done, there'd be nothing left to rise from the ashes.

CHAPTER 10
LINA

The thought of that future—of any future—with Mikel in power had Lina's berserker shrieking in fury. For a second, she was lost to the frenzy, her rage so intense she couldn't quite draw a breath through the whirling ball of emotion building in her chest. Spots danced in her eyes as she struggled to breathe.

"Lina?" Quinn asked, sounding worried.

But even if she wanted to explain what was happening, Lina couldn't form an answer. She was gasping now, her mouth tasting of ash as her lungs began to seize.

In response to her panic, or perhaps in an attempt to save her, her magic surged. The space around her crackled with energy as Lina's berserker tried to break free while her Animagi's power fought to shove it back down. It was an odd, entirely autonomic battle of wills as the two halves of her nature fought for dominance.

"Lina!" Quinn shouted, jumping to her feet.

As her magic continued to build and her berserker refused to retreat, her skin prickled, the pins-and-needles sensation so intense it bordered on painful. There simply wasn't enough room within her body to contain the opposing magical forces. It was as if she was being stretched from within like a balloon on the cusp of being over-filled. If one of them didn't back down—now—Lina feared she might explode.

"Stay back," Finley called out. "She's surging."

But then he ignored his own advice and reached out for her.

"What are you doing?" Quinn asked, her voice high and strained. "You just told us to stay back."

"I think I can help her," he murmured, his eyes blazing silver as his hand just grazed her shoulder.

It was too much.

Everything was too much.

The air rent in two, and Lina let out an inadvertent scream as her power swelled and finally tipped the balance. Her berserker ceded control, and without anything to resist it, her magic slipped free. With nothing to give it shape, it burst from her as a pure bolt of wild energy flying straight at Quinn and Cora. The women dove for the ground as her power slammed into the abstract painting right behind them.

Finley was also tossed back by the mini shock wave, along with the Codex and two small pillows resting beside her.

As one, Cora, Quinn, and Finley pushed off of the floor, glancing first at the smoking crater in the wall and then back up at her.

"What the hell just happened?" Quinn asked.

"Are you all right?" Cora asked in a softer, albeit no less intense, manner than her daughter.

Quinn blew out a breath as she helped her mother stand. "Yeah, that too."

Lina sagged against her chair, still trembling from the unexpected surge. "I think so?"

"What set you off?" Finley asked, handing her the Codex.

She accepted it with a soft thank-you and shook her head. "I'm not entirely sure. I was just so pissed about Mikel, and I think I tripped my bloodlust. It happened so fast, I just wasn't prepared, and I guess my magic was trying to help me regain control? It was . . . intense."

"It was something," Quinn murmured, hitching a finger toward the hole just behind her head. "You going to do something about that?"

Lina winced, looking at the charred remains of the painting. "I probably should. Do you think it's safe to try using my magic so soon after a surge?" she asked Finley.

"Since it was a response to your emotions, as long as you feel in control, I don't see why not."

Lina wasn't sure 'in control' was how she'd categorize herself, more like shaken and emotionally drained, but it was probably as close as she was going to get.

"Guess it'll be a good test, huh?" she said, feeling more cautious than usual when she reached out for her power. She let out an internal sigh of relief when it responded immediately, reminding her of an affectionate cat as it brushed against her senses and began bending to her will.

When she opened her eyes, the hole was gone and the painting restored, though she'd taken some liberties with its design since she couldn't recall what it looked like before. Hopefully, no one noticed.

"Nice work," Quinn said, giving the picture a once-over before settling back in her seat.

"I wish dealing with Mikel was that simple," Lina said with a heavy sigh. "Do you think I could turn him into a piece of art?"

Quinn shuddered. "Who the hell would want his scary ass hanging on their wall?"

"You might be surprised," Finley said. "People collect all sorts of obscure items. There are entire museums dedicated to serial killers and ancient torture methods. I'm sure he'd fit in at a place like that."

"Yeah, but he'd be one of those paintings where the eyes follow you around wherever you go. Until eventually, he'd find a way to possess his owners and make them do despicable things and start his cycle of torment all over again. Hard pass."

"No one said anything about displaying it. My vote is to lock it away in some hidden vault and then throw away the key. Or burn it! You know, purify his soul through fire, or something like that," Lina said, getting into the idea.

"Or if you turned him to stone, we could toss him off the roof and watch him shatter," Cora said, joining in on their wishful thinking.

"God, if only beating him was that easy." Lina's smile dimmed at the edges, and her mood plummeted as the reality of what they were up against came crashing back down. "Seriously, guys. What the hell are we going to do? I mean, we got lucky today, but we were only dealing with a fraction of his forces. Did you notice that even the Thortons were fighting for him? I thought Natalia, at least, would side with us."

"If he's not above manipulating his closest friend, I don't see why he wouldn't stoop to something equally awful to persuade her," Quinn said.

Cora nodded, adding, "And Nico's already made it clear that when called upon, the Cuskas will fight at his side."

"Great, and that leaves who exactly to stand against him?" Lina asked.

"The people in this room," Finley answered.

"And the rest of the Satori, though our numbers are few," Cora added.

"We're yours until the bitter, bloody end," Quinn said.

Lina offered them a fleeting smile she knew didn't reach her eyes. "I appreciate that more than you'll ever know, but it's not going to be enough. It would be a different story if we were at least fighting with fair numbers, but not even our combined power will be enough to stop him—not without serious help. The next time Mikel comes for us, he's not going to hold anything back. Especially not after today. I don't think we're going to get away with only one casualty next time."

Cora's expression was grim as she nodded. "I have a feeling you might be right."

Lina felt the color drain from her face. It was one thing to say the words, but having them confirmed by Cora was far worse. They'd lost too many people already—friends and allies they couldn't begin to replace. She didn't think her heart could stand to lose anyone else, not without breaking completely. And if that happened, no Animagi magic, or any amount of king's men, would ever be able to put it back together again.

"Doesn't your fancy book have something in it we can use?" Quinn asked, gesturing toward the Codex she still held.

"How the hell should I know? I've barely made a dent in the translations, even with Alistair's notes. It's like this thing is encrypted on top of being written in a different language. I need a damn cipher."

Finley gave her an odd look at that. "Lina, have you ever tried telling it to translate itself?"

She raised a brow and barked out a little laugh. "It's not a computer, Fin. I can't just press a button and expect it to print out a perfect translation."

"No, but you could use your magic. And, you know"—he wiggled his fingers—"will it to translate."

"You think I can actually use my power to turn the words in this book into their English equivalents?"

He gave her an eager nod. "I don't see why not. I mean, you basically played a game of magical hide and seek with it once before by making it reappear after Alistair hid it. It stands to reason you'd be able to make it do other things."

"Finley, that's a brilliant suggestion," Cora said, sounding excited. "Our Codexes are infused with our ancestor's magic, each one unique because of our family's varying gifts. Of course the books will respond to our use of it. You should try it, Lina. Especially since the nature of your gift is manifesting change."

Finley sat up straighter at Cora's praise, giving Quinn a smug smile. "You hear that? Your mum thinks I'm brilliant."

"Only because she doesn't know you better. Don't worry, Batman. You'll disappoint her soon enough."

Finley raised a brow. "Just wait, Satori. Mums love me. Given enough time, yours will too."

"Who says she doesn't already?" Cora asked with a cheeky smile.

"Traitor," Quinn muttered.

"What? It's not like I said I loved him more than you. But it's hard not to be impressed by a man who has made a habit out of saving my daughter's life, despite her every effort to send him running in the opposite direction."

Finley winked at Cora. "I don't scare easy."

"Good, because you'll certainly have your hands full with this one," she said, tipping her head in Quinn's direction. "I should probably apologize for that, by the way. I'm sure I'm at least partially at fault for it."

"Partially?" Quinn said, sounding sullen.

"No need to apologize. You raised an incredible woman, one who deserves to be properly wooed and fought for. It's her way of weeding out the unworthy. I appreciate that and find myself more than up to the challenge of winning her over."

The words were for Cora, who was absolutely beaming, but he delivered them while looking straight at Quinn.

"Is that what you're doing?" Quinn drawled, her flushed cheeks completely undermining her unaffected tone.

Finley gave her a wolfish grin. "Is it working?"

"Shut up," she growled, looking flustered as she tucked some of her hair behind her ear and shifted so she was looking directly at Lina.

"That's a yes," Finley stage whispered to Cora, who nodded her agreement.

"Keep it up," she whispered back encouragingly.

Quinn loudly cleared her throat. "Aren't you supposed to be

doing something to help us rid the world of a madman?" she accused, ignoring the others and giving Lina a pointed stare.

Lina glanced around. "Um, yes?"

"Well, get on with it."

Trying not to laugh at Quinn's transparent attempt to change the subject, Lina flipped the Codex open to a random page. She took a deep breath, trying to center herself and feeling like there was absolutely no way this was going to work. Still, she couldn't deny there was more than a little bit of hope present as well.

"Here goes nothing," she said.

Quinn raised both her hands and crossed her fingers in a sign of solidarity.

Summoning her power, Lina willed the letters on the pages of the heavy tome to rearrange themselves into words she could read, but without them losing their original meaning.

It was a different way of using her power. Usually, she focused on specific, tangible things she wanted to happen. But ever since the Transference, she'd found she could mold her magic in a more abstract way. Which was a blessing, honestly, because for what she was attempting to work, she couldn't imagine something specific.

For a few reasons.

One, she didn't know what more than half of the Codex actually said—if she did, she wouldn't be doing this in the first place. And two, any words she might imagine could inadvertently be the ones she transcribed onto the pages, leaving her with a book filled with nonsense.

So instead, she focused on her intent rather than the final physical product.

In a matter of seconds, power poured from her hands, making them tingle as it moved through her and settled into the book in her lap. Lina waited several heartbeats before looking down, too afraid of what she might find. Taking a deep, steadying breath, she finally dropped her gaze, her eyes skimming a few lines before a smile stretched across her face and she finally allowed herself to believe what was literally in front of her.

"Holy shit. It worked."

The voices around her faded away as Lina became absorbed by the newly translated words. Thankfully, her friends were understanding enough not to mind her essentially ditching them mid-conversation, keeping each other company while her eyes greedily consumed page after page.

There was just so much here. Too much, realistically, for her to read it all in one sitting. That didn't stop her from trying, though. Not with a treasure trove of ancient arcane information at her fingertips.

She flipped through the history section, planning on coming back to it after reviewing the other two sections outlining her line's powers and the various spells and rituals. But as she was jumping ahead, a word caught her eye, making her gasp.

Prism.

No. It can't be.

What are the odds . . .

She'd been flipping so fast her brain hadn't registered the word right away, so she had to go back a few pages to be sure, but there it was in black and white. An entire chapter dedicated to the Ouroboros Prism, AKA the source of nearly endless magical power disguised as an innocent-looking crystal on her forearm.

This was it. The answer she'd be searching for. She could feel it.

If she could figure out how to draw on and use the energy stored in the Prism, maybe, just maybe, it would be enough to offset their lack of numbers. She may have just found a way to legitimately beat Mikel.

Her hands shook with nervous excitement, and her heart raced as adrenaline shot through her. It almost felt like she was entering dangerous territory, and her body wasn't sure whether it wanted to stay and fight or prepare for flight.

Lina started to read like her life depended on it, which, frankly, it did. Her eyes devoured the words so fast she had to stop herself and go back and start at the beginning twice, just to make sure she actually comprehended them. After she finished her second readthrough, she sat back in stunned disbelief.

Holy.

Fucking.

Shit.

She hadn't realized she'd said the words out loud until Quinn's concerned voice pierced her mental fog.

"Lina? What's wrong?"

"I-I found it."

"Found what?" Finley asked.

"A way to defeat Mikel."

"Lina, that's amazing!" Quinn said, her excitement flagging when Lina didn't immediately agree with her. "Isn't it?"

Lina opened and closed her mouth, not sure how to condense everything she'd just read into bite-sized chunks.

"You're freaking me out," Quinn said, coming to stand next to her.

Finley followed suit, reclaiming his perch on the arm of her chair and resting a hand on her shoulder. "Just start talking, and we'll make sense of it after," he gently ordered, perhaps understanding better than the others the information overload she was trying to wade through.

"Alistair was wrong about the Prism," she said.

"Wrong? How?" Cora asked.

"Well, first off, it's not a prism at all. It's a prison."

Quinn blinked a few times, looking between her mother and then back at Lina. "A prison?"

Lina licked her lips and then swallowed, trying to force some moisture back into her mouth as she continued, "The Prism was created due to an absence of magic. It's a husk." Lina stopped, shaking her head. "I'm not explaining this well. Okay, let me back up. Remember how there used to be more than just our five Animagi families?"

The others nodded.

"All of them, in some fashion or another, were gifted with the powers of the Ancient Ones. Well, apparently, not all of those eternal beings followed the same moral code."

"You're saying one or more of them was corrupt—at least by our definition," Finley said.

"Exactly."

"Shocker," Quinn muttered, crossing her arms. "That goes a long way to explain how Mikel ended up like he did."

"Well, eventually there was a divide, and the good guys teamed up to prune the source of the corruption."

"This is all sounding eerily familiar," Quinn said.

"History has a funny way of repeating itself," Finley said.

"Hush," Cora scolded, her attention focused on Lina. "What happened then?"

"Well, they won. But in order to win, they had to rip out the source of his power so he'd be made mortal and could then be killed."

"What happened to his power?" Quinn asked.

"That's where the Prism—prison comes into play. The Ancient Ones created it to hold and store their brother's power."

Finley pointed to Lina's forearm. "You're telling me you have the equivalent of a god's power trapped in that thing."

Lina nodded, feeling a bit sick as she said, "Yeah, but that's not all. The Ancient Ones didn't realize it at the time, but their prison wasn't perfect. Or it was, but once it was filled with endless, corrupted power, it changed, becoming sentient and hungry. It started to . . . feed off their power. In order to stop the drain, they had to reinforce the prison, strengthening its walls so that it would no longer siphon their magic at will."

"And that worked?" Cora asked.

"It did, but it wasn't perfect. If anyone came into contact with the prison directly, it could still consume their magic. But that wasn't all. They soon discovered that anyone connected to the prison would also draw on the power contained within. Meaning the corruption they'd tried so hard to extinguish could still be accessed. So to save not just themselves, but the realm they were bound to protect, they sealed the prison away in a special box, and over time, the truth of what it was has been forgotten."

Quinn shook her head. "That seems like the kind of thing you'd want to make a point to remember. Why didn't they, I don't know, put a little disclaimer on it that said, 'Danger! Do not open! World-destroying power-sucking crystal inside.'"

Lina smirked. "Because telling someone not to touch the red button always works."

"Well, I mean . . . at least those guys try to warn you. It's not their fault humankind is flawed."

Finley scrubbed a hand over his jaw. "But isn't the Prism—prison—in contact with you right now?"

"Not directly, no. Alistair left it in its box when he disguised it, remember? He didn't want to tempt himself by opening it. But . . ." Lina blew out a breath. "Well, this is the tricky part. In order to use the prison against Mikel, it's going to need to be in contact with him for an extended period of time. The Codex referred to it as an attunement."

"I thought you just said it can feed off whoever is in contact with it," Quinn said with a frown.

"It can, but only after it's attuned. You see, it was created specifically for the brother, and it was made out of the others' magic, so it was attuned to them from the beginning. Stealing more of their power was never an issue. And once the prison became sentient, it learned how to attune itself to new hosts to feed from them as well."

"Oh great. A smart parasite. My favorite," Quinn said.

Finley crossed his arms. "So how are you proposing to complete this attunement?"

Lina shook her head. "I don't know. What if I can make it appear to be something else? Something he wants?"

"Such as?"

"I haven't thought that far ahead. The Codex, maybe?" She shrugged. "We know he wants that."

"He's not going to trust anything you give him willingly," Cora pointed out.

"So we make him think I'm unwilling," Lina said.

"How are you going to do that?" Finley asked.

Lina bit her lip, her mind racing.

"All right, well, assuming you figure that out. How long does the attunement take? And how can you be sure he'll spend the required time in its presence?" Finley pressed, poking yet more holes in her admittedly not very well-thought-out plan.

When the answer came to her, it brought with it a sense of euphoric triumph, which was immediately followed by utter dread.

"I know that look. You're plotting something. Spill it," Quinn said.

Lina scowled at her. "Do you always have to be so bossy?"

"Yes."

"All right, fine. But you aren't going to like it."

"When do we ever like your plans?" Quinn asked.

"Fair." Lina sighed, sitting up a little straighter as she solidified things in her mind. "You heard Mikel today. He wants me alive. I propose we let him take me. Then once I'm captured, I'll be in his presence and able to ensure—"

"What? Lina, no!" Quinn said.

"Absolutely not," Finley said, adamantly shaking his head.

"Lina, dear. That's suicide," Cora said. "You've seen firsthand how the Drakes treat their prisoners."

"Yes, but I survived."

"No, actually, you didn't," Quinn said. "The last time you were one-on-one with a Drake, you ended up spending a few decades as a ghost."

"Okay, you've got me there. But back then I wasn't a berserker, didn't have access to the power I have now, and we were all caught unaware. No one suspected Mataius would try to kill me. This time around, we know what to expect. More importantly, it's our plan, and we can use my time with Mikel to our advantage. Think about it. I'm the perfect distraction. While he thinks he's gotten what he wanted, I'll be secretly working on the attunement and giving you guys the time you need to stage your attack. Then, once enough time has passed, I can use the Prism, and you guys can strike. Bing, bam, boom, the dick is dead."

"Bing bam boom?" Quinn asked.

"Exactly."

"Just like that?"

"Well, yeah."

Quinn sighed. "Lina, when do things *ever* go according to plan?"

"Almost never," she admitted, feeling her cheeks heat.

"So how will this time be any different?"

"It has to be."

Quinn's smug smile warned Lina she wasn't going to like whatever came next.

"All right, Napoleon. Assuming that's even a real strategy—which it's not in case you were wondering—how the hell are you going to get Nord to agree to any of this?"

"Get me to agree to what?"

Oh, for fuck's sake.

Lina squeezed her eyes shut, her stomach immediately sinking. She'd been so caught up in her scheming, she hadn't heard him come in. But Quinn clearly had, the sneak. She probably watched him walk through the door and saw it as her opportunity to go for the jugular. Those two had a whole bad cop, worse cop routine they loved to pull out whenever it came time to try to talk her out of something. Which, come to think of it, happened a lot. Not that she usually listened, but still, siccing Nord on her was a pretty effective counter-measure—and that was when she legitimately had a well-thought-out plan.

This one? Not well thought out. Not even much of a plan, really. More of a throwing-spaghetti-at-the-wall-to-see-what-might-stick approach.

When he found out what she wanted to do, Nord was going to go absolutely berserk on her ass.

And not in the fun way.

CHAPTER 11
NORD

Lina was slow to turn around. When she finally did, her shoulders were stiff and her smile strained. "Oh hey, you're back. How'd the chat with Astrid go?"

Nord cocked a brow, not needing their connection to sense the anxiety pouring off her. "Why are you avoiding the question?"

"I'm not," she insisted, just a shade too quickly.

"Now you're lying to me."

Lina tipped her head back and groaned. "You make it sound so awful. I'm just trying to delay an inevitable blowup."

Nord glanced at Finley, knowing his friend's answer would help him gauge just how worried he should be. "That bad?"

"Worse," he answered, adding on a private thread, *"Brace yourself. She intends to act as bait and let herself get taken by Mikel. There's more to it, but I'll let her explain the details."*

His berserker roared in immediate protest, but Nord clamped down hard on the impulse to dive headfirst into the rage. "I see."

Though his voice was even, there was no way Lina could mistake the angry surge of his emotions due to their bond, and her exasperated outburst confirmed it.

"Oh great, now he's mad, and he doesn't even know why."

"Isn't that sort of the status quo for a berserker?" Quinn asked.

"Hush, you've already caused enough trouble," Lina said, pointing at her. Then she scowled at Finley. "Couldn't you let me ease him into it?"

"Trust me, I did you a favor. Now he's prepared and less likely to rage out on you."

"Did me a favor? All you did was—" Lina narrowed her eyes. "Finley, did you just tattle on me with your stupid mind whispers?"

"I have no idea what you're talking about," he said, crossing his arms.

She lobbed a pillow at his head. "You dick. You totally did."

"Prove it."

Nord might have been amused by their sibling-like bickering, if not for the fact that his mate wanted to play fast and loose with her life. Again. If he didn't intervene, Lina would just keep going after Finley as a means of delaying this conversation as long as possible. And from the sound of things, it was one they needed to have. The moon had better odds of falling from the sky than he did of allowing her to willingly sacrifice herself to that sadist.

"This seems like something we should discuss without an audience. Come," he said, holding out a hand, "walk with me, Kærasta."

To her credit, she only hesitated for a second before standing and placing her hand in his. "You're not just saying that because you don't want any witnesses when you start yelling at me, are you?"

"And if I am?" he asked, weaving his fingers through hers.

"I'd feel obligated to remind you that I'm just going to start shouting right back."

He lifted their joined hands, pressing a kiss to the back of hers. "I'd expect nothing less."

"You know, if we're busy being all ragey and snarly with each other, we're really just wasting time we could be using to do other things," she pointed out.

"Then let's try to be quick about it," he said, pulling her out the door and leading her out of the building. Instead of laughing as he hoped, she just bit down on her bottom lip, looking resigned. "What's this sudden fixation of yours about me yelling? When do I ever yell—"

She opened her mouth to chime in, but he spoke right over her.

"—*at* you? Did you ever stop to consider that maybe I asked you to come with me because I want to spend some time alone with my future wife?"

She stopped, pulling him up short so she could peer up at him. "Is that what this is?"

He squeezed her hand. "Why can't it be both?"

"A shouting match and a romantic stroll? Yeah, that does sort of sound like perfect foreplay for a berserker." She laughed a little and resumed walking.

"If you're so worried about me losing my temper, maybe you should just tell me what you're planning so we can deal with it and move on to more pleasant matters."

"You mean so you can try to talk me out of it by distracting me with sex?"

"That's not what I said." Though the thought had merit, now that she mentioned it.

"Maybe not, but I know how you work, Bloodaxe. If you can't beat a problem to death, you fuck it out instead."

Nord laughed at her overly simplistic, albeit not entirely inaccurate, assessment. "I don't recall you having any complaints about my problem-solving skills, Kærasta. Also, I'm pretty sure that's not true."

"Isn't it, though?" she asked, a smile tugging at her lips when she glanced back his way.

They'd made it down into the heart of the city by then. It was late afternoon, and there weren't many people milling around, though there were a few who shot curious glances their way or blatantly stopped to stare as Nord and Lina walked past. When he noticed the first stirrings of recognition in the Novasgardians' eyes, he gave Lina's hand a tug and led her to a small park Astrid had pointed out earlier. Given what they had to discuss, it was probably best if they went somewhere out of earshot.

After following a short path that wove up a hill on the easternmost side of the city, they found a small cliff with scattered benches and picnic tables overlooking the harbor below. Without a word, they both veered to the right, heading for the furthest bench. Once they were both seated, Nord rested one arm along the back of the bench and faced her.

"Lina."

The smile slipped from her lips, and she continued to stare out at the glistening water, her eyes tracking a passing ship instead of looking at him.

He brushed a lock of hair away from her face. "Are you really that afraid to share your thoughts with me?"

"Afraid of you? Never."

"Then talk to me."

"And ruin this incredible view? Why bother getting into it at all? I know Finley already told you my plan."

"Maybe so—"

"I *knew* it! That crumpet-eating weasel."

"—but I rather hear it from you."

Lina lifted both her feet, hugging her arms around her shins and resting her heels on the bench. Then she laid her cheek on top of her knees and finally met his gaze.

He noted the protective nature of her chosen position and the wariness tingeing her eyes. She seemed to be bracing herself for whatever explosion she believed would follow on the heels of her explanation.

While it was inevitable that they'd find themselves on opposite sides of an argument from time to time, he didn't ever want her to worry about what such a disagreement meant for them. He should be the one person, above all others, she knew she could come to. Because when it really came down to it, whether he agreed with her or not, if Lina insisted on walking straight into the bowels of hell, he'd be right there, walking alongside her.

Nord decided to change tactics. He skimmed his fingers over her hair and down her spine, causing her to shiver slightly. "Would it help set your mind at ease if I told you what Astrid and I spoke about first?"

Her relief was palpable. "I'd love that."

"Well, after I told her about all that had come to pass since the moment we saw her last up through Mikel's attack at the penthouse today, Astrid pledged the people of Novasgard to our cause."

Emotions passed so swiftly across Lina's face it was hard to catalog them all. Shock. Amazement. Hope. She straightened and turned to face him fully, one of her legs folded in front of her on the bench, the other anchoring her to the ground. Grasping his wrist, she gave it a tight squeeze.

"Nord, that's incredible." Then she shook her head as breathless laughter escaped, pressing her free hand to the space just above her heart.

The sight of her unimpeded joy warmed him from the inside out. This was the look he'd been waiting for, the moment he'd been anticipating ever since leaving Astrid's home.

"I thought that might cheer you up."

"I never allowed myself to really believe she'd agree to help us. How did you manage to convince her?"

"She volunteered."

"Just like that? No questions asked?"

"Well, I wouldn't say it was quite that open and shut. She has her reasons for wanting to assist us in ridding the world of such filth. And a request, actually."

"Did she tell you what it was?"

Nord ran a hand over his beard, trying to hide his smile. "She did."

"And?" Lina shoved his chest lightly. "Don't leave me hanging. What does she want?"

"Well, it has to do with you."

Her eyes flew wide. "Me? I mean, I don't see what I can possibly offer her, but of course. Whatever she wants."

"I'm glad you feel that way because I already committed on your behalf. And you need to stop selling yourself short. There is much you have to offer."

Lina waved the compliment away, leaning forward to dig her finger into his chest. "Are you going to tell me what she wants, or am I going to have to beat it out of you?"

He grasped her finger and pulled her hand up to press a kiss into her palm, enjoying the way her eyes went liquid when he traced one of the lines with his tongue.

"And by beat, I meant wrestle," she added a little hoarsely.

He nipped the tip of the finger she'd used to poke him.

"Naked."

"Obviously," he deadpanned, though he could feel the corner of his mouth tug up. "That goes without saying."

Lina blinked a few times and shook her head as if to clear it. "See. I told you you'd try to distract me with sex."

"Are you sure? From where I'm sitting, you're the one talking about getting naked."

"How do you expect me to think about anything else when you're doing those things to me with your mouth?" He grinned at her, and her eyes narrowed playfully. "Sheath your smile, Viking, and tell me what I owe your cousin in exchange for her army."

"Oh, that," he said, sitting back to put some distance between them, before casually answering. "She wants us to get married here, honoring the old ways, in three days' time."

Lina made a strangled sound in the back of her throat before letting out an incredulous laugh. "Married? In three days? Is that even enough time to plan an entire wedding?"

"Astrid told me to leave it up to her, and I knew better than to start asking questions. The way I see it, the smartest thing I can do right now is show up when and where she tells me to. You'd be wise to do the same," he warned her with a laugh.

"Considering I wouldn't even know where to start, that seems like solid advice." Lina's laughter joined his. "I'll admit, I sort of assumed Quinn would be the one to take charge of our wedding and boss us both around. I wonder what she'll say when she finds out Astrid beat her to it."

Nord shuddered. "The thought of those two joining forces is mildly terrifying."

"It really is, isn't it?" She fell silent then, but he could feel ripples of her excitement fluttering around in his chest. Her silence only lasted thirty seconds at most before she blurted, "I can't believe we get to have a Viking wedding! I mean, obviously that's what we wanted and talked about. I just never thought it'd happen so soon. And definitely not before Mikel was dealt with. I figured our wedding would be the kind of thing we'd have to wait for and earn, you know? Like it would be our reward when all of this was over."

Nord wrapped his arm around her and reeled her body in until it was curled into his. "In that way, her price is really more of a gift, isn't it?"

"She's giving us more than she could ever realize," Lina agreed, her smile radiant as she snuggled deeper into him.

He pressed his lips to the crown of her head. "I have a feeling Astrid knows exactly what she's giving us. Anyone familiar with the realities of war knows better than to put off something so important."

He didn't need to explain why. The way Lina's arms banded around him as if they alone would be enough to keep him safe told him she already knew.

The silence that settled around them was heavier now, still comfortable, but filled with the weight of everything waiting for them once they returned home.

"If you would have told me we'd save Crombie's life, fend off an Animagi invasion, and travel back to the land of the lost Vikings, all in the course of a single day, I don't think I'd have believed you. One of those things, maybe two, but not all of them. And never in my wildest dreams would I have guessed we'd have an entire army trained in magic and warfare prepared to return home with us."

"You never allowed yourself to consider the possibility?"

"I'd hoped, obviously. But after what Astrid said last time, I never let myself believe it. Certainly not enough to make any plans hinging on their aid." She was quiet for a second before snorting. "Mikel is going to shit his pants when he sees them. Can't you just imagine his expression when a full swarm of Vikings comes bursting in?"

Nord's chest rumbled as the mental image came to life in his mind. "Powerful allies have a way of changing things." Then, seeing his opening, he added, "So much so they sometimes require you to change your strategy entirely."

Her attention had returned to the water, but he sensed her happiness dim at his words. When she shifted to look up at him, her smile was apologetic. "True, but not this time."

Desperate fury swelled within him, but Nord knew he needed to hear her out before trying to press her into making a different decision. While she appreciated his protective nature, she'd made it abundantly clear how she felt about his heavy-handed approach where her safety was concerned. Whatever she was planning, she believed in it, and he didn't want her to misinterpret his need to keep her safe as a lack of faith in her abilities. And to do that, he needed to hear the idea in full before shooting it down out of hand.

"I'm listening."

She stiffened in his arms and the underlying command in his words, but then as she released the breath she'd been holding, all the tension melted out of her. "Did you know Finley can be quite clever when he wants to be?"

"I'm familiar with the phenomenon, yes. But I prefer to claim ignorance in his presence."

She chuckled. "Me too. Well, today while you were off with Astrid, he suggested that I use my power to translate the Codex."

"And?" Nord prompted.

"And it actually worked."

"Here I was thinking I was the only one with exciting news today."

Lina then filled him in, giving him an abbreviated history regarding the Prism and how it had been created with the intention of being a prison for an Ancient Ones' source of power.

"So, you see," she said, looking adorably earnest as she peered up at him. "It can render an Animagi powerless once fully attuned to them."

Nord could already see the value of such an artifact. Relieving Mikel of his power would cut their enemy off at the knees, essentially winning the final battle for them before it could really start. Once he fell, any others standing with him would come toppling down right after. But even better, for a man such as him, there would be no fate worse than discovering he was utterly without power.

Even so, Finley's warning about her intentions echoed in his mind, so he refrained from commenting, waiting for her to explain why exactly she felt the need to barter with her life in order for them to claim Mikel's.

She'd fallen silent, clearly hoping he'd give her some indication as to where his thoughts lay. When he didn't, her smile faltered and she started to fidget. "There is a downside," she admitted. "In order for it to work, we need the Prism to be in contact with Mikel."

"How are you proposing to accomplish that?"

This was the part she'd been avoiding. He could tell that she'd hoped hearing the benefits would make him agree that the risk was necessary. And he did agree. But not about her being the one to take it.

When she spoke, the words fell out of her in a rush. "I'd let him take me so I could ensure the attunement was complete."

It was a battle to contain his berserker's roar. Nord knew Lina felt him grappling for control, the surge of his emotions mirrored inside her through their bond. But even if they weren't, it was easy enough to see in the white-knuckled grip he had on the back of the bench and the labored turn of his breathing.

Her voice was gentle. Pleading. "Nord, it's the only way."

"No, Lina, it's not. You may believe it is. But there's always another option."

"Not one that would work," she insisted. "The only thing Mikel wants more than the Codex is me. He knows, or at least he suspects, that I have the Prism. If I can trick him and access it without him realizing I've learned how to use it, I can begin to attune it without him ever even knowing it was there."

"Lina—"

"No, listen. We know he's after the Codex, right? What if I make the Prism look like it? He'll be so eager to learn its secrets, he'll be in direct contact with it from the second I hand it over. And if not, then it will definitely be somewhere nearby. He's not going to let it out of his sight, and he certainly isn't going to hand it over to anybody else. Just his proximity alone is enough to kick-start the process."

"How long?" Nord gritted out, his voice harsh due to his internal battle for control.

"The Codex said half a day, if there's constant, direct contact."

"And if there isn't?"

"A day, maybe two, if it's proximity alone."

His control snapped. Frankly, he was proud of himself for lasting this long.

"Two days? You want me to leave you alone at the hands of that monster for two. Fucking. Days?"

She winced.

"How are we even supposed to know when it's complete?"

"The crystal changes color—"

"But it won't be a crystal, will it? It will look like a Codex. Also, did you ever stop to think about what the prison could do to you? If proximity is enough to complete the attunement process, how will *you* remain safe? What good is your plan if it handicaps you as well?"

"Nord," she said, resting a hand just above his racing heart. "If he acts the way I believe he will, it should only take a day at most. That's not long at all."

"You saw what he did to Cora, to her sister—"

"You're forgetting, this time he'll be distracted by the Codex. Oh, I'm sure he'll slap me around. But I'm not some helpless damsel in distress. I'm a berserker, just like you. If it gets too bad, I'll give in to the lust so that I thrive on the pain and bloodshed. You know how it works. I won't feel a thing."

He clenched his jaw so hard he heard his teeth grinding together.

"And, while I'm busy distracting him, you, with the aid of Astrid and all the others, can lay your trap."

"How will we know when it's time to strike? If we burst in and the attunement isn't complete, you've done this all for nothing, and we lose the advantage. How will we even know where to find you? Lina," he said desperately, taking her hand in his, "this isn't even a plan. It's the barest hint of one. And even if it was, there are too many things that can go wrong."

She pressed her free hand to his cheek. "Then help me make it one."

"Lina," he groaned, his eyes falling closed as he rested his forehead against hers. "Ask me for anything else, and it's yours, but please, don't ask me for this. Not when you know how the thought of you in danger tears me apart."

"What if we could stay in contact so you'd know I was safe? And if something went wrong, you can pull the plug and come get me."

"How?"

"Fin—"

"His gift doesn't work like that. Unless you're a Guardian, it's only one way, and it doesn't work past a certain distance, and definitely not across realms."

She frowned, biting her lip.

"Okay, so we use mortal means. An earpiece, or I don't know, a disguised clip I hide in my hair. With our gift, we could make it look like literally anything, and then I can use a code word so you'd know if I need help, or when it's time to attack."

She shifted so her hands were clenched around his, right between their hearts. Her voice was raw with emotion when she resumed her impassioned speech.

"Nord, we *have* to find a way to make this work because if we strip Mikel of his power, we win. All this would be over, and we could actually start our life together. Wouldn't you like that? Don't you want us to be able to live happily ever after? To come back here and have that vacation house Astrid promised you? Somewhere safe and beautiful, where we could raise a brood of our own little blond Vikings?" Her eyes were wet with tears as they searched his for an answer. "Because that's what I want. More than anything, I want those things with you. I want a future spent loving you where we can finally be free from all these burdens and obligations. But the only way we get that is if Mikel is gone. Neither of us, nor any of the people we love, are safe while he lives."

She may as well have gutted him, her words cutting him to the core and flaying him open. If he dared glance down, he was almost certain he'd find his heart lying in her palm.

He wanted those things too. Desperately.

They were the dreams he never dared speak. A life he'd once made peace with never having, but now wanted more fiercely than ever before.

"You know the desires of my heart more clearly than I do, Kærasta. And you're right, we will not be free until Mikel is dead, but I cannot agree to this plan." A tear splashed down her cheek, and he brushed it away with his thumb. "How can you ask me to risk the one person my every dream centers on?"

"Nord—"

"I do not trust him, Lina. He's unpredictable. You may think you know how he'll act, but he has proven time and again we don't. I cannot bear the thought of him harming a hair on your head while I stood by doing nothing. Allowing it. You are the star my universe revolves around. Do not ask me for this."

"It's the only way."

He felt as if something within him was splintering. Not his heart, exactly, more like his sanity. And with each affirmation of her intent, he felt more desperately out of control.

"What if someone went in your place?"

"No. It has to be me. I'm the one who's responsible for his son's death. I'm the one he fears. He has to think he's bested me. It's the only way he'll let his guard down long enough to enjoy the spoils of his victory."

"I'll go. You or I can use our power to make me appear as you. I have the same gifts, so if anyone checked for traces of your magic, they'd still sense them in me. And I can obviously tap into them if necessary."

"And then who would lead the others? I understand why you're fighting this. Why you want to be the one to put yourself at risk when the others need you to coordinate the attack. No one else can do what you do."

"Astrid—"

"Doesn't know what she's up against. You do."

He closed his eyes, despair eating at him as he ran out of alternatives.

"Nord, my love, look at me."

He obeyed, shielding nothing of what he felt as he did.

She sucked in a breath. "If we've learned anything about our power, it's that what we will, and what we believe, becomes real. Maybe it's time we start believing we're going to win. We have two things right now that we didn't wake up with this morning: a weapon and an army. We can do this. We can beat him. And then, we can be free."

The sun dipped low in the sky, painting her in its gold and amber light. For a second, she appeared as if she'd been crafted from the rays of the sun itself. A gilded goddess sent down from the heavens themselves to guide him. And as her hope-filled eyes held his, he could feel her devotion and love for him pouring through their bond. In that moment, there was nothing he could deny her.

And though he still despised her plan, after listening to her reasons, it really did seem to be their best shot. So, he'd do what she asked. He'd help plot her capture so she could distract Mikel long enough for the prison to do its job.

He'd help her play the most dangerous game of her life.

Nord just hoped while he was at it, he also found a way to ensure it was one she wouldn't lose.

CHAPTER 12
LINA

"I'm thinking about getting bangs," Quinn said when Lina waved her hand in front of the panel on the wall that unlocked the door.

"Good morning to you, too."

Quinn made a face and then blew her a kiss. "Hi. So what do you think?" she asked, moving into their suite and heading to her usual spot on the sofa.

"About you with bangs? Did you forget fourth grade?"

"No, not like those. I mean sexy femme domme pin-up bangs. Just imagine me in some fishnets, skin-tight black leather, and six-inch stilettos, maybe holding a crop or whip or something."

Finley had just walked into the living room, a cup of tea raised to his mouth when she'd made her announcement. Lina watched as his hand jerked and tea went sloshing everywhere. Quinn smirked, and Lina couldn't help but wonder how much of that little description had been for his benefit.

"So basically, what you wear on Wednesdays?" Lina teased.

"Exactly," Quinn said.

"Where the hell have I been on Wednesdays?" Finley muttered.

Quinn winked at Lina, who was quietly shaking her head and laughing.

"Sounds like you have it all figured out."

"Yeah," Quinn said with a shrug. "Just thought it might be fun to change it up."

"I can help with that if you ever want to test it out before committing."

Quinn snapped her fingers and aimed a finger gun Lina's way. "Oooh, yes. Now you're talking. Maybe for the wedding?"

That brought Lina up short. She didn't consider herself a high-maintenance bride, but she just wanted to make sure she'd understood correctly because with Quinn, you could never be too sure. "You want to dress up like a dominatrix . . . at my traditional Novasgardian wedding?"

"What? Too much? I thought it was white guests weren't allowed to wear. Is bondage gear out too?"

Finley dropped all pretense of not eavesdropping at this point. He'd made himself a towel and had been wiping up the spilt tea when she threw that bomb. "Jesus wept," he groaned.

Lina held up her hands. "Whatever makes you happy. But if someone asks you to spank them, can you at least do me a favor and take it outside?"

"No promises."

"What in God's name did I do to deserve this?" Finley asked, straightening.

"Sounds like somebody woke up on the wrong side of the bed this morning. Or is it that you're the one who wants to volunteer to be spanked?" Quinn chirped.

Finley opened and closed his mouth, looking like there were so many things he wanted to say at that moment and not able to give voice to any of them. Finally, he shook his head, spun around, and headed back into the kitchen.

"Too bad," Quinn purred as he disappeared into the other room. "I bet he'd look pretty all tied up."

"I think you broke him," Lina said.

"Nah. It would take more than that with a man like him. This is just foreplay."

"Is that so?"

"Oh yeah. He won't be able to get that image out of his head for weeks. Maybe even months. I wouldn't be surprised if he headed straight for the shower as soon as we leave so he can take matters into his own hands."

"You're terrible."

She lifted a shoulder in an unrepentant shrug. "He baited me in front of my mother. He deserves to suffer a little."

"Ah, so that's what this is about. Revenge."

"Love *is* a battlefield. And he might have won a couple battles, but I'll win the war."

"Don't be so sure about that."

"What? You don't think I can outlast him?"

"Sweetie," Lina said, moving until she was standing next to her and leaning down to kiss her cheek, "I don't think you know what winning really looks like."

"What's that supposed to mean?"

Lina stood and shrugged. "You two will figure it out. But until you do, I'll just start making myself popcorn for these little showdowns."

Quinn narrowed her eyes. "Traitor."

Lina was still laughing when Nord walked out with the Codex in hand. He'd been reading it since they'd gotten back last night, trying to see if there was anything else they might be able to use in the days to come.

"What did I miss?" he asked, giving Lina a quick kiss on the cheek before sliding into a seat at the table.

"Quinn broke Finley."

"I did not. I just played with him a little."

Nord raised a brow. "I'm sure he deserved it."

"I knew I loved you, big guy," Quinn said, blowing him a kiss. "So, what time do we need to meet with Astrid?"

Lina glanced at the clock. "We should head out now. Probably best we don't keep her waiting."

"Just let me finish this chapter, and we'll be off," Nord said.

"Sure," Lina agreed, claiming the seat beside Quinn while they waited.

"Does anyone else think it's a little rude she's making us come to her instead of the other way around? No? Just me?"

"Quinn, she's a busy woman. She runs this entire city. It's a lot harder for her to drop everything and swing by for a visit."

"Yeah, well. I'm just saying. It would have been nice to at least offer."

Lina bit her cheek, knowing Quinn's ire had more to do with the fact that Astrid was in charge of planning the wedding than any real frustration.

She didn't think the news Quinn and Finley had been expecting when Nord and Lina returned from their walk the other night was that they had three days to throw a wedding together. But you'd never know it by the way they'd whole-heartedly jumped on board. From that moment on, all talk of Mikel, voluntary capture, and the Prism were tabled in honor of the big day. Everyone seemed to silently agree that the specter of war didn't have a place here. At least, not until after the nuptials when the official war council would gather.

"I know Novasgard is a little lacking in the nightlife department, but it's not too late to organize that naked hot oil wrestling pit," Quinn said.

Nord interrupted his reading of the Codex only long enough to look up and say, "Yes, it is."

Lina snorted. "I appreciate the offer, but I'm good."

"We'll discuss it more later," Quinn said, as if they hadn't both just shot her down. "My mom mentioned something about how women and men go their separate ways the day before the wedding. We'll have a whole window of time to make it happen tomorrow."

"Did she now?" Lina asked, wondering what other sorts of traditions she might be asked to partake in.

"Oh, that reminds me. She said you should bring Alistair's cane with us today."

Lina frowned. "Why?"

Quinn shrugged. "Don't know. She just had a feeling it might be useful."

"Useful? For wedding planning? You know what, never mind," Lina said, standing once more to go and grab it. "If she made a point to have you pass it along, I'm sure I'll work it out."

On her way back from the bedroom, cane in hand, she heard running water coming from the suite's second bathroom.

"Guess Quinn was right about the shower," Lina said with a snicker, though since she was secretly on Team Finley, she wasn't about to tell her so.

Nord and Quinn looked over as she walked back into the room. The Codex was lying closed on the kitchen table, and they were both standing near the door, so she assumed they'd just been waiting on her.

"Mission accomplished," she said, holding the cane out and executing a quasi-baton twirl which made Nord smile and Quinn roll her eyes heavenward. "You guys ready to go?"

As they trailed up the winding path leading to Astrid's home, Lina allowed herself to take in the majestic beauty of the modern Dragestil longhouse—something she hadn't had time to do during their previous visits. The sprawling mansion was an exquisite blend of contemporary and traditional architecture. Rows of windows were set into sleek ebony timber topped with a steeply angled gable roof that curved into peaks that mirrored the prows of the famed Viking ships, right down to the snarling creatures adorning them. Lina was thankful, and somewhat comforted, to discover the beasts were serpents rather than dragons. She took it as a sign from the universe good things were headed their way.

Though, as lovely as the structure itself was, there was no denying that the real showstopper was the land framing it. From the endless stretch of sapphire water to the kaleidoscope of blooming wildflowers and the soaring mountains jutting across the horizon— it was an experience to be savored. One no photograph or artist's rendering could ever fully capture.

The more she saw of Novasgard, the more she wanted the opportunity to make it her home.

Lina slipped her hand into Nord's. "I love it here. The way it smells, the weather, the views." She sighed wistfully.

"The way it smells?"

"Yeah, all briny with just a hint of snow and pine. It's my favorite."

His eyes sparkled at her description, but she was pretty sure it was with affection rather than amusement at her expense. He leaned down and nipped at her ear, growling playfully, "It's pleasant, but if I had to choose a favorite, I much prefer your scent, Kærasta."

"Keep it in your pants, you two. Yeah, that's right," Quinn said when Lina broke away from Nord with a giggle. "I'm still here. You invited me to come along, remember?"

Lina moved to wrap her arms around Quinn's waist. "As if I could ever forget you."

"You were doing a pretty good impression of it a second ago," Quinn sulked, but Lina knew there was no real weight to it.

"Are you jealous? Do you need smoochies too, my wittle Quinnie-poo?"

And that's how Astrid found them when she opened her door. Nord silently chuckling while Lina peppered loud-smacking kisses all over the side of a squirming Quinn's face.

"Are you sure you're the one getting married?" Astrid asked, her eyes squinted in mock suspicion as she looked at her cousin.

"Unequivocally," Nord said with a wide grin.

Lina flushed and let go of Quinn with an embarrassed chuckle. "Hello again."

Astrid opened the door wider, her smile warm and welcoming. "Come on in and make yourselves at home."

"Thanks. You really do have a beautiful home."

Astrid glanced around. "Yes, I've always loved it here. The house has been in my family since the exodus. As it's passed down through the generations, we all leave our mark on it."

"Oh? What did you add?" Lina asked curiously as she stepped inside.

"I have a fondness for European wine and bubble baths, so I insisted on a proper wine cellar and remodeled the master bathroom so I can enjoy the sunset while indulging in both. It's one of the few luxuries I afford myself."

"It sounds divine."

"It is," she agreed, closing the door behind Nord as he joined them in her foyer.

"I take it your mother decided not to join us?" Astrid asked Quinn conversationally as she led them through the front of the house, past her formal living room, and into a much more intimate space with a stone hearth and crackling fire. Though more casual a setting than the room they walked by, the furnishings were no less sumptuous. And there was no beating the one-hundred-and-eighty-degree view of the mountains.

"Unfortunately, she received another offer she couldn't refuse." At Astrid's raised brows, Quinn explained, "Strega offered to show her and my aunt around today."

"Ah, well, that's understandable. But I'd hoped to get to speak with her some more. She seems like such an interesting woman."

"She said the same about you."

Astrid smiled as they funneled into the room. "Please, make

yourselves comfortable. I took the liberty of setting out some tea and small snacks. I wasn't sure what you might like, but these are some of my favorites."

"That was so thoughtful. Thank you, Astrid," Lina said.

She shrugged, waving off the words of gratitude. "It's the least I could do. I truly appreciate you indulging me and coming here. As you can imagine, there's much to do and little time to do it."

"In that case, we should probably get started," Lina said. "I don't want to take up any more of your time than necessary."

"Don't be silly. You're family. There's nothing more important than that."

Lina was oddly touched by the casual inclusion. Seeing as her track record with most blood relatives was fraught at best, it was surprisingly uplifting to find herself so easily welcomed into a new one, especially by someone as fiercely loyal as the Novasgardian leader.

After Astrid made sure they'd all loaded up with refreshments, she dove straight into what they should expect over the course of the next few days. Starting with Lina's ritual hair washing at the bath-house and all the way through the details of the ceremony. Lina's head was spinning in a matter of minutes, and she was beyond grateful she'd begged Quinn to come with them. With her perfect recall, she'd ensure Lina didn't accidentally make a fool of herself or Nord by forgetting some essential detail.

"So that brings us to the last thing I wanted to discuss with you," Astrid said, clapping her hands together.

Lina shot Nord a panicked glance. "There's more?" she mouthed.

He reached out and gave her hand a reassuring squeeze.

"I have something for you," Astrid continued, seeming almost nervous as she fully faced her cousin.

Lina slumped back, relieved that, at least for the moment, this didn't seem to involve her.

"For me?" Nord asked, his gaze dropping automatically to her empty hands. His expression turned quizzical as he lifted his eyes back to hers.

Astrid gestured to the wooden coffee table. Lina had assumed the stretch of black fabric along the center was some sort of simple table runner, but now that Astrid had drawn attention to it, she realized it concealed something long and rectangular. While Nord inspected the sheet, Astrid gave Lina a conspiratorial smile—as if she was somehow in on the secret.

"What's this?" he asked.

"As you know, many of our ancestor's valuables were lost because they were only able to take that which they could carry when they fled through the gateway."

Nord nodded, though his face was still creased with confusion.

"That," she said significantly, "is a little piece of our history I thought you might appreciate. It's not your father's but . . ." Astrid shrugged as she let her words hang.

Nord wasted no more time, grasping an edge of the sheet and giving it a sharp tug. There was a sharp intake of breath, and then he breathed her name. "Astrid."

Hand trembling slightly, Nord reached out and picked up the ancient blade. The sword was massive, the blade thicker and almost twice as long as any she'd seen in person. The steel was a gray so dark it was nearly black, with a series of runes etched down its center. Nord tipped the sword toward the fireplace, and the runes seemed to alight and radiate the absorbed firelight. The hilt was a lighter metal, appearing almost white set as it was against the dark blade, and it was rich with its own intricately carved details.

"It belonged to—"

"Brynhild. My grandmother," Nord supplied, his voice thick with emotion.

Astrid nodded, a small smile still playing about her lips. "I know it is customary to visit an ancestral tomb to retrieve your matrimonial weapon, but as we seem to be in short supply of those, at least this way you can still offer your new bride a piece of your family's heritage as you welcome her to its fold."

The others might be unaware of how deeply affected he was by his cousin's poignant gift, but not Lina. Even if she couldn't feel the waves of his turbulent emotions echoing inside of her, she could see them in the wet shine of his eyes and the slight tremor of his hand as he reverently held and inspected the weapon.

Nord cleared his throat, jerking his chin in a sharp nod. "That is . . . I . . ." Unable to find the words, he settled for a hoarse, "Thank you, cousin."

"It is my pleasure to be able to offer it to you."

"I'll make sure it's returned after the ceremony."

"You'll do no such thing," she said, her blue eyes flashing.

"You don't want it?" Nord asked.

"I've got many blades which hold special meaning. I can let go of one. And I can think of no better owner than a berserker for a weapon with a history such as that. Besides, you couldn't return it if you wanted to. After the ceremony, it will be Lina's."

Lina, who'd been trying to discreetly wipe the tears from her cheeks, looked up. "M-mine?"

Quinn brushed the back of her fingers against Lina's, and suddenly, Astrid's explanation was there, in perfect detail.

Right. They exchanged weapons in addition to rings. It had once represented the guardianship and protection of the wife over to the husband, while she would safeguard her husband's blade until she bore him a son. Now it represented the joining of two families and their acceptance of each other.

"Thank you," Lina mouthed.

Quinn winked.

"Um, Astrid, I don't have a family weapon to offer Nord." A soft tapping against her shoe pulled Lina's attention down. Using the tip of her boot, Quinn gently pushed Alistair's cane into Lina's line of sight. "Unless a cane counts?" she added with a little laugh. But even as she said it, it was suddenly overwhelmingly obvious what she was supposed to do and why Cora had insisted she bring it. Before she put her plan into action, she just wanted to clarify one point. "It wouldn't be offensive if I offer Nord something that wasn't originally a sword, would it?"

"I don't see why it would," Astrid said.

Taking a deep breath, Lina held the image she wanted in her mind. By the time she'd fully released the air in her lungs, Alistair's cane had been transformed. The handle with the Cuska crest remained mostly untouched. Though the hissing serpent had gone from a hooked upside-down u to more of a lowercase t-shape with the intersecting line curving slightly down, so it would still rest over her hand. The wood had been turned into a blade, similar in design and color to the one Nord held, though significantly shorter.

"Will this do?" she asked when she was done, holding her newly forged blade out for Astrid's inspection.

"Oh yes. That will do very nicely indeed."

For a second, it felt as if her uncle was right there, standing just out of sight behind her and whispering in her ear how proud he was of her. Something unfurled in Lina's chest, and a relieved smile stretched across her face as a weight she hadn't realized she'd been carrying fell away. Still beaming, she turned to Nord, her voice a little wobbly as she said, "Now it'll be like Alistair's there with us, watching the whole thing."

"You know he'd never let something as silly as death allow him to miss your wedding," Quinn said, her husky voice even deeper with emotion.

"Or the chance to walk you down the aisle," Nord added, brushing his knuckles over her cheek to sweep away the fresh tears that had fallen without her realizing it.

Astrid handed Lina back the sword. "And now, it seems, he doesn't have to."

CHAPTER 13
FINLEY

Finley adjusted his cufflink, the slight pounding at his temples a reminder that attempting to drink his body weight in aged whisky the night before hadn't been his finest idea. No matter how easy the Vikings made it look.

There was a slight knock at the door. "Fin? You decent?"

He glanced up at the clock on the bedside table. He wasn't running that late, was he? Surely not enough for the bride herself to come hunting him down.

"Yes, but—"

Lina pushed open the door.

"Wait!" Finley blurted, slamming a hand over his eyes. "I'm not supposed to see the bride before the ceremony."

She laughed, her mirth suffusing his room. "Fin, that only applies to the groom."

"Oh. Right." He let out an embarrassed chuckle and lowered his hand. "It's been a while since I've been to one of these." The rest of his words fell away as he took in the vision before him. "Lina . . ."

She'd chosen a dress made of delicate white lace, which covered her from the collarbone down. Though the conservative nature of its cut was belied by the way it molded to her body from her shoulders to her knees, where it flared out in a pool around her feet. The only other adornment she wore was a belt at her hips, a series of interconnected silver disks decorated with Norse runes.

It was traditional. Elegant. And all the more stunning for its simplicity. Just like the woman who wore it.

She blushed and did a little twirl for him, holding out her arms. "You think he'll like it?"

The show of nerves was endearing and wholly unnecessary. He didn't think he'd ever come across a man who loved his woman more than Nord did Lina. She could walk down that aisle in a bathrobe, and he'd be entranced.

"Darling, he's going to absolutely lose his mind. If he manages not to throw you over his shoulder and storm off before the end of the ceremony, I'll be impressed." Finley crossed the room and pressed a kiss to her cheek. "Truly. You might be the most beautiful bride I've ever seen."

"You're looking pretty dapper yourself, Fin. Nice tux."

"Well, the occasion seemed to call for something special."

"Quinn's going to die when she sees you."

It was on the tip of his tongue to ask if she'd made good on her threat about the fishnets and leather, but he decided it was best for his sanity not to know. That way he didn't drive himself mental at the thought of all the men undressing her and fucking her with their eyes—or worse, following through on the desire. It was hard enough for him to resist the impulse himself. His cock was already twitching at the mere thought.

Thankfully, Lina came to his rescue, bringing his attention back to the present.

"Should I add a veil? Strega said that the bride's hair was the most important feature. I wasn't sure if I should hide it."

Finley found it endlessly amusing that she'd come to him of all people for advice, but as the only person around who'd known Nord longer than her, he supposed he was the closest thing to an expert on the berserker's tastes.

"Turn around; let's take a look."

She obeyed, and Finley studied the jeweled hairpiece she'd nestled in a complicated series of twists and braids which looped together and fell down her back in a golden cascade. "Leave it. It's perfect. And am I wrong, or is it longer?"

"I, uh, may have added a few inches."

"Took Strega's words to heart, did you?"

She blushed. "When in Vikingland . . ."

"Well, in that case, here. You'll want this as well."

Finley picked up a towel he'd hung on the back of his door and summoned his power. When he was finished, he held a fur wrap in the same tawny hues as the mantle Nord had been presented with the night before. He settled it about her shoulders, using another surge of magic to create a smaller version of one of the disks at her hips to act as a clasp.

"Now you're a perfect Norse bride."

She beamed at him. "I'm so glad I decided to be on your team. Quinn needs to hurry up and get her head out of her ass."

Finley's chest hollowed out as the air fled from his lungs. "What was that?"

"Nothing," she said breezily. "Actually, there's one more thing I need that I was hoping you'd help me with."

"So you didn't pop in just for my fashion tips? I'm crushed."

She chuckled. "No, though they are much appreciated. I did have an actual reason for bothering you."

"You could never be a bother. What's on your mind?"

Lina turned suddenly shy. "It's okay if you want to say no after you hear it. I know it's sort of sentimental and outdated, but I was hoping you might be willing to . . ."

Her rambling was bordering on painful, so he placed his hands on either of her shoulders to help reassure her. "Whatever it is, you only need ask, and it's yours."

That seemed to bolster her because she blew out her breath and asked on a rush, "Fin, will you walk me down the aisle?"

Now the wind really felt as if it'd been knocked out of him. "Me?"

She nodded, her eyes not quite meeting his. "It's okay if you don't want to."

His hands flexed on her shoulders. "Of course, I do. I'd be absolutely honored. I'm just surprised you want me to."

Lina had no trouble meeting his gaze now. "Well, you're the closest thing I have to a brother, and today is about family—"

Her words were cut off as his arms banded around her back, crushing her to his chest. He couldn't seem to find his voice over the unexpected ball of emotion lodged in his throat. Finley didn't consider himself a particularly sentimental or maudlin man, but it had been a long time, longer than he cared to admit, since someone wanted him to be recognized as belonging to their family.

After being cast out from his own after his mother died, he'd been left to fend for himself until finding and joining the Brotherhood. But that was a family built out of duty and honor. What Lina offered was a family built on nothing more than genuine, no-strings-attached affection. She was the first person in his entire life to willingly make such an offer. Even his grandfather, who'd been the only person besides his mother to take more than a begrudging interest in him, couldn't say the same. But then, the aristocracy was nothing but a series of complicated relationships tied up in messy strings.

The shock of her offhand admission, so matter-of-fact and sweetly delivered, cut him to the marrow.

She tapped him on the shoulder. "Fin, I can't breathe," she gasped.

Finley jerked back. "Sorry, um . . ." He had to stop to clear his throat. "You just caught me by surprise."

"I can see that. So does that mean you'll do it?"

"Yes. Absolutely. As long as you're certain Quinn won't mind. I know she's like a sister to you; I wouldn't want to step on any toes."

"It was her idea, actually."

Finley staggered back and sat down on the edge of the bed. "Really?"

She nodded, grinning at whatever she read in his expression. He could only imagine he looked as bowled-over as he felt. It was certainly a novel experience. One he had absolutely no idea what to do with.

The Satori heir loved nothing more than to keep him guessing, but this was something new. Outside the one time she admitted not enjoying watching him get hurt, she'd kept her feelings about him close to her chest. He knew she was attracted to him. Whenever he got close, it was there in her sharp inhale of breath and the delicate flutter of her pulse against the velvety hollow of her throat. But she also used her attraction as an excuse to keep him at arm's length. Like a double-sided weapon she exploited to systematically disarm and cut him.

To find out she might actually take his feelings into account, that she thought of him at all outside their little game . . . that spoke to something else. Something that went far deeper than mere attraction.

Something that, if given the chance, could change everything.

"Well," Finley said, running his hands down his thighs as he rose back to his feet. "I guess we'd better get you to that altar before we have a raging beast to contend with."

"Oh, I'm sure Astrid will keep Nord in check until we get there."

Finley raised a brow. "Who said I was talking about him? He's not the only berserker in town."

Lina playfully slapped his arm. "If that's your way of calling me a Bridezilla, you better take it back. I've been nothing but a delight, and you know it."

"Ow," Finley moaned theatrically. "See? There you go mistaking violence for affection again. Best we hurry. I'd hate to see what state you devolve into if we let this go on unchecked for much longer."

"Keep talking like that, Fin, and I'll change my mind about this escort thing."

Finley took her arm, weaving it through his. "I thought brothers were supposed to tease their little sisters. I'm just playing my part. You know, really giving you the full experience."

Lina's eyes grew misty. "Oh. Well, in that case, carry on."

They shared a smile as he led her out of the room. "I suppose I could do more of the obligatory, 'you can change your mind, and I'll get you out of here no questions asked' speech, but I feel like that ship has long sailed."

"Yeah," Lina agreed. "If I tried to run, he'd find me. And he'd probably murder you, so best not to risk it. Even though I'm sure I'd have the night of my life once he found me."

"Disgusting. I don't want to think about my sister being ravaged by my best mate. Listening to it nightly is bad enough."

"I'd apologize, but that would mean I'm sorry, and I am definitely not."

Finley laughed. "Fair enough."

They'd just about reached the front door when she called his name. "Hey, Fin?"

"Yes, love?"

"Thank you for doing this. It means a lot to me."

He gave her hand a squeeze where it curled around his bicep. "I'm the one who should be thanking you."

Her head canted to the side. "How do you figure?"

"Because until I saw it with my own eyes, I didn't believe love was real. Watching you two together proved to me that it is. And that it's worth fighting for."

"Does that mean what I think it does?" she asked, her eyes bright with hope.

Finley winked at her. "Today's about you and your happily ever after. We'll worry about mine another day."

CHAPTER 14
NORD

Astrid smirked knowingly as Nord shifted impatiently beside her. He ignored his cousin, his eyes never straying from the other end of the dock where the faering would arrive with his mate in tow. So far, there was no sign of the small canoe-like vessel or its passengers.

He hadn't seen Lina since yesterday morning, and he felt every excruciating second of it. Nord knew she was safe, that there was no logical need for the anxiety caused by their separation. But that restless gnawing in his chest, the one that built the longer they were apart, didn't defer to something as trivial as logic. Until she was beside him, her body safely tucked in his, Nord knew he wouldn't feel whole or remotely steady. And so he continued to fidget, which only made Astrid's smirk deepen.

"Peace, cousin. She'll be here."

He growled in answer, not trusting himself to speak and not wanting to insult the woman who'd made this ceremony possible in the first place.

She'd certainly outdone herself. Not usually one to notice or care about such details, even Nord had to admit the transformation was nothing short of impressive. Astrid had managed to take a simple forest clearing and convert it into a place teeming with romance and magic in the span of only a few days.

The site was located on the western side of town, nestled between the mountains and sea. Towering conifers wrapped around almost half of the ceremony site, leaving the back half exposed to the lapping waves and the sun slowly sinking in the sky. The dock acted as an aisle, with small lanterns lining its sides and balls of brilliant violet light flickering within. Hundreds of flower petals were strewn across the sun-bleached wood and forest floor, creating a path that would lead his bride to him.

A stunning arbor had been erected for them, created with fallen branches from the surrounding trees and decorated with fragrant blooms and countless motes of twinkling purple light. He recognized the motes as the magical source that powered much of this place, but Astrid had yet to explain how they'd come by it.

A large crowd had already gathered, more than a little eager to bear witness to the union of the first female berserker in known history and their hero, the notorious Gunnar Bloodaxe.

All that was missing was her.

"They're here!" Strega shouted, a dull roar sounding as everyone rose to their feet and turned as one to face the small seacraft rowing up to the dock.

Time seemed to slow, all sound fading away until all Nord could hear was the uneven beat of his own heart. Finley disembarked first, twisting and offering Lina a hand as she climbed out. Nord couldn't seem to draw a full breath as she straightened and lifted her head, her eyes immediately finding his.

He'd never given much thought to his wedding or his future bride. When he'd been young, such things held no interest to him, and by the time he was old enough to care, he'd been too seduced by bloodshed to pay them any mind.

But now . . . Now that he'd found the woman who'd been made solely for him, he knew his lack of interest had been a gift from the gods. A way to ensure this exact moment came to be. Because nothing in his wildest imaginings could have prepared him for the reality of her. And the beauty of it, the sheer wonder, made his heart stutter in his chest as if learning how to beat for the very first time.

It should have been impossible for one such as her to exist. A woman who was both as regal as a queen and as tempting as a siren. Bloodthirsty as a warrior, yet still retaining the unmarred purity of someone who'd never set foot in battle. More loyal than any man he'd ever known and just as fiercely protective of the ones she loved as the mother he hoped she'd one day be.

She was exquisite. Utterly without equal. And she was his.

Lina's lips curled up in a slow, sensual smile, letting him know she'd felt every raw inch of his reaction, and it pleased her.

Music swelled, but he barely heard it. He was too busy tracking her steps, counting each breath until he could touch her. It was the struggle of his life not to move, to go to her. He thought waiting before had been agony, but these last few seconds might actually kill him.

Lina began to walk down the aisle, her steps sure, her smile only for him. One of her hands remained clasped in Finley's, and in the other held the sword she'd made from Alistair's cane, though she'd hung flowers from the hilt so they cascaded over the blade, thus turning the weapon into her bridal bouquet.

He'd never been more jealous of his friend in his life. He wanted to rip off the hand that held hers and then fling it and Finley into the sea.

Nord felt Lina's laughter bubbling up in his chest. The minx. She knew what the berserker was like. How reason played no part in its rationalizing. She, better than anyone, should understand how tenuous his hold was and how goading him was a recipe for disaster. At least, generally speaking. Today, her amusement tempered his anger, and he found himself returning her smile.

It felt like a thousand years had passed by the time they reached him. Once they stopped, Finley lifted Lina's hand to his lips, winked at her as he pressed a gentle kiss to the back of it, and then took her hand and set it in Nord's.

Before he stepped away, Finley caught and held Nord's gaze. "I know it goes without saying, but if you ever hurt her, I will make it my life's mission to destroy you."

Nord would have laughed. The thought of anyone thinking to threaten a berserker with violence was endlessly entertaining. But the sentiment behind the words checked the instinctive reaction. Here was a man who recognized the value of the woman whose hand he held. Who would guard and protect her with his dying breath. A man he'd trust with her life, which made Nord love him even more.

"Thank you, brother." With his free hand, he wrapped it around Finley's head, pulling him close and pressing a brusque kiss on his cheek. "And if the day ever arises where you need to follow through on your warning, I'll welcome the blade you drive through my heart."

They shared a one-armed embrace, and then Finley joined Quinn and the other Satori in the front row.

Nord's eyes returned to his bride. "Kærasta, you undo me."

"And you me, Ástvinur."

His brows flew up, though his surprise at her use of the endearment was eclipsed by his joy at hearing her call him her beloved in his native tongue.

"I see you've been busy since I saw you last."

She grinned. "That's not all Strega taught me how to say. You look so very handsome in your leather and fur, elskan mín."

My love.

It did something to him, hearing those words fall from her lips while she looked like a Norse goddess. She'd learned them for him. Dressed with care. For him. Each deliberate choice was like a love letter. A way for Lina to tell him how much she loved him. To show him she understood what his culture meant to him and how deeply ingrained in him it was. And how she'd embraced it, and him, absolutely.

And then she went and proved that not only was she a perfect match for the man, but his beast as well. Dropping her voice low to ensure her next words were for him alone, she said, "I can't wait to rip those clothes off and take you for a ride."

His berserker roared to life, urging Nord to grab her and take her somewhere she could do just that. Cock straining against his pants, he let out a strangled laugh. "I think that's supposed to be my line."

Lina shrugged as they turned and rejoined Astrid, her voice still pitched low. "Guess we'll have to wait to wrestle it out and see which one of us gets to be on top."

He couldn't contain his low, approving growl. Even when she looked like an angel, his mate invited him to sin.

So. Fucking. Perfect.

Without thought, he leaned forward to catch her lips with his, only to be pulled up short by Astrid's low cough.

"Forgetting something?" she teased. "Traditionally, we do the handfasting and vows before you kiss her."

The crowd burst into raucous cheers and appreciative laughter.

Björn's booming voice rang out, "Hopefully your restraint proves greater in the marriage bed, Gunnar, or your bride is in for a disappointing night."

Nord's eyes cut toward the bear of a man, but Lina stopped him by squeezing the fingers still gripped in his, calling out sweetly, "After what Strega told me, Björn, you do seem to be quite the expert when it comes to premature ends to an evening."

The guests whooped and hollered while Strega walloped a crimson Björn on the back of his head and ordered him to sit down and shut up.

Astrid held up her hands, and the crowd died back down. "Shall we begin?"

"Just get on with it," Nord said, not even bothering to curb his impatience. He knew the wedding had been his idea, but he couldn't seem to remember why he'd wanted to suffer through this spectacle in the first place. Resisting the call of his beast and keeping his hands off Lina was proving to be the sweetest torture. Having to share her and this moment with a herd of rabid hyenas was even worse.

Nord was only half-listening as Astrid officially started the ceremony by opening the 'circle.' She did this by picking up one of the three horns of mead set beside her and asking Nord and Lina to turn with her as she poured a little mead on the ground in each direction as an invitation for the various gods to join and bless them.

When they'd done this four times, Astrid asked Nord and Lina to raise their joined hands and look into each other's eyes. As they moved to obey, just as it had when she stepped off the boat, everything faded away but her.

Her eyes were wide and shining, staring into his with absolute devotion. The echo of what she was feeling swept through him, filling him with a joy so sweet he felt high with it. Once again, his mate had managed to wash him free of any residual temper. All he could feel—all he wanted—was her.

With that thought forefront in his mind, Astrid lifted a red cord and began binding their hands as she spoke.

"You begin your journey bound together by the vows of this rite. No matter the number of years you will share or the moons you may watch, if you keep your vows, your sacred trust, blessed and happy will be your days.

"May the keepers of the sacred winds whisper joy into your life. The past is in flames, as you are forever changed from this day forward. May those fires of love kindle your passions for each other. And the waters of life help you discover the reflection of your love in one another's soul. Together, explore the laughter of rain and share the tears of life. Plant your roots together in the earth. Grow old and wise. And may the future you build bring you happiness and peace strong enough to chase you from this life into the next."

Tears burned in his throat, though Nord managed to hold them at bay. Lina was less successful. She was crying freely, though her smile only grew more radiant as Astrid continued with her blessing.

When she was finished, Astrid said, "Will you both repeat after me."

Nord had already decided he would make his vows to Lina in his native tongue since he considered it the language of his heart. There was no worry of her understanding since her vows would be the same. And, even if that hadn't been the case, he knew their bond would ensure she felt every single word.

Staring deep into her eyes, Nord began to speak. "Beloved, I seek to know you, and ask the gods and goddesses above to grant me the wisdom to see you as you are and love you without condition. I will take joy in you, delight in my love for you. For you are the whispering of the tides, the seduction of summer's warmth, a temptation impossible to resist. You are my greatest adventure and my most cherished memory. You are my friend, my lover, my equal in every way."

He'd lost the battle to his emotion somewhere in the middle, his voice husky but no less steady because of it.

Lina's lower lip trembled as she repeated his words back to him. He lifted his free hand and brushed away a few of her tears, but more only splashed down to take their place. Her voice hitched and went threadbare as she struggled to breathe through the depth of her emotion.

Quinn, ever the savior, crept forward waving a white handkerchief at her, which Lina accepted with a watery laugh that was echoed by the guests. The moment of levity helped her regain herself enough to deliver the last lines without issue.

"Phew," she joked, "I almost really made a mess of those."

The crowd laughed, and Nord's heart squeezed. He couldn't love her any more than he did in that moment.

He almost leaned down to kiss her again, but Astrid reined him in by saying, "And now we will signify these sacred vows with the exchanging of rings. Gunnar . . ."

Nord used his free hand to unsheathe the sword at his back.

Lina's ring, a slender silver band of Norse knots, had been tied to the pommel.

Quinn stepped forward to untie the ring and take the sword. She staggered when Nord released it, her eyes flaring comedically. "Christ, couldn't you do something about the weight?"

Lina bit down on her bottom lip as she tried to contain her laugh.

"Fucking Vikings," Quinn sniped as she readjusted her hold and then carried the sword over to a small table that had been set aside for that purpose. There were a few more grumbles as she hefted it up, but she managed, turning to give them a thumbs-up as she moved to reclaim her seat.

Small chuckles rang out from the crowd, and Quinn flipped them off. "Not all of us are disgustingly strong, okay? Deal with it."

Cora rolled her eyes and tugged on the bottom of her daughter's dress. "Just sit down, dear."

"Shall we proceed?" Astrid asked, amusement coloring her tone.

"Yes," Lina said, still smiling as she lifted her unbound hand.

After pressing a kiss to her knuckles, Nord slid the ring onto her finger, speaking in Norse once again as he did. "Just like this ring, there shall be no end for us; from this life, into the next and every one hereafter, you and I will be one."

He watched her throat bob as she fought against a fresh wave of tears.

"I love you," she mouthed.

He winked at her.

"And now, Lina," Astrid gently prompted.

Finley stepped forward, having held onto Lina's bouquet for her. Just like with her ring, Nord's had been tied to her weapon. Finley untied it and then held the band out to Lina before turning to lay her sword in its place beside Nord's on the table.

"I could have made it look easy if I got to carry the little one too," Quinn griped under her breath.

Nord shook his head as he caught Finley's whispered reply. "Darling, I make everything look good. But I make it feel even better."

Quinn's face flushed, but Nord's attention returned to Lina, leaving those two to their games.

His bride cleared her throat, her hand trembling as she guided the ring onto his only naked finger. And though he hadn't earned this ring in battle, he knew the moment she slid it into place, there'd never be one he valued more.

Her voice trembled as she repeated his earlier vow. "Just like this ring, there shall be no end for us; from this life, into the next and every one hereafter, you and I will be one."

The feel of that ring combined with those ancient words soothed a wild part of his soul, even as it lured the berserker back out of hiding.

Finally. It was done. She belonged to him in every possible way. And no one, not even the gods themselves, could do anything about it.

"You have declared your consent before your gods and goddesses within this holy circle. May our Mother Goddess Frigga strengthen your consent and fill you both with her blessings. We wish the two of you as many days of perfect love and perfect trust as life can bring you. By the witness of our gods, goddesses, and ancestors, may these sacred vows manifest. I hereby pronounce you man and wife. You may now kiss the bride."

Nord's mouth was on Lina's long before Astrid finished speaking. A low growl sounded in his throat as she wove her newly ringed hand through his hair and yanked him closer. The kiss spiraled out of control, need and lust winding tighter as she nipped and licked at him, her berserker spurring his own.

Astrid tried to get their attention, but Nord was done. They'd spoken their vows, and she'd said the words. Their obligation to anyone but each other was complete.

It was time for him to fuck his wife.

Calling on his strength, he ripped his hand free of the rope binding their hands and swooped Lina up in his arms. She looped her arms around his neck without hesitation, still kissing him as he turned and stalked toward the edge of the forest.

"What about the reception?" Astrid shouted after them. "You still have to drink the mead!"

Nord pulled away from Lina only far enough to lift his head and call back, "No, what I need to do is for my wife and I alone. If any of you bother us before sunrise, know that I will kill first and ask questions later. So if you value your limbs or your life, I suggest you reconsider and enjoy the party on our behalf."

Loud cheers rang out at his words, but Nord only cared about resuming where he and Lina had left off.

Her eyes were soft and her smile dreamy as his gaze dropped back to her face.

"Is that smile for me?"

"All my smiles are for you," she said, her fingers playing in his hair. "But that one's because you called me your wife."

"That's what you are."

He could feel the explosion of her wonder and lust as she raised her lips to his. "I love you, ektemann."

Those feelings became his own, hearing her call him husband for the first time.

"And I you, eiginkona."

Before their lips could meet, she moved her mouth to his ear. "Now, be a good husband and take me somewhere you can fuck me until I forget my name again. For the rest of the night, the only thing I want to know is the feel of you moving inside me."

His cock wept at the command. "Be careful what you wish for, Kærasta. It just might be more than you can handle."

"That's what I'm counting on."

CHAPTER 15
LINA

There was something about the sight of a man—her man—in muscle-hugging leather and draped in a mantle of fur that made her think of presents on Christmas morning. Her mind was consumed with thoughts of unwrapping him. Of taking her very favorite toy out of its packaging and discovering each and every one of its secrets.

She'd already done that, of course. Plenty of times. But it never got old, letting her hands roam across the broad expanse of his chest, over the ridges of his abs until they closed over the velvety steel of his arousal. Taking him in her mouth or aching cunt. Feeling the flex of his ass as he drove into her without mercy. Hearing the throaty growl of her name as he spilled inside of her.

Lina knew he'd picked up on the decidedly filthy turn of her thoughts when his husky chuckle washed over her. "Something on your mind?"

"I think I might have been a shield-maiden in a past life."

Nord's steps faltered as he looked down at her. He hadn't been expecting her to say that, and she secretly rejoiced at being able to keep him on his toes. "*That's* what you're thinking about right now?"

Lina ran a hand down his jaw, letting the tips of her fingers move over one of the decorative beads he'd worn in his beard before she answered. "There's just something about seeing you in your element like this. It's doing it for me in the biggest fucking way. From the second I saw you waiting for me at the end of the aisle, all I could think about was getting my hands on you. I'm pretty sure brides aren't supposed to have the kind of thoughts I was having. A porn star, maybe, but definitely not a bride. Good thing we weren't in an actual church. I might have been smited."

Nord laughed, a deep, masculine rumble filled with approval. "First of all, if I was in my element, I'd be naked and inside you. Second, it's a good thing our gods approve of lusty brides. No smiting required."

"First of all," she mocked, "what the hell are you waiting for? And second, same question."

The look he shot her could have converted an entire abbey of nuns. "Privacy for the things I'm going to do to you."

Her stomach took a low, toe-curling swoop as heat began to pool in her core. She squirmed in his arms as she said, "We're in the middle of a Novasgardian forest. I think we're as private as it's going to get, so you might as well pick a tree and get on with the doing."

"If I can still hear them, they can hear us. And I don't intend for anyone but the two of us to be part of tonight's festivities."

Need stabbed at her, and it took considerable effort for her to breathe through the anticipation of him following through on that promise, let alone string together an entire coherent sentence. The best she could manage was a breathy, "Hurry, Viking. Or I might just have to start without you."

"I'd like to see you manage that in this dress."

"Oh, that's easily fixed," she said, ready to call on her power and nix it completely.

He stopped her with a low warning growl. "Don't you fucking dare. I've waited what felt like an eternity for the honor of removing you from that lace. Do not rob me of the privilege."

Lina's heart leapt, and she was half-convinced it was trying to escape the confines of her chest and return to the man it belonged to.

"Then do it. Or I will, because one way or the other, I'm going to have you naked and inside me in the next five seconds."

Pressed against him as she was, Lina felt Nord's body react to her demand. His arms spasmed around her, his muscles swelled, and when his eyes met hers, the black of his berserker was already bleeding into the icy blue. He was hanging onto his control by a thread, and it was her sudden mission to cut it and send him free-falling until he was nothing more than a slave to his body's desire. She wanted him as desperate and mindless as he made her.

She wanted him at his purest, most primal state.

She wanted it all. No holds barred.

Finesse and bedroom games were fun, and they had their place, but when she'd become a berserker, she'd been reborn. Something wild and untamed lived inside her, a creature every bit as savage and feral as his. And she needed her mate to come out and play.

"I don't care who hears us. Let them listen. Let them learn what it sounds like when a berserker claims his mate. And then let them live the rest of their lives knowing what they have with their partner doesn't come fucking close to what exists between us."

"Lina," he growled a second before his lips descended over hers.

Mission accomplished.

There was a sudden shift in gravity as he set her down and then walked her backward until her back crashed into a tree. Before her mind could make sense of her change in position, his fingers were skimming over her collarbone before grasping the edge of her dress with each hand and rending it in two.

"Gods, if I'd known you weren't wearing anything under your dress . . ." He didn't finish the sentence, his chest rising and falling in erratic pants as he raked his gaze over her body.

The look was so potent, so filled with need, she could feel it wash over her. She had to clench her thighs and lock her knees to remain standing. Holding his gaze, Lina let what was left of her wedding dress drop to the forest floor. Cool air washed over her desire-warmed skin, and goosebumps formed in its wake.

"Time's up, Viking."

She'd intended to return the favor and use her berserker-enhanced strength to rip him free of his leathers, but at her words, he let out a low snarl.

"You don't issue the commands."

Usually, that alone would be enough to render her little more than a quivering pool of desire, but Lina wasn't in the driver's seat right now. Her berserker was—and she was a mouthy bitch.

"Not only will I be making demands, mate, but you're going to obey them. Ensuring my pleasure is one of your sole functions. And a surefire way for you to please me is to fuck me. So do it."

Nord bared his teeth, slamming her into the tree and lifting her up so her legs wound around his waist in one fluid move. Thankfully, berserkers thrived on pain, because the scrape of bark against her back only enhanced her pleasure.

"Yes," she purred, grinding herself over his erection and sending delicious tingles racing across her body. "Now you're getting the idea. Free that massive cock, Viking, and fuck me like you were born to do it."

"Keep it up, and I won't let you come."

"My orgasms are not dependent on your permission."

His hand snaked out, grasping her around the jaw and forcing her head back as his fingers dug into her cheeks. "Your orgasms belong to me. All of them. Every. Single. One." He brought his mouth to her ear. "You will not come until I tell you that you can. Do you understand?"

Lust spiraled through her at the display of domination, and she could feel herself dripping with arousal. This was a mate worthy of her. One who would cherish and protect her but also never let her forget who she'd bound her soul to. She was looking forward to the reminder, but she was also enjoying this too much to let him know her surrender was assured.

"Earn them first, Viking. And then maybe I'll let you control them."

"Let me?"

She felt the punch of his need as it rolled through her and joined her own. She loved that he was enjoying this as much as she was. That he was as eager to prove his dominance as she was to revel in it.

Lina hadn't been prepared for their berserkers to take over, though she supposed the traditions they'd taken part in today were as much theirs as the other Novasgardians. Perhaps it was only appropriate they'd want to partake in some of their own. She certainly wasn't complaining.

While this was no bridal night in the traditional sense—filled with sweet words and tender caresses—it *was* a mating dance. A rite of passage for two predators intent on laying permanent claim to each other. Instead of vows, they exchanged ultimatums. Instead of rings, they drew blood. In the end, it was every bit as sacred, as vital, as what had taken place in front of their family and friends.

Nord pressed into her, making it impossible for her to focus on anything but the feel of his body against hers as he slid his rock-hard length along her slick center.

"Understand this, mate. There's not an inch of your body that does not belong to me. Your lips" —he punctuated the words with a deep kiss—"your breasts."

He dropped his hold on her face as he feathered his knuckles down her chest. She let out a wanton moan when his fingers grazed her nipple and then gripped and twisted. He released her sooner than she'd have liked, his hand continuing its journey south. When he reached the apex of her thighs, he rotated his wrist so that his hand could slide between her legs. Then he spread her wide and swiped his thumb over her throbbing center. As he did, he growled, "Your pussy."

She groaned and rocked her hips against his hand, silently demanding more.

Despite the inky color of his eyes, they burned with sexual

promise as his hooded gaze met hers. "See, Lina. Every fucking inch of you is mine. Your body knows it, even if you still try to pretend otherwise."

It was a struggle to draw breath, but Lina somehow managed, looking him straight in the eyes as she said, "Prove it."

The smile he gave her was sin and sex. "I was hoping you'd say that."

There was no room for talking after that. His lips claimed hers in a kiss that robbed her of breath and all conscious thought. He pinned her body between his and the tree, one hand working her center while he fucked her mouth with his tongue. Just when she was on the cusp, little fireworks building in her periphery and the sensation between her legs burning white-hot, he pulled back.

"Ah ah ah," he tutted. "Did I say you could come?"

"Fucker," she breathed, her hips humping the air as they tried to reestablish the delicious friction he'd been providing mere seconds earlier.

"Say it, Lina. Say that your pussy and all your orgasms belong to me."

"I don't remember that being one of the vows."

"Funny, I do."

She raised a brow and started to slide one of the arms she'd wound around his neck between them. His pulse leapt in his throat when she grasped her breast, pinching and twisting its pebbled tip. She was trying to make a point, teasing him as she did, but the move was doing just as much, if not more, to tease her. With a half-sob, she dropped her hand lower. She barely made it down to the space between her dripping core and his throbbing length when he reacted.

He immediately dropped her, his hands catching her hips before she could fall to the ground and spinning her around to face the tree. With one hand at the base of her spine, he gently but firmly captured one of her wrists in the other hand and lifted it, pressing it into the bark above her head.

"If you move this hand, you will not be able to sit for a week."

That shouldn't have been sexy, but the words alone were enough to send sparks of sensation rippling out from the place longing for his most intimate touch.

He released her slowly, one finger peeling back at a time. When she didn't make a move, his lips brushed the back of her neck where it met her shoulder. "Good girl." Then he took her other hand and laid it on top of the first. "Stay," he ordered.

She was trembling, but she obeyed. Gone was the need to provoke and push back. All she wanted now was whatever he was planning. When she heard the rustling of fabric, she peeked over her shoulder, but he growled out another command.

"Face forward."

Lina obeyed with another quaking breath. She almost groaned when she heard his pants join the rest of his clothes on the floor. She pictured him towering over her, his perfect, masculine body tense with his desire for her. His proud erection jutting out. His face flushed, eyes hooded. All of it because of what he was feeling for her. The image of him alone was almost enough to tip her over the edge.

When his hand curled over her hip and slipped back between her legs, she could have wept, but her pleasure was short-lived. Although he ran his fingers through her folds, gathering her slickness, his hand fell away from her body almost as quickly as it appeared.

"No," she protested weakly. "Don't stop."

Then she heard his soft groan as he took himself in his hand and began to slowly slide her wetness up and down his length.

"You bastard," she growled. "If my pussy is yours, then your cock is mine."

"Is that so?"

She could hear the smile in his voice, along with the slow, even strokes of his hand. Her fingers clenched, digging into the tree as she fought the desperate impulse to return them to her aching clit.

Sensing her loss of control, Nord wrapped his free hand around her wrists, anchoring her in place.

"If you want my cock, mate, you know what you have to say."

"I want it."

"I know you do, but that's not what I meant. Tell me who your pussy belongs to."

While he'd been talking, he'd lined himself up with her entrance, and now he slowly ran his tip through her slippery folds.

Lina's eyes rolled back in her head. "Y-you."

"I didn't quite catch that. Come again?"

"I'm still trying to come the first time."

He laughed. "Good girls get to come. Naughty girls get left on the edge. Which do you want to be?"

"Both," she groaned when he slid into her that first delicious inch. Her body tried to chase him when he pulled right back out.

"Say it and mean it, Lina. And I'll give you what you so clearly crave."

Her words were frantic, leaving her in a rush. "My pussy is yours. All of me is yours. My orgasms. My heart. You can have whatever you want. Just, please, fuck me. I need you. Oooooh."

He slammed into her before she finished speaking.

"All of you, Lina. I want it all. Nothing less than everything. You are mine. My mate. My wife. My reason for existence. Never. Fucking. Forget it."

His thrusts were relentless, wild. It was like her admission had set something free within him, and whatever control he might have retained until now vanished. He fucked her with abandon. Claiming her body every bit as much as he had with his words.

She was sobbing. Crying out his name. Pleading for something. Her body chasing its climax but never quite reaching that last, exquisite inch. It was as he'd said. She belonged to him. She couldn't come until he told her to.

Lina lost track of everything but the feel of him, helpless to do anything but exist in a sea of sensation—just like she'd asked. There was nothing but her, Nord, and the forest around them as he worked her body, imprinting the feel of him on her very soul.

And when that growled command finally came, stars exploded behind her eyes, entire worlds rising and falling as she shook with the force of her release. She screamed so loud she thought the tree trembled from the strength of it. And when Nord sank his teeth into that spot on the back of her neck, grunting his own climax, it triggered a second, more powerful orgasm. Her vision went black, and there was no doubt that the tremors that ran through her body were passing into the tree she'd been clutching for dear life.

A crack sounded far above her, and if not for Nord's arm around her waist tugging her back, she might have been hit by the branch they'd somehow shaken free with their vigorous lovemaking.

"Well," she said, when she was able to speak again, "I guess this means we've upgraded from breaking the furniture."

Nord laughed, kissing her hard. "Yes, we did."

"At least we didn't make the whole tree topple over. That would have been hard to explain."

He raised a brow. "Is that a challenge?"

"No," she laughed. "Not at all. I'm just saying it's probably safer for everyone involved if we stick to flat surfaces from now on. Beds. Floors. Those sorts of things."

Nord eyed the fur spread out on the ground beside them, then looked back at her with a roguish grin. "Don't be so sure about that. Trees are known to fall when the earth quakes. I bet we could manage to knock down one or two."

Lina followed his gaze, her lips curling. "I guess there's only one way to find out."

CHAPTER 16
QUINN

The party had been raging for hours, and people's inhibitions were starting to fall by the wayside. With each twirl around the dance floor, or new cask of mead, eyes got brighter and hands more adventurous.

Quinn watched it all unfold from the sidelines, eyeing the revelers with interest while nursing her own drink. She envied their freedom. Freedom to live in the moment. To love without fear, whether the person in their arms was theirs for the night or a lifetime. They didn't seem weighed down with anything more complicated than finding happiness wherever and however they could.

Longing, fierce and hungry, swept through her. She wished she could be more like them. Less bogged down by the reality of who and what she was. Free to take what she wanted without apology. To live solely for the moment with no worry of what the morning would bring.

She'd briefly contemplated finding a Viking of her own to sneak off with and scratch a particular itch, but every time one caught her eye, there'd be a flash of black tux in her periphery, and she knew it was useless. There was only one man her body craved, and he just happened to be the one she couldn't dare to have.

Not even if she could afford the price of such freedom. Which she absolutely could not. Certainly not while Mikel lived. He'd made damn sure of that.

But he isn't here now. How would he ever know?

"Shut up, you hussy," Quinn hissed. Such indulgence would only end in heartache—hers—and more pain than the human body could withstand—theirs.

"Talking to yourself is rarely a good sign."

Quinn startled and glanced over to find Søren had joined her. The man cleaned up nicely. He'd swept his dark hair up into a half-pony-tail, letting the rest fall to his shoulders in soft waves. And he'd shaved his beard so only a dark stubble remained on his strong jaw. The combination made him look years younger and far more approachable.

"That's a hell of a warning coming from a gregarious fellow such as yourself."

He flashed her a smile that would have shocked the panties off her had she been wearing any. "People talk too much and say too little. I reserve my words for when they hold actual weight."

She lifted her brows. "And coming over to save me from a solo conversation counts, huh? Wow. Low bar."

He chuckled.

"Who are you, and what did you do with the broody asshole I met last time? The real Søren doesn't smile, and he sure as hell never laughs."

His glower was instant, and Quinn wasn't faking when she shivered. Geez, but he could be a scary fucker when he wanted to be. Then he broke out into another grin. "Was that better?"

She placed a hand over her heart. "Just promise me you won't go jumping out from any dark corners, and we should be fine."

"Deal."

They lapsed back into silence, and Quinn's eyes returned to the dance floor. Her lips lifted in a smile when she found her mother being dipped by a man who'd introduced himself as Sten. He was a distinguished-looking fisherman with laugh lines at his eyes, silver at his temples and his beard, and the deepest growl of a voice she'd ever heard. Her mother had blushed like a schoolgirl when he asked her to dance. Quinn couldn't remember the last time her mom had looked so carefree and alive.

Even Sheridan had set aside her grief tonight to dance with Björn, whose wife watched from the other side of the room. Strega's eyes sparkled with amusement as her husband tried to make her jealous by dancing with another woman. He might have been onto something if his method of seduction didn't involve jumping from one leg to the other while raising the opposite arm in the air. Every now and then, he'd stop to point in a random direction and thrust his hips a few times before resuming his enthusiastic hops. What he lacked in technique, he made up for in sheer charisma. Sheridan's face was flushed with laughter, and she was constantly stopping to either clutch her sides or wipe away the tears streaming down her cheeks.

"You know, you can join them instead of just watching from way over here."

"Still worrying about me, are you? And here I was thinking you were over there trying to figure out how to teach that bird of yours Björn's sweet moves."

Søren shook his head. "I'm not even sure what he's doing counts as dancing."

"Are you kidding? That's a one-man-discotheque if I ever saw it."

"A what?"

"Disco? Stayin' alive. Stayin' alive." She pointed her finger up to the right and then brought it across her body and down to the left. "You know what, never mind. Not important."

"Well, whatever you call it, Huginn doesn't much care for dancing."

"Who?"

"My raven."

"I *knew* it."

Søren raised his brows. "Knew what?"

"Everyone said he was too big to be a raven, but I just had a feeling. What other black bird would a Viking own, you know, with the Odin thing and all?"

His lips twitched. "What can I say? We grow them big here."

Quinn gave him an appreciative once-over. "Yeah, you do."

"So what do you think, häxa? Shall we dance?"

"You want . . ." Quinn pointed between the two of them. "Me and you?"

"Is that so hard to believe?"

"Have you looked at yourself in a mirror? Men like you aren't known for cutting a rug."

"What does a rug have to do with it?"

"It's an expression for dancing."

He made a face.

"Okay, I'll admit, not our best, but there are far worse ones. Trust me." Quinn narrowed her eyes. "Do you know how to find and keep a beat? Because I really don't want to go all the way over there if we're just going to awkwardly shuffle side to side."

"I've been known to cut rugs," he said with heavy emphasis, giving her a look that clearly conveyed it was the most asinine thing he'd ever said, "when the occasion calls for it."

Quinn pitched her voice low. "Is this one of those times?"

He crossed his arms over his chest, making his muscles flex in a way she couldn't help but appreciate. "We're on the eve of war. Is there a better occasion to celebrate being alive?"

"Well, when you put it that way, Viking. How can I refuse?" She held out her hand, pulling it back before he could grasp it. "But take a good look at these stilettos before you dare step on my feet, because I will return the favor."

He looked confused again, his eyes roaming over her body. "You're hiding blades in that dress?"

"Oh, for fuck's sake. Let's go."

Søren led her to the edge of the dance floor, taking her hand and pulling her into his body like he'd done it a thousand times before. Quinn was soon lost to the feverish beat of the music, her partner expertly guiding her through the moves of the unfamiliar dance. And when he gripped her hips and lifted her up to spin her around, she let her head fall back and held out her arms, feeling as though she was soaring just like that raven of his.

Dancing with Søren was the most liberated she'd felt in years, her heart floating in the way only genuine euphoria achieved instead of anchored in chains of grief and duty. He may never realize what a gift he'd given her through a single dance. The release of such heavy emotions had her nearly in tears, though Quinn furiously blinked them away, not wanting to scare off her partner. She had a feeling out of all the things he'd faced without flinching, a woman's tears were not one of them.

The song was over before she was ready, its fast pace shifting to something slow and romantic. Søren stared at her like he wasn't sure what to do next. Then with a slight roll of his eyes, he tugged her close until her arms were resting on his shoulders.

She tipped her head back, ready to say something outlandish and overly flirtatious, as was her specialty, when there was a slight tap on her shoulder.

"I believe this dance is mine."

Finley.

She'd been avoiding him all night, and the look of challenge in his eyes told her he knew it. The air in her chest condensed and then expanded so fast she couldn't quite hide the soft hitch of her breath.

Søren took one look at Finley and then at Quinn before dropping the hands that rested on her waist.

"You could have at least pretended to fight for me."

He bent low, giving her a brotherly peck on the cheek. "Live while you can, häxa. Tomorrow is never guaranteed. But it's even less likely you'll live to greet the dawn when battle looms." And with that profound, albeit incredibly depressing bit of parting wisdom, he gave Finley a nod and took off in the direction of the dark-haired bartender Quinn assumed was his lover.

Finley looked mildly impatient, teeming with a restless sort of energy she wasn't used to from him. "Well?" he demanded, holding out his hand for her.

"I'm starting to see why the whole nobility thing didn't work out for you. Your manners are lacking, darling. 'Well' isn't an invitation."

"Dance with me, Satori."

The husky cast of his voice, combined with the banked heat in his hazel eyes, was the most delicious temptation. She didn't think she'd ever heard a man make something so innocent sound quite so delightfully filthy.

"Is this the part where I'm supposed to curtsy, because I'm not sure I can manage that in this dress."

His gaze swept over the deep purple cocktail dress with its scoop neck and black-beaded overlay. While modest from the front, the back was open, leaving her skin exposed from her shoulders down to the base of her spine. When Finley's eyes returned to hers, there was no mistaking his hunger. Or the way his scorching gaze seared her with its heat. How could any woman resist a man who looked at her like he wanted to destroy her and save her in the same breath? Quinn's nipples drew into tight peaks, and damp heat pooled in her core at the thought of how he'd manage just that.

"Must you make everything so damned difficult? Just get over here," he growled, grabbing her wrist and pulling her close so not even a sliver of space was left between them.

Unlike Søren, who'd been a perfect gentleman, Finley left no doubt that his intentions were anything but platonic. His touch was possessive, imprinting itself on her soul as he molded her body to his, running one hand down the ridges of her spine and bringing their hips into direct contact.

She gasped at the feel of his arousal pressing insistently against her belly. Learning he was just as affected as she was made it even harder to behave and not cross the tenuous line she'd drawn between them. She might step right to the edge of it more often than not, but since putting it there, she hadn't dared take the final, damning step.

Taking one of her arms, he ran his fingers along the underside as he lifted it up and draped it over his shoulder. Then he repeated the move with her other. Once he had her positioned the way he wanted, he trailed the tips of his fingers over her spine before splaying both of his palms as low as they could go on her back without being completely indecent. Though, with the cut of her dress, his fingers still grazed the bare flesh of her ass when they slid beneath the fabric.

He wanted there to be no room for doubt that she was spoken for if any other man looked her way. And she kind of loved it.

Quinn's breath stuttered at the unexpected flurry of longing that rolled through her at the casual act of possession. She ached for his hands to slide lower, to delve between the shadowy cleft between her legs and—God, she'd never needed anyone the way she needed this man.

As they began to sway in time to the beat, he held her in his arms like she was something precious. Someone he'd never let go. The realization left her off-kilter. Attraction was hard enough to fight, but genuine emotion? It threatened to undo her completely.

Needing to reestablish their usual dynamic, she opted for the blandest tone she could manage. "Didn't know you could dance, Batman."

"There's a lot of things you don't know about me, Satori."

"Is that so? And I was so sure I had you all figured out. Tell me something I don't know, British Man of Mystery. Really shock me."

He seemed to consider her teasing command for a minute before lowering his head so his mouth hovered just beside her ear. His whispered confession caressed her skin like crushed velvet.

"I was really hoping you'd opt for the leather and fishnets."

The tingles that set off had her clenching her thighs. "Oh? Were you hoping for a spanking?"

She heard the smugness in his grin, even though his cheek was pressed to hers. "I'm the one who does the spanking, princess."

Lord have mercy.

Arousal, potent and electric, coursed through her at the image of him bending her over his knee and pinkening her ass with his palm. Quinn's reaction shocked her. She craved control, needed it even, because her life so often felt completely out of her own. It was rare that she found a partner she was willing to cede control to. Rarer still to find one strong enough to tame her. There hadn't been one yet who could.

The idea of Finley, proper, polished Finley, being the man that would succeed? Now that was damn near irresistible. After the blatant way he'd claimed her mouth in that alley, she was under no illusions about what it would be like if she ever gave him the opportunity to do the same to the rest of her body. Just the thought did all sorts of wicked things to her lady parts.

Finley pulled back. The silver specks ringing his pupils seemed to glow as they scanned her face. "I see you like the sound of that. Have you been naughty, princess? Is that what you need? The feel of my hand raining down on that ass till you're dripping for me? Begging me to fill you?"

Yes! Fuck yes! Sign me up. I'll take ten in every color.

Despite her racing heart and the way she was all but panting for him to do just that, she raised a brow. "Sorry, handsome, I'm not in the market for a daddy. Not even one as sexy as you."

"How do you know? Have you had one? Someone who took care of you? Really took care of you. A man who saw to your needs—the emotional and physical ones?" His eyes glittered as they studied her. "No, I didn't think so. Don't be so quick to say no to something you don't understand, Quinn. It might be the very thing you've been searching for."

"I doubt that."

"Liar. Your body gives you away. Your skin is flushed, your pupils blown wide, breaths shallow—and I haven't even touched you yet. Give me one night. I bet I'll change your mind."

God but she wanted to say yes. If not for the fact she knew one night would be nowhere near enough she might just have.

"I won't crawl for any man, Batman. You're barking up the wrong tree if you think I'm that kind of girl."

"I don't think, I know. I know *exactly* what kind of woman you are."

"Is that so? Enlighten me."

"You're the kind of woman who's so trapped in her own head, she craves release. She craves someone to release her from the overwhelming burden. To pleasure her so thoroughly she's helpless to do anything but exist in that moment, free from the weight of the world crushing her. Be brought to a place where nothing exists but the feel of his hands on your body . . . his tongue in your mouth . . . between your legs . . . his cock driving into your aching cunt. That's the kind of woman you are."

Quinn's mouth fell open, but there was no smart-ass rebuff at the ready. Finley had thoroughly and utterly shocked her. Not only that, but the infuriating man *saw* her. Better than anyone ever had.

"So what if he helps you find peace by tying you to his bed or spanking your pert little ass until you're floating in a sea of sensation? There's nothing wrong with that. There's nothing wrong with needing someone to help you learn how to be free. To help you become who you truly are."

She was so turned on she could hardly see straight. She couldn't manage to look him in the eyes, so she settled for the hollow of his throat. It was a second before she gathered herself enough to say, "And I assume you think you're that man?"

"Oh, princess. I know I am."

She forced a hollow laugh through the constriction in her throat. "You just want to tie me up as payback for that serious case of blue balls you've been sporting since we met."

"You've got it all wrong. I don't want to humiliate you. I want to free you."

"Do I look like I'm in chains to you?"

"Princess, you're bound so tight you're suffocating, and you don't even realize it."

"And you really think you're the answer? The key to my proverbial lock?"

"I know I am. And so do you. You're just too scared to admit it."

"I'm not scared of anything."

"So prove it. Spend the night with me."

The temptation to give in was beyond anything she'd ever experienced.

Finley leaned down, his lips just grazing hers as he whispered, "I bet if I were to touch you right now, you'd be dripping. That perfect little cunt of yours is more than ready for me to slide my cock in where it belongs. You were made to be mine, Quinn. Let me prove what your body already knows."

Her eyes fluttered closed, and Finley moved his lips over hers, his sweet, teasing kisses so at odds with his carnal words.

"Just say the word. I can make it all go away. I can set you free."

"Fin—"

He kissed her again, this time sliding one of his hands into the hair at the nape of her neck and giving a light tug. "Say yes, Quinn. Put us both out of our misery."

She groaned, forcing her hands between their chests. "Fin, you know why we can't. Mikel—"

"There's no need for you to worry, princess. Nothing's going to happen to me." He dipped his face low until his lips brushed over the shell of her ear as he growled, "I'm Batman." Then he pulled back and flashed her his most charming, dimpled grin. "Remember?"

His playful words shattered her. It was the absolute worst and most heart-wrenchingly perfect thing he could have said.

It went against her nature to deny herself—unless it was necessary to protect someone she cared about. Usually it was no trouble.

Her heart was rarely at risk of lingering attachment. Until Finley. And knowing what Mikel would do to him if she gave in to the feelings he'd threaten to unleash inside her? There had never been anyone more in need of protection.

The thought of what Mikel would do to Lina or her mother was awful enough, but if he got his hands on her dark knight . . .

There'd be no coming back from that.

A sob climbed up her throat.

"Quinn?" he asked, his brows dropping low as he searched her face.

"I can't do this," she sobbed, pulling free.

He caught her arm before she could flee. "Quinn, wait. Don't run away, damnit. I know you feel this thing between us too. You think that comes around more than once in a lifetime? Stop fighting yourself and just give in because this, you and me, it's going to happen."

She squeezed her eyes shut, a tear spilling free. He was killing her with his stubborn persistence and certainty. She wanted what he offered, all of it. More than anything. There'd never been anything in her life she'd wanted more desperately. But desire wasn't enough to offset reality. Which was why, no matter how badly she wished it could be otherwise, Finley was the one thing she'd never let herself have.

"You're wrong. You and me? We were over before we began."

"Quinn—"

"Don't. Don't follow me, Finley. Please."

CHAPTER 17
NORD

The fire had long since burned to embers, and the moon given way to the sun. His wife laid on her side, cradled by his body, her head pillowed by his arm. She looked like an angel lying there, her golden hair spilling between them, cheeks flushed with sleep, and lips softly parted. He couldn't think of a more beautiful vision to wake up to.

Their appetites for each other the night before had been insatiable, lasting many rounds in the forest and culminating in one memorable chase. While they hadn't managed to fell a tree, their vigorous lovemaking had startled a cougar who'd taken one look at them and wisely went off in search of new hunting grounds.

They never made it to a bed. Though sometime in the early morning, they did finally stumble back into the private suite of rooms Astrid had arranged for them. The candles and fireplace must have been spelled because they'd flickered to life as soon as the bride and groom crossed the threshold, illuminating the fur rug covered in rose petals and the two horns of matrimonial mead they'd yet to consume, along with various other refreshments.

Lina had taken one look at the romantic setup and pounced on him, thus continuing the voracious cycle for several hours more.

Despite all of it, his cock still stirred to life at the sight of her snuggled beside him.

"You can't be serious," she murmured sleepily.

Nord trailed his fingers down her side and over the rise of her hip. "About loving you? Deadly."

She chuckled, her laughter puffing over his inner arm. "If by that you mean you're seeking to kill me through an overdose of pleasure, you may just get your wish. Especially if you attempt what I think you're going to attempt."

He pressed a kiss to the back of her neck. "Do not think to escape me so easily, wife. Die if you must, but I will simply follow you into the next life and then set about doing it all over again."

"Mmm," she murmured. "Sounds like heaven to me."

Nord grinned, his fingers sliding down her hip to settle between her legs. Initial protest aside, Lina's thighs fell open immediately, welcoming his touch. As his fingers parted her slick folds, he found her more than ready for him. Lina shifted in his grasp, tilting her head back so her lips could meet his.

Before they got any further, a loud knock sounded at the door.

He growled as Lina pulled away. "Where do you think you're going?"

"Someone's at the door."

"So?"

"You did tell everybody they were allowed to bother us again once the sun was up." She gestured to the window. "At least whoever it is listened."

"I've waited centuries for you. It's my wedding night until I decide otherwise. Whoever it is can fuck off."

"I heard that," came Finley's voice.

Nord grabbed the first thing within reach—which ended up being a fire poker—and flung it at the door, where it sank into the wood and vibrated with a resounding thrum. "You of all people should know better."

Finley's laughter traveled through the door. "Astrid's busy welcoming back the last of the war party, so she asked me to do the honors. She had the misguided notion you'd be less upset about a wake-up call if it came from me instead of one of the Novasgardians."

"She was wrong."

"That's what I told her, but she pulled rank on me. Since she's the one who runs the place and is ultimately responsible for setting the terms of our asylum, it didn't seem prudent to argue the point."

Lina giggled and squirmed in his arms, trying to stand up, but Nord rolled and pressed her back into the rug with his body. "Not so fast. I'm not finished with you, Kærasta."

"I can feel that, but you heard him. The war party's here."

"And?" he countered, holding himself up on his arms as he trailed kisses from one side of her neck to the other.

"And as much as I love what you're implying," she teased with a delicious wriggle of her hips, "this meeting is what we've been waiting for. We shouldn't leave the troops waiting when they're the ones doing us a favor."

He dropped his forehead to hers with a growl of defeat. She was right, but he wasn't happy about it. Duty and honor had been drilled into him long ago. So long, it was nearly impossible to separate the lessons from his personal desires, even with his mate naked and squirming beneath him.

Lina threaded her fingers through his hair, which she'd asked him to grow out last night so she could 'see what he looked like with authentic Viking locks.' She hadn't stopped playing with it since, so he could only assume she was a fan.

"I know, my love," she murmured, brushing her lips against his. "I don't want to leave our little love nest any more than you do. But we talked about this. The only way we can get to work on making those dreams of ours come true is to remove Mikel from the board. Permanently. He's the only thing standing in the way of our dreams becoming reality, and today's meeting is the first step in making that happen."

Twisting his head toward the door, Nord called out, "We'll be ready in an hour."

"Got it," Finley answered.

"Nord—"

"No, Kærasta. If you're going to insist we spend the rest of our time here planning a war, I'm damn sure going to take my fill of you first."

Her eyes turned liquid as they stared into his. "Okay." Then she wrinkled her nose. "But can we do that in the shower?"

He chuckled as he leaned down to nip the side of her neck. "If you're looking to get clean, I should probably ensure you're nice and dirty first."

"Isn't that what we've been doing?" she asked breathlessly as he rocked into her.

He smiled against her skin, slowly drawing himself out. "Just once more to ensure you're well and truly defiled."

Lina moaned, scoring her nails down his back. "Maybe twice. Just in case."

"I thought there'd be more people," Lina whispered two hours later as they stood in the assembly room, or museum, as she'd taken to calling it.

"More people means more opinions. In matters such as these, it's best to limit the number of decision makers," Nord answered, matching her low tone.

"I thought Astrid was the decision maker?"

"She's the deciding factor, but a good jarl always takes the wishes of their people into consideration before settling on a path."

"Which means she trusts them," Lina murmured, her eyes scanning the assembled Novasgardians.

Nord grunted an assent while allowing himself to do the same. Most of the usual suspects were accounted for, namely himself, Lina, Finley, and Cora. Quinn was suspiciously absent, and when pressed, Cora said only that she was sleeping off the effects of the night before. The slight tensing of Finley's jaw when she'd given the excuse told Nord the story was nowhere near that simple, but now was not the time to get into it.

Astrid, Søren, Björn, and Strega were also present for the meeting, but they'd been joined by four new additions whose faces he set to memorizing. One Nord recognized from their arrival, the mage Arrick. He stood to the far side of the room, shadows clinging to him as he clutched a wooden staff that housed an orb filled with crackling violet light.

Nearest to him, though clustered more in the center of the room, were the two sisters: Revna and Ruhla. Both women wore blades strapped to almost every visible inch of their bodies, black paint decorating their faces. The only noticeable difference in their appearance, at least from where he was standing, was that one wore her long wheat-colored hair in a thick braid over her shoulder while the other let hers hang free.

The last of the newcomers introduced himself as Ulf. He was built like Søren, tall and heavily muscled, with swirling tattoos decorating his arms. It was hard to make out much more detail than that, as he wore a hooded wolf pelt that left much of his face hidden.

Astrid and Arrick had been the last of their ranks to arrive, the former nodding along at whatever report the mage had been relaying. She'd dismissed him with a hand on the arm and then moved to stand beside her antlered throne. Attention focused on a small stack of papers in her hand, she'd yet to address the room and formally start the meeting.

"Is this some kind of power play?" Lina asked, keeping her voice pitched low.

Nord hid his smile behind his hand. "Not an intentional one. My cousin strikes me as the kind of woman without a moment's peace, always running from one crisis to the other."

"Ah. She's taking a couple minutes to get her thoughts in order before her next crisis of the day," Lina surmised with a nod. "Good on her for making sure she's up to speed before diving straight in."

There was a hint of admiration in her voice, but something else too. Nord glanced down at his mate. "Taking notes for when you reclaim the Council?"

She blushed. "How could you tell?"

"Astrid is one of the few uncorrupted leaders you've seen in action. It makes sense you'd note her leadership style as you begin to develop your own."

Lina shrugged. "I respect her, is all. She knows how to command a room without stepping all over other people. There are worse role models to have."

"She'll be glad to hear you think so highly of her."

Lina gripped his arm. "For the love of God, please don't tell her. The woman makes me feel inferior just by standing in the same room with her. It's bad enough I know it, but she doesn't need to know it too."

"Really? Why?"

"Have you seen her? She's the female version of you. Who in their right mind wouldn't be intimidated by someone like that? Seriously. I bet there's not a person in here, save yourself, she couldn't successfully take on."

Nord's lips twitched up. "I think you dismiss your own accomplishments too easily."

"You're biased."

"So you keep reminding me. But I've also lived a long time. I've seen plenty of leaders in action, and you, Kærasta, have only begun to tap into your potential. And that's not bias, it's fact."

"Ugh," she groaned. "Just when I think it's not possible to love you any more, you go and say something like that and make me all squishy inside."

His smile stretched, and he placed his hand on her back as he leaned down. "Then I'll say one thing more, just to push you over the edge."

"I'm listening."

"There's only one woman in this room who's my equal, and she's standing beside me."

Her emotions crashed into him, so it came as no surprise when she looked up, blinking away tears. "Are you trying to make me cry in front of all the big bad Vikings? Because it's working."

He cupped her cheek. "Just helping you remember who you are and why there's no reason for you to ever feel less than anyone else."

She took a shuddering breath, her eyes searching his for a second before he turned away. When she reached out to take his hand in hers, he noticed she stood taller, her shoulders squared, her chin raised.

Pride wormed its way through him, and there was no restraining his smile as his eyes found his cousin's across the room. She smirked at him before her expression returned to her usual stoic mask.

"I believe you all know why we're here," she intoned.

There were a few murmurs of agreement around the room. Nord searched each person's face, looking for any sign of dissent or resentment, but there were none. Only the anticipatory buzz he'd become accustomed to whenever facing an impending battle. When his gaze found Finley's, they nodded at each other as if mentally agreeing that this was it. The point of no return.

"I've briefed everybody on what we discussed, Gunnar. Unless there's anything else you'd like to add, I suggest we get straight down to it."

Nord tried not to tense at the use of his birth name. His cousin loved to whip it out and toss it around whenever she needed to make a point, but he was no more comfortable with its use now than he was the first time. Still, recognizing the strategy behind it, he did his best not to grimace as he stepped forward to address the room.

"I would only reiterate that our enemy is not to be underestimated. They are magic users unlike anything you'll be accustomed to. I'll let Cora elaborate on what we can expect to encounter, as she is the most well-versed in the specifics. Mikel Drake, especially, is an unknown quantity. He is powerful, without a doubt, but no one in this room has witnessed the full extent of what he can do, which means we are walking into this battle half-prepared at best. What we do know is the man will stop at nothing to win. Once he realizes we have no intention of allowing that to happen, he'll likely do everything in his power to bring each and every one of us down with him. That includes the people allied with him. A man who values so little is the most dangerous enemy of all because nothing short of death will stop him."

The room had been silent before, but the weight of the silence became something new in the face of Nord's warning. It was equal parts bated breath and dread. A weary sort of acceptance that not everybody standing here now would still be with them when this was over. Death no longer lurked on the horizon; she stood here in this room. And when the time came, she would show no mercy.

Astrid was the first to speak. Her smile was razor sharp and no less cutting. "You forget, cousin, that he has never encountered the likes of us either. The killing field will be more level than he's used to, which gives us quite an advantage."

"True, which is why we must strike hard and fast. We cannot give the enemy time to adapt."

"The floor is yours," Astrid said, settling back in her chair. "What do you have in mind?"

Nord began to outline the details of the plan that had been solidifying in his mind since his cousin first agreed to help them. He was no stranger to the finer points of strategy, but the last time he'd had to account for the kind of expert fighters he knew the Novasgardians to be, it had been the battle that led their ancestors here.

As he spoke, the others made suggestions, highlighting their skill sets and how their various squadrons could best aid the overall mission. Hours passed in a blur until it came down to the final pertinent details.

"How are we going to get that many people into Bell Falls without notice?" Cora asked. "Mikel may be tied up with Lina, but you can be sure if an army descends on the town, his spies will notify him."

"I could summon a portal at a predetermined time," Finley offered.

"With the time differential, and our inability to stay in contact across realms, it's not ideal. Too many things could go wrong," Nord pointed out.

"Actually, I have something that can help with that," Astrid said, catching her son's eyes and giving him a slight nod. Björn stepped forward, handing his mother a black velvet sack about the size of a large shoebox. As Astrid pulled the item free of its bag, a frisson of recognition shot through Nord, sending the hair on his arms and neck to stand on end.

It can't be.

But there was no mistaking it.

With its silver edges and faintly glowing runes, the curved object could only be one thing: The Horn of Odin.

The air left him in a stunned whoosh, and Lina's hand clasped around his more tightly as she shot him a worried look.

"I thought it was lost," he managed.

Astrid's lips tipped up smugly. "That which is lost can always be found."

"How?"

"Men grow careless with their secrets over time. All it required was patience and a few well-aimed daggers."

Revna and Ruhla laughed softly at her words, and after eyeing their blades, Nord wondered if the assassins had been involved in its recovery. But regardless of how the artifact had come back into their possession, it was an incredible boon.

The horn was said to be god-touched, believed to belong to the Allfather himself. As the legend goes, it had been bestowed by Odin to the first of his berserkers. When activated by a true Warrior of Odin, the horn not only called the berserkers to war, it could also rip open a portal through space and time, allowing an entire Viking army to arrive at their commander's side in seconds. The last time Nord had seen it in person, his father carried it into battle, neither to return.

And now Astrid was presenting it to him.

"Since the last heirloom I returned to you now belongs to your wife, it only seemed fair to gift you with one you could keep."

The significance of that statement was not lost on him, nor any other Novasgardian in the room. Astrid had just officially deferred to him. By presenting him with the horn, she'd declared him leader of her military and placed his authority above her own. She'd all but proclaimed him acting leader of Novasgard itself.

"I . . ." Nord shook his head, at an absolute loss. It was more than he'd expected. More than he likely deserved. But this artifact was the very thing they needed to ensure the Novasgardians' entry into their realm would be a surprise. It could be the difference in whether they won this war.

Astrid rolled her eyes. "Oh, just take it. No one in this room is under any illusions as to who they're following. I've just made it slightly more official."

Lina was looking between Astrid and Nord with wide eyes. "What am I missing?"

"Your husband's just been promoted," Astrid informed her.

"Promoted? To what?"

One by one, the Novasgardians bent the knee. First the sisters, then the mage and the wolf, followed by a grinning bear and less impressed worg. Astrid was the last to drop, and she did so intentionally, holding his gaze the entire time, still wearing her smug little grin.

"Nord, what is happening right now?" Lina asked.

He shook his head, too overcome to explain.

When Astrid spoke, her voice rang out loud with authority and jubilation, "All hail, Gunnar Bloodaxe, Warrior of Odin, last of the berserkers and rightful jarl of Novasgard. Long may he reign!"

As one, the rest of the people in the room cried out, "Long may he reign!"

A grinning Finley and misty-eyed Cora joined in the chorus. But it was the voice beside him, the one filled with awestruck pride, which resonated within him like the sweetest caress that threatened to unman him.

"Long may he reign," Lina whispered.

When she started to kneel, Nord's hand snaked out, grasping her arm before her knee touched the floor. Lifting her back up, he said, "You do not kneel to me, Kærasta. Ever."

"But—"

"Your place is at my side."

His words echoed around the room, and after a beat of silence, Astrid called out, "Long may they reign!"

This time, when the others repeated her cheer, Finley's voice edged out everyone else's in sheer volume.

"Long may *she* reign!"

At which point, Lina promptly burst into tears, and even Søren, the most hardened of warriors, cracked an approving smile.

CHAPTER 18
LINA

"You're sure about this?" Quinn asked, leaning against the doorframe while Lina stared unseeing into the closet. She'd come in here to change clothes but was—perhaps unsurprisingly—having an impossible time deciding on what to wear for her upcoming torture date with Mikel.

Leather maybe? It would be harder to cut through than denim or cotton . . . though if he opts for fire, all bets are off.

"Are you even listening to me?"

"Hmm?" she asked distractedly, half glancing over her shoulder.

There was no mistaking the worry in her best friend's eyes. "Just . . . come sit down with me for a minute, okay?"

Lina dropped the shirt she'd been debating and did as she was asked.

"It's not too late to change your mind."

Her lips twitched. "Fin said the same thing when he came by. So did your mom when she left twenty minutes ago."

Quinn didn't match her smile, opting instead to take her hand. "Because we love you and the thought of what that sadistic bastard is going to do to you makes us sick."

Lina steeled herself against the emotion threatening to break free. She knew this would be the hardest part—the goodbyes. But the reality was far worse than she imagined. "I love you too. But you don't need to worry. Pain is sort of my thing these days."

"He won't stop until he breaks you," she whispered.

"I can't be broken."

Quinn's hand spasmed in hers. "I wish I could believe that, but I've seen how Mikel operates. He will pick at you until he finds the one thread that will unravel you entirely. If he can't do it with his fists, or a blade, or his magic, he'll do it with his words. Please don't let him. Please, if you're going to do this, just…hold on until we get there. I can't lose you too."

"Quinn—"

She turned away, the hand not squeezing Lina's lifting to discreetly wipe away the tears spilling down her cheeks. Then she cleared her throat, her eyes still watery, but her voice even as she asked, "When do you leave?"

Understanding the question was Quinn's way of requesting Lina not acknowledge her emotional plea, she sighed and answered, "About an hour."

"So soon?"

"All of us want this over with. Nord and I didn't see the value in delaying."

"Not even to give everyone more time to prep?"

"If by everyone you mean the Novasgardians, war is their bread and butter. Don't let their sleepy little town fool you. They're warriors through and through. It runs in their blood every bit as much as being a pain in the ass runs through yours."

Quinn's mouth opened in mock outrage. "Bitch."

Lina grinned. "Ass."

Quinn smiled back, but it quickly started to wobble at the edges, and she pulled Lina into a bone-crushing hug. "I'm not going to be here when you leave, okay? I can't . . ." She sucked in a quavering breath. "I'm done saying goodbye to you, so do whatever the fuck you have to do. Just come back in one piece, and for the love of God, don't die."

"I won't," Lina promised, squeezing her eyes shut and holding her best friend just as tightly. "I'll see you in a couple days, and then we'll end this together."

Quinn pulled back, her face tear-streaked and blotchy. "My plan is to stay *away* from the sharp, pointy things. Unlike you, I don't have a hard-on for blood play. I'm one of the smart people. We tend to run in the opposite direction when things like death and dismemberment are on the table."

Just like that, they were back to normal.

Lina laughed, a deep rolling belly laugh. "I can't help it if the berserker embraces all things violent. But I wouldn't go as far as to say I'm turned on by the thought of . . ." She was going to say violence, but watching Nord in action was her personal wet dream. "Um, blood."

Quinn's quirked brow spoke volumes. "Uh-huh. Sure."

"You're the one with a lifetime supply of latex catsuits. Don't kink shame me, Satori."

"I would never. As long as it's consensual and he makes you come like a class five hurricane, I say let your freak flag fly, Mrs. B."

Lina shook her head. "How did we go from not saying goodbye to talking about this?"

Quinn shrugged. "What can I say? Stimulating conversations are one of my specialties."

They shared a smile.

"If you aren't planning on fighting, where will you be?" Lina asked.

Quinn's smile turned wicked. "Oh, I'll be there, fighting in my own way. I have some debts to repay, and I intend to do so with interest."

"That's my girl."

Quinn exhaled. "Well, I guess I should be going. You have things you probably need to do, and frankly, I want to be anywhere but here while you do them."

"Okay."

She stood and started walking for the door, pausing just before she crossed the threshold. "Hey, Lina?"

"Hmm?"

"No matter what he says or does, don't allow Mikel to make you forget who you are. If anyone stands a chance against that twat waffle, it's you."

Then, with a small smile, she was gone.

"She's right, you know," Nord said, filling the doorway Quinn had just vacated.

Lina shook her head ruefully at his sudden appearance. She wasn't surprised exactly; the taut rubber band feeling that sat in her chest whenever they were apart for too long had started to ease, which typically meant he was nearby. But she did think it was sweet of him to give her and Quinn time alone when she knew he must have been just as keen to spend these final moments with her.

"How long have you been standing there eavesdropping?"

He shrugged, his lips twitching. "Long enough."

She stared at her husband, drinking in the sight of him. He'd left his hair long since the wedding, wearing it loose around his shoulders and making her fingers itch with the need to run through it. It was darker than usual, wet from the shower he'd likely taken after finishing the drills he'd run with the others. He was wearing a pair of black pants she didn't recognize and a long-sleeve shirt that hugged his muscled torso, the sleeves pulled up to reveal the inked skin of his forearms. His pose was deceptively casual—hands in his pockets, legs crossed at the ankles. But she could feel the coiled tension snaking through him. He'd been gone for the better part of the day training with his new raiders and coordinating the last of the battle plans with Søren. She hadn't realized how much she'd missed his steady presence in just those handful of hours. How was she supposed to go without it for two whole days?

Out of all of today's goodbyes, this was the one she was most torn up over. Nord was the absolute last person she ever wanted to part with. Her heart rejected the very thought of it. Leaving him was the least natural thing in the world. Like a jellyfish trying to fly. Or a parakeet taking up ballroom dancing lessons. It just wasn't coded into her DNA.

"Keep looking at me like that, and I'll pull the plug on this thing here and now," he warned her.

"No, you won't."

"No, I won't," he agreed with a sigh. He took in her appearance as she rose to her feet. "Almost ready?"

"Unless I'm popping by Hope Street in my jammies, no. Not quite."

He chuckled. "You're overthinking it."

"Am I?"

"It's not like you can show up in tactical gear. He'll sense the trap. If you want him to believe he caught you off guard, you need to wear something that won't arouse suspicion."

"Well, when you put it that way, it sounds obvious."

"Because it is."

Lina waved her arm toward the closet in exasperation. "Then by all means, almighty Novasgardian overlord. Please, do the honors."

Nord snorted and pushed off the doorframe, prowling toward her. When he reached her, he gave the end of her ponytail a tug, tipping her head back.

"Always happy to help when you ask so sweetly," he teased, brushing a kiss to her lips.

Lina wrinkled her nose. "You're lucky I said please."

He laughed as he grabbed a pair of jeans at random and a shirt that looked like a smaller version of his own and tossed them both onto the bed in less than twenty seconds. "All done."

She glanced between the clothes and the closet, then back at him. "And to think, I wasted an hour of my life trying to make that same decision."

Nord curled an arm around her waist, towing her back into his body so he could hug her. "You have a lot on your mind. It can be hard to make decisions, even small ones, at times like this."

"But you said—"

"I was being an ass." He kissed her forehead. "What else is left?"

"Retrieving the Prism, implanting the tracker, and disguising the little radio thing."

"You mean the comm?"

"Isn't that what I said?"

His chest vibrated with laughter. "So, what you're telling me is everything's left?"

"Pretty much. It's been a little . . . hard to focus today."

His eyes softened. "Well, let's get to work. Here, take this off," he said, tugging at the hem of her tank top.

"I don't think we have time for that."

Nord raised a brow. "I could prove you wrong about that as well, but I won't. Now take it off."

"So bossy," she muttered, lifting the pink cotton over her head and letting it drop to the floor.

"Where'd you leave the tracker?"

"Beside the bed."

She'd put everything there the night before, afraid to leave anything too far out of reach. It had been a group effort preparing all the mortal spy gadgets she'd need for her mission. While Nord explained what they were looking for, Finley would make a recommendation, and Quinn and Sheridan would work together to show the others exactly what Finley was thinking about. Then Cora would weigh in on whether it 'felt' right, and if she gave her thumbs-up, Lina and Nord would recreate the item. It was like their very own Animagi production line.

Nord scooped it up and returned to her, his warm hands skimming up her sides. Pushing her hair over her shoulder, he pressed the tracker against her spine, right in the center of her Helm of Awe tattoo.

"Remember how this works?" he asked as the tingle of his magic spread across her back.

"As soon as you are back in our realm, you'll be able to pick up its signal and, with Finley's help, be within range almost instantly."

"Exactly. Fin and I will portal back to Bell Falls exactly twenty-four hours after you leave to find out where Mikel's keeping you. Then, unless we hear from you sooner, we'll strike at the forty-eight-hour mark."

Hearing him sound so calm sent a wave of reassurance through her. She might be on her own for the first part of this mission, but she was not alone. Her Viking would be right behind her.

Nord kissed the top of her tattoo. "All done."

She glanced at him over her shoulder. "You're sure Mikel won't be able to detect it?"

"As sure as I can be. I used the same magic Alistair did with the Prism. It should appear to be nothing more than a tattoo."

Lina let out a breath she hadn't realized she was holding. "Right. Should we take care of the comm next?"

He held out his hand, a pair of black diamond earrings glittering in his palm. "Way ahead of you."

She looked from his outstretched hand up to his face, smirking. "You keep crossing items off the to-do list like this, we might have time for you to-do me, after all."

His eyes twinkled. "That's always the hope."

Smiling, Lina put the little studs in, her confidence lifting as they slid into place. "How will I know when you arrive?"

"Our bond should alert you as soon as I'm near. That will be your signal." Nord tapped the comm concealed as the gemstone. "And this will link up with mine as soon as we're within range. All you need to do is talk when you feel the shift in the bond, and I'll hear everything that's happening from that point on."

"But I won't be able to hear you, right?"

"No. It's a one-way signal."

Lina nodded. They'd already been over all of this—more than

once—but it helped her ground herself by going over it again. Before grabbing the fresh shirt off the bed, she looked down at the crystal inked into her skin. "I guess there's only one thing left."

There was no missing the way her fingers trembled as they hovered over her arm.

"Want me to do it?"

"No. I just feel like I'm about to break a promise. Is that weird? After everything Alistair did to hide it, it seems . . . wrong somehow."

Nord shifted so he was standing with his chest pressed to her back and his hands resting on her shoulders. "He also told you to study and use the Codex. I can't imagine he'd fault you for following where it led you. Especially not after telling you to trust your instincts."

"Right. Of course." She forced herself to take a deep breath. "I'm just being silly."

Still feeling anxious, Lina shook out her fingers and stretched her neck. Nord aided the process, digging his thumbs into the corded muscles and helping her work out more of the tension. Feeling slightly more relaxed, Lina settled back into her original position.

"Okay, one Prism, coming up."

Just like she had when bringing the Codex out of hiding, Lina envisioned what she wanted and willed it into being. This time, however, instead of a book tucked into a secret cubbyhole, she imagined the Prism locked safely in its box, resting in the palm of her hand. When the weight solidified, she opened her eyes and let out a breath that could have been relief or resignation.

The clock was really ticking now. As soon as she opened that box and turned the actual Prism into a fake Codex, she'd have to leave. There was no other way for her to limit her, as well as everybody else's, interaction with the magic-siphoning prison.

"Wait," Nord said, his breath stirring the hair at the back of her neck. "Give me a few more minutes before you do it. I want to hold you just a little bit longer."

Lina set the box on the dresser and turned to face him, wrapping her arms around his hips and resting her head over his heart. They held each other like that for countless heartbeats, neither ready to let go nor wanting to fill the silence with words.

There was no need when their emotions flowed freely through the bond. It was all right there. The fear. The hope. The love.

Finally, they pulled apart, and Nord helped her finish getting dressed before they turned as one back to the unassuming little box. He tensed beside her, and she knew he wanted to tell her not to do it. But he resisted. He knew she needed to do this. They'd come too far, and even if it failed, she had to at least try.

"You have forty-eight hours starting the moment you step through the portal," he said instead. "Not a second more. If you need to use your codeword, do it, and I'll be there. If I don't hear from you at all, or if something goes wrong and the tracker fails, all bets are off."

Lina swallowed and nodded. "I know."

"Repeat your codewords so I know you remember them."

She fought the urge to roll her eyes, understanding that this was his way of ensuring her safety while he couldn't be with her. "If everything is going according to plan, I'll call Mikel a sniveling lick-spittle. If shit hits the fan hard, I'll call him a preening cockalorum. Or any other type of cockalorum because really, what doesn't go with an insult that glorious? And in that case, I'm probably about to die, so I may as well make my final words the verbal equivalent of a blaze of glory."

"Don't even joke about it." He stared at her, his expression tortured. She could feel the conflict roiling within him, her berserker growing restless as Nord's surfaced in response to his tempestuous emotions.

"I'm sorry. Jokes are how I'm dealing with my nerves. I didn't mean to make light of the situation. But, honestly, with codewords like that, how can you not? Come to think of it, you really ought to blame Fin. He's the one that came up with them."

Nord snorted, and she could feel the peppering of his amusement fluttering in her chest. She gave him a soft smile, much preferring his amusement to his fear, even if her next words would ensure it would be short-lived.

"Speaking of our favorite Brit, you should go get him. It's time."

"Lina—"

She stood on her tiptoes and cut him off with a swift kiss. "Go, so you can come rescue me, Viking. You're not the only one who's going to be counting down every second we're apart."

He swallowed, giving her a tight nod and a last lingering look before going off in search of Finley.

Lina stood in the center of the room, staring after Nord and feeling as if he'd taken her heart with him. She hated that this was the way it had to be, and she ached knowing he'd be suffering even more than her while they were apart.

Her pain was nothing. It was a fleeting, temporary thing, limited only to her body. But his? It tore at her soul. And being the reason behind it? The knowledge gutted her. Not even reminding herself she was doing this to save him, save all of them, made it any easier to bear.

Her fingers went immediately to the ring he'd slid onto her finger only a couple days earlier. With a small wave of magic, she turned it invisible, so its weight could comfort her without alerting Mikel to its presence or meaning. If she was going to subject them to this, then she was damn well going to ensure it wasn't for fucking nothing.

And with that thought in mind, Lina laid the final piece of her trap.

CHAPTER 19
LINA

Even though the portal had long since closed, Lina could still feel the weight of Nord's gaze pinned between her shoulder blades. The ghost of it steadied her, reminding her of her reason for being here, even as blades of anxiety worked to shred her resolve.

Two days. That's it. You only need to get through the next two days, and then all of this will be over.

Or . . . you'll be dead, and it won't matter anymore.

One fear Lina hadn't voiced, especially not to Nord, was she didn't know what it meant for her immortality now that the Prism had been removed from her body. After what happened to him in the alley with the Director, she was pretty confident her healing powers were strong enough to counter the worst kinds of injuries. But there was always a chance—now more than ever—that they still might not be enough.

She *really* didn't want to find herself in a situation where she would have to put that to the test. That's probably the reason she was still standing out here in the park instead of already inside her uncle's house.

Come on, Cuska. You're an honorary Viking now. Show no fear and all that.

Lina took a shaky breath, glancing left and right to see if she was still alone. She had no way of knowing what day it was. She recalled how a full day in Novasgard was an entire week on Earth, but all she had to go off of was that she'd slept in Novasgard four times, and tonight would have made the fifth. So, as far as Mikel was concerned, they'd been missing in action anywhere from four to five weeks. Definitely long enough for him to set up surveillance at the locations he knew she had ties to. Which was what she was counting on.

The Prism—now concealed as a fake Codex—was safely tucked into a small knapsack she'd slung over her shoulder. She needed something that wouldn't draw too much attention but would still be large enough to keep the book hidden. Even though she wanted to be seen entering the house, she didn't want it to be obvious what she'd brought with her. Her guise for returning to Hope Street was that she needed to retrieve the Codex, so getting caught with it before entering the building would be a major fail. She hoped her attention to detail paid off.

Just trust the plan. You may not be able to see them, but the Drakes are here. They're watching. It's time to start the show.

Lina made her steps short and quick as she crossed the street, trying to appear as though she was in a hurry, but not necessarily worried about being followed. She forced herself not to look over her shoulder as she unlocked the door and stepped inside.

At first glance, the house was much as they'd left it. She could still smell the faint amber and clove scent of Finley's cologne—which made sense because he'd technically been the last one here. It was also comforting. If her chosen family couldn't be with her, at least she'd be surrounded by subtle reminders of them. Lina smiled to herself. Even from an entire world away, they were still lending her their strength.

It was tempting to move through the house in the dark, to use the darkness as an added layer of protection. Lina knew that was her internal defense system talking—the part of her trained by Nord to avoid ending up in potentially dangerous situations. It was surprisingly difficult to ignore the now instinctive habits he'd helped her hone. But if she wasn't afraid of detection, there'd be no reason for her not to flip on the lights. So she did.

She couldn't, not even for a second, drop her act. She had to play this perfectly.

Too many lives depended on it.

The next phase of her plan was a little trickier. It required her to stage the scene where she'd be 'caught unaware.' That meant she needed to get both herself and the forged Codex in place. Since she didn't know how much time she'd have before the Drakes made their move, she had to assume it would be minutes at most.

In case they were already here watching her—which she assumed they most likely were—she needed to make a show of beelining to grab what she'd come for. As that item was currently tucked into her bag and not actually secured somewhere in the house, she'd need to perform a little sleight of hand.

Luckily, Nord had helped her with that as well.

Dropping her keys in the metal bowl by the door, Lina moved into the living room off to the left of the entryway. As she walked toward the painted portrait of Alistair she'd hung beside a replica of his favorite armchair, she called on her power, willing a safe into being just behind it. Once there, she lifted the portrait off its nail and set it gently against the wall so she could access her fancy new wall safe.

Having never attempted to create something with a functioning locking mechanism, Lina didn't want to test one now. Which was why she'd opted for something less risky and easier to fake.

Pressing her thumb against a scanner, she 'unlocked' her safe and pulled open the metal door. Then, letting out a sigh of relief that wasn't entirely for show, she grabbed her knapsack and lifted it up so it was concealed by the door panel. The idea was to make it seem like she was emptying the contents of the safe into her bag. She'd just shoved a handful of notepads and loose-leaf paper into her sack when she heard the soft scrape of furniture sliding against the wooden floor.

For a second, all she could hear was the roar of blood through her veins and the heavy thump of her heart.

This was it.

Showtime.

Lina took a slow step back, allowing her hand to visibly shake as she closed the door to the safe. But when she turned, the man sitting on the far side of the room with his ankle propped on his knee and his blond head resting against the fist of one hand wasn't Mikel, as she'd expected. She crossed her arms, thankful that nothing about interacting with Nico required her to play scared or dumb—she simply wasn't that talented an actress.

"Weird, I don't recall ordering a taxidermy asshole when I spoke with the decorator. How ever did you get here?"

Nico made a show of slowly clapping. "Your wit is as sharp as always, cousin. I'm glad to learn living in exile hasn't snuffed that delightful spark out of you yet. I am so hoping to claim the honor for myself."

"Like there's a chance in hell that's ever going to happen. I could be knocking on death's door and still wipe the floor with you."

"Is that so?"

"It is, actually. What you can't seem to comprehend is that I'm a pretty fucking big deal now, and the angrier you make me, the more creative I become."

He shrugged, his eyes dropping to his hands as he inspected his nails. "Maybe you are. But you know what else you are, Evalina?"

"I'm sure you're going to inform me."

"You're predictable."

She barked out a laugh. "Me? You think I'm the predictable one? Funny, Nic."

"Perhaps you don't understand the meaning of the word. I suppose that tracks, since it would require you to actually pay attention to anyone other than yourself for longer than thirty seconds at a time. A skill you've always seemed to lack."

Lina rolled her eyes. "Oh, go hump a cactus, Nico. No one wants to hear your sob story. We both had fucked-up childhoods."

"You?" he scoffed. "What could you possibly know about miserable childhoods? You were the perfect little princess. Everything you could ever want was handed to you."

Lina laughed at that. Loud, belly-aching guffaws that sent tears streaming down her face. Nico scowled at her over-the-top display of mirth, a muscle ticking in his jaw.

"Oh, oh wow," she wheezed, brushing a stray tear away. "Thanks, I really needed that. I can't remember the last time I laughed that hard." Then her smile fell, and she shook her head, dropping all pretense. "I hate to break it to you, Nico, but clearly you weren't paying as close attention as you think. I promise, life with Anatoly Cuska as a father was nowhere near the cakewalk you seem to believe. And yet, you still don't see me rooting around Mikel's ass looking for handouts like a filthy traitor."

"Loyalty is earned, cousin. What the hell has anyone in the Cuska line ever done for me?"

"Besides birth you, feed and clothe you, put a roof over your head, pay for that fancy education of yours—"

"None of those things replace actual regard or affection."

"And you think your—I don't even know what to call it—your partnership with Mikel exemplifies those qualities?"

"It's a damn sight better than what I endured at home living in your shadow."

Lina rolled her eyes. "Okay, Nico. Sure. Mikel Drake is a pillar of paternal love and support. The wind beneath your fucking wings. Is this your way of telling me you're finally going to change your name and make your status as his bitch official?"

"Now, why would I go and do something foolish like that?"

His eyes glinted dangerously, and the first frisson of fear spiked through her. She wasn't talking to her reject of a relative any longer. This was Mikel's rabid dog.

All bets were off.

Lina continued to meet Nico's gaze, her chin jutting up as she said, "Because you want to replace Mikel's heir. Isn't that what all of this is really about?"

Nico smiled, and the sight of it made her blood run cold.

"Why would I settle for being an heir when I'm already the head of a family? A few more tragic accidents, and I'll be surrounded by people loyal only to me. And then, finally, poor little Evalina can be laid to rest, and that embarrassing hiccup in our family's legacy will be over."

"Is that really what you think is going to happen, Nico? Mikel is never going to willingly give you anything. You might be a head of Mobius in name, but it will always be an empty title."

He leaned forward, his face obscured by shadows as he rested his elbows on his knees. "That is what I *know*. I do not intend to sit around and wait for Mikel to allow me to do anything. My days of seeking permission and obeying orders are numbered. But that's really none of your concern, dear cousin, because now it's time to bid you adieu."

Lina opened her mouth, ready to tell him what a fucking idiot he was if he thought Mikel would ever let that happen. But then something solid and heavy crashed into the side of her head, and she was out cold before the first syllable ever left her lips.

***

Consciousness returned in stages. First, there was the taste of blood. Then a throbbing ache behind her eyes so acute and piercing she wondered if someone had stabbed through the top of her head with an ice pick. Next was the wet rattle of her breath and the all-too-familiar chafing of metal at her wrists, which left her limbs heavy, immobile, and rigid with pain.

She'd woken like this before. Bound and bloodied, with no memory of either. First in a warehouse and then in her dreams. Finding herself in such a position again was a bit like realizing she was trapped on a macabre carousel. One she'd never be able to get off.

No matter how far she went, she always seemed to find herself right back here.

Lina groaned and shifted, testing her bindings to see if there was any give. There wasn't.

"Oh good, you're awake."

She cracked her eyes open, groaning again when only one obeyed. Her right eye seemed to be swollen or caked shut. She was guessing it was a bit of both.

Mikel was staring at her from a heavily cushioned armchair about ten feet away. The Prism-Codex lay open in his lap. The sole part of her not currently moaning in extreme discomfort cheered to see he'd taken the bait. But that was all she could really see. There was a lone lamp casting him in a circle of yellow light, its bulb naked and placed right behind his chair. The rest of the room, as far as she could tell, was cast in darkness.

Even so, Lina knew she'd been here before. A girl never forgot her first time.

Being tortured, that is.

Apparently, Papa Drake had a flair for the dramatic. Mikel had brought her to his son's warehouse. Looks like she wasn't the only one intending to put on a show today.

As the thought crossed her mind, she internally jolted.

Is it still today, or is it already tomorrow? How long have I been out? Is Nord here? Fuck me sideways, we're only who knows how long into my brilliant plan, and things are already going off the rails.

She blamed the blow to her head for the somewhat disjointed and slaphappy nature of her thoughts. Thankfully, the longer she was awake, the clearer they were becoming. Forcing herself to slow down and take a deep breath, Lina tried to get her thoughts in order.

There was too much riding on this for her to start spiraling now. And the only way she'd remotely get back on track was if she figured out when Mikel first came into contact with the Prism.

Given the venue change from Hope Street back to Bell Falls, she had to assume a plane was involved. Unless Mikel recently added a Guardian to his payroll, which she doubted. But had Mikel been on the plane? Or had he been waiting for them here?

Shit. There were too many variables. Her best bet was to assume the minimum amount of contact. And if a direct flight between cities took about twelve hours, she'd already used up at least half a day.

This was far from good news, but maybe things weren't quite as fucked as they appeared. If Mikel had been sitting there with the book in his lap since he'd found it, there was still a chance the attunement would be complete before Nord's deadline. But if she wanted to know for sure, she needed to find out how many of her forty-eight hours had been lost.

"How long?" she croaked, her tongue darting out to wet her lips, finding them both split and swollen.

He didn't bother answering her, but she hadn't actually expected him to. That wasn't the game Mikel played. He didn't give anything away, and especially not for free.

She gingerly investigated her lip with the tip of her tongue. Somebody'd been busy while she'd been out. Her injuries resulted from far more than a single crack to the head. What was less obvious was who was responsible. For all she knew, it could have been Mikel, her favorite cousin, or someone else entirely. Not that it really mattered. It's what she signed up for.

Far more concerning was the fact the injuries hadn't seemed to trigger her berserker or her Animagi healing. Which meant these nifty bracelets of hers were of the magic-binding variety.

Fucking perfect.

Things were just getting better and better.

At the sound of a page being flipped, Lina's attention refocused on the man in the chair. Without looking up, he said, "You're joining us just in time."

Joining us. As if they were attending a damn dinner party.

Lina snorted, causing Mikel to lift his gaze. It crawled over her, and his lips tilted up with dark amusement. "I'd say you look well, but it would be a lie."

"And you *never* lie."

"Never." His teeth flashed as he smiled, and Lina would have sworn she caught the tiniest hint of fang.

"Good book?" she asked, wondering if she could piece together a timeline based on how far into the false Codex he'd gotten.

She'd been careful to model it as closely as she dared to the real thing. Quinn had tried to trick him before and failed, so Lina wanted it to look and read authentic. Besides creating fake spells and passages, the only liberty she'd taken was to leave the book decoded, so Mikel would be tempted to spend time reading its pages.

"Fascinating."

"And utterly useless to you."

His gaze sharpened on hers.

"Oh, haven't you gotten to that part? Oops. Guess I should have warned you by saying 'spoilers' first."

Mikel tried to act unaffected, but she noticed the slight twitch of his eye as he looked back down. Lina inwardly grinned. There was nothing more appealing than the lure of the forbidden. It was the red button theory she and Quinn talked about all over again. Tell someone they can't have or do something, and they'll quickly fixate on it.

That's right, asshole. Take the bait. Your hubris will be the very thing that kills you.

She couldn't resist goading him further. "By all means, keep reading. But unless you find a way to become a Cuska, there's not a damn thing in there you can use."

Instead of responding, Mikel smiled to himself, as if he'd been hoping she'd say something like that. It was the single creepiest thing he could have done, and it threw her completely. Because why would he smile . . . unless he already had something in mind which would allow him to do just that?

Lina shivered, her body simultaneously hot and cold. She had the sudden, horrifying realization she'd missed something vital. That instead of being the one who'd laid the trap, she'd inadvertently landed straight in the middle of his.

Somewhere behind her, there was the scratch and hiss of a match being lit, and then row upon row of candles blazed to life, casting the hangar-sized warehouse into flickering relief.

That's when she could see what she'd so obviously missed.

She and Mikel had never been alone. When he'd said 'us' he hadn't been using it in the royal sense; he'd quite literally been referring to the hundred or so robed figures scattered throughout the room.

This was all becoming terrifyingly familiar.

The robed figures. The candles. Even the storm that chose that moment to make itself known with a bright flash of lightning and distant roll of thunder.

It was Mataius' ritual all over again.

After everything she'd overcome, Lina considered herself a pretty badass woman. But when brought face-to-face with an exact repeat of the night she'd been murdered, that strong, powerful, alpha female was nowhere to be found. In her place, all that remained was endless, hope-shattering dread.

Not again. Not again. Please, not again.

And then the chanting started.

What was it she'd told Quinn? 'I can't be broken?' In one fell swoop, Mikel had proven her so very wrong.

Lina shook, the chains hanging from her manacles rattling and betraying her distress.

Mikel's smile stretched as he slowly closed the book in his lap and rose to his feet.

She whimpered, nothing about her display of fear an act as he set the Codex down, his long fingers trailing across its cover before plucking something else up from beside it on the table.

Something long, silver, and wickedly sharp.

As the first of her tears rolled down her cheek, Mikel's smile widened. This time, there was no missing the pointed incisors or the reptilian slant of his pupils. Where a man once sat, a monster now stood.

Rolling the dagger in his fingers, Mikel started toward her, his steps practically languid as he closed the distance between them. In one impossibly fast move, he slashed out, cutting her shirt up the middle and pressing the tip of the dagger against the hollow of her throat.

"Time to finish what my son began." Mikel grasped her hair with his free hand and jerked her head back, pressing the dagger deeper into her neck. "And make no mistake, Evalina. Unlike Mataius, I will not fail." Then he leaned forward, his lips brushing against the shell of her ear. "And by the time I'm through with you, there will be nothing left for your friends to resurrect."

CHAPTER 20
NORD

"Are you sure we got the calculation right?" Quinn asked, her voice high and tense. "What if we fuck up and leave her there for half a week instead of a couple days? We're fools for thinking Mikel will leave her alive for a single day as it is. Anything more than that is just sheer idiocy."

"Hush, mon coeur. You're not helping anyone asking questions like that right now. We've already been over this. Mikel needs Lina alive for whatever he's planning. He won't kill her before we get there. I'm certain of it."

Cora's feelings on the matter were one of the only reasons Nord had given in. Had she suggested otherwise, he didn't think there was a force on this world or any other that would have convinced him to let Lina go alone.

Finley rested a hand on Nord's shoulder, his words as much a reassurance for him as they were an answer to Quinn. "We are as sure as we can be. Given the passage of time in these two realms, three and a half hours here should be just about a day there."

Quinn turned on Nord, her voice ringing with accusation. "How could you let her do this? How could you let her just hand herself over to that monster?"

Nord hadn't moved since Lina stepped through the portal. He'd sat in the same chair with his eyes glued to the clock as he counted down the seconds until he could rejoin her. At Quinn's demand, he slowly lifted his head up, his eyes meeting hers. She flinched at whatever she found there, and he did absolutely nothing to spare her from it. If she thought any of this was easy for him, she didn't know him at all.

Quinn spun away from Nord, muttering under her breath, "I still think someone should have gone with her. I mean, Lina just magically popping up on her own after weeks of being gone? Could she be any more obvious?"

Once again, it was Finley who answered. He seemed uniquely suited for the task, getting through to Quinn where the others couldn't with just the right blend of logic and exasperation.

"Mikel's too egotistical to sense a trap. He's used to luck working in his favor. He probably thinks it's simply a matter of course he would stumble across her on her own when no one else would. And he's certainly not the type of man who would question his good fortune. He'd take the gift and run without a moment's hesitation."

Quinn worried at her bottom lip, but eventually nodded. "You're probably right."

Nord's eyes had already returned to the clock. His control over his berserker was strained at best. The only thing keeping him put was that he'd given Lina his word. She was counting on him to provide her with the time she needed to see her plan through.

The problem was, since the second she'd vanished, he couldn't escape the raw ache in his chest or the oily, unsettled feeling slithering around in his stomach. No matter how many times he or one of the others tried to reassure him, Nord just couldn't shake the belief that something was about to go horribly wrong.

No one was under any illusion that their plan was foolproof. If anything, everyone agreed it was bound to fail, if only because of the unpredictable nature of the man they were up against. But since the entire point of this scheme was to force Mikel to spend the requisite amount of time in the presence of the Prism, they'd decided to risk it.

If Lina pulled this off, it would be the coup to end all others. But if not, they were still prepared to bring this war to an end. One way or another.

They already had strategies mapped out for what to do if—when —the attunement failed. Stripping Mikel of his power was the only path resulting in a low body count, which was how Lina had convinced them to at least let her try it before they made the streets run red with blood. It was an effective means of distracting him while they got into place, if nothing else.

All that was left to do was wait. Astrid and the others were already gathering to wait for his signal. They knew to be ready in case whatever he found when he arrived in Bell Falls was the worst-case scenario.

Even so, that same relentless anxiety tore at him.

There were only ten minutes left on his countdown, but what if those minutes were the difference in whether he was *too* late? What if Lina needed him now?

Nord had spent far too much of his life learning to trust his instinct, to discern the difference between emotion and intuition. Those lessons were failing him now. He knew he was irrational when it came to matters of her safety. That his berserker's possessive nature and their bond's reaction to physical separation were potent influencers. So was what he felt now merely a result of their combined effect? Or was it something more?

Fuck it.

Maybe it was just him overreacting, but he couldn't live with himself if he sat here and was wrong. Even if it put their entire plan in jeopardy, he'd risk it all to save her.

"Finley, open the portal."

"But—"

"Open. The. Fucking. Portal."

Quinn released a heavy breath. "Finally." She glanced at her mother. "I love it when the berserker comes out to play. That's how you know things are about to get handled."

"That's not what you said last time," Finley muttered, eyes glowing silver. "In fact, I distinctly remember you trying to stop him from raging out and storming off after her."

"Yeah, well. Our goals are aligned this time."

"Convenient."

"Maybe for me," Quinn agreed with a dark smile. "But not Mikel."

Nord dismissed their voices, his focus settled on the spot beside Finley where the air started to shimmer and move. Pausing only long enough to ensure that the horn was strapped to his belt, Nord was halfway across the room and striding through the portal before Finley had a chance to say he was finished.

Finley's voice traveled through the portal as he called back to the Satori women, "Go and join the others. Let them know the timeline's moved up and to be ready."

By the time Finley joined him, Nord's phone was in hand, and he'd already pulled up the app that would provide him with Lina's tracker location.

"Find her?"

Nord squinted at the small screen. "It says she's in Bell Falls, but I'm not familiar with that part of town. It looks like she's in the middle of some kind of nature reserve."

"Let me see."

Nord handed him the phone.

"That's not a reserve," Finley said. "It's a private vineyard. Lots of land and no neighbors for miles. There are also a couple of big warehouses for their winemaking and storage. Perfect place to go if you're looking not to be overheard."

"Have you been there?"

"I have."

"Then what the fuck are you waiting for? Summon the damn portal."

Finley raised a brow. "If you were anyone else, I'd tell you to fucking walk."

Nord grabbed his friend by the neck of his shirt. "Do you really want to test me right now?"

It was likely only due to the strength of their friendship—and his familiarity with Nord's temper after these past few months—but Finley didn't so much as flinch. "I get that you're worried, mate, but don't let your emotion cloud your judgment. This is still a mission, and we have a job to do. You need to be smart. Don't forget who owns that land. I wouldn't be surprised if it's under heavy guard and surveillance, or if we set off some sort of proximity alarm when we get there. There's a very good chance we're going to be discovered—and likely outnumbered—within minutes. And after seeing how the Animagi hid their meeting space, I'd also bet the place will be riddled with tunnels and all sorts of things we won't be able to detect."

Nord dropped his hold. "I know all that, but something's not right. I can feel it." The sensation that had been unsettling in Novasgard was now a full-scale prickling running the entire length of his body. He felt seconds away from crawling out of his own damned skin.

"The bond?" Fin asked, concern sharpening his gaze.

"I can't feel her yet, if that's what you're asking."

Finley looked back at the phone in his hand, seeming to reach a decision. "If we're not going for stealth, then I can get us here"—he pointed to a blank patch on the screen in the middle of two gray rectangles—"that will put us between the two warehouses. In terms of where they are keeping her, it's the most likely spot. That we know of, anyway. And it'll cut down on any additional travel time if things really have gone bad."

Nord nodded, ready for him to just get on with it. At this point, he didn't care if they portaled in on Mikel's head. He'd probably prefer it, to be honest. Would make it that much easier to slip a dagger between the fucker's ribs.

Thirty seconds later, they were both crouching behind the smaller of the two rectangles from the map, already soaked through by a raging storm that appeared to be centered directly overhead.

Finley glanced at the sky, his eyes flashing silver as he confirmed what Nord suspected. "This is no natural downpour. It reeks of magic."

Nord couldn't care less about the rain. He was too busy listening to the comm crackle to life in his ear. He held his breath, his berserker clawing restlessly beneath his ribs. For a second, there was nothing. Not so much as the hitch of an inhale, but then low guttural chanting came through.

A shiver raced down his spine, chilling him more thoroughly than the storm.

He recognized that sound. He'd heard it once before while trapped in the worst of Lina's nightmares.

Before he could open his mouth to tell Finley they were going in, something far worse echoed in his ear, only to be immediately underscored by an icy wave born of Lina's terror.

"Time to finish what my son began."

Nord. Fucking. Snapped.

The berserker came roaring to life, a bellow of primal rage building deep in his belly and exploding out of him to join the tempest above. He started running, intent only on reaching her.

"Nord, wait." Finley grasped his arm, trying to rein him in.

The berserker rounded on him, baring his teeth in a warning snarl.

"The horn! Use the bloody horn!"

There was a brief flicker of clarity, and he yanked it free. Raising his face to the sky, he lifted the rune-forged horn to his lips and blew until his lungs were depleted. Nord poured every ounce of his desperation and need into his call, praying the Allfather would heed his plea.

He gasped for breath, his lungs burning in protest as the sound of his bugle was swallowed by the wind.

One heartbeat.

A second.

And then . . . an answer.

Lightning webbed across the sky, one bolt forking down to strike right at his feet. Instead of fading, the bolt of electric energy stretched and grew, rapidly expanding until it was no longer a bolt, but a doorway.

And standing in that doorway, their expressions as savage as the fury pumping wildly through his veins, was the entire fighting force of the lost Viking city and three very pissed-off Satori.

His heart stuttered at the sight of them, clad in their magic-infused armor, paint decorating their faces and arms. Even though Astrid had given them the option, not one able-bodied person had remained behind, save those watching over the children. All others were here, answering his call and ready to put their lives on the line to help him save his mate.

"No one escapes," Nord commanded, his voice booming like thunder as he used magic to call his grandmother's sword. Lightning ran down the blade as it formed in his hand, causing the runes to blaze to life with vibrant white light. Feeling the power of Odin himself coursing through his body, Nord tipped his head back and let out a mighty battle cry.

"Óðinn á yðr alla!"

The Novasgardians took up the cry, raising their weapons high and shouting back, "Odin owns you all!"

And then all he knew was the eternal fury of a vengeful god.

CHAPTER 21
LINA

Mikel dragged the tip of his dagger across her chest, carving his sinister symbol into her flesh with little finesse. So far, Lina had managed to swallow her screams, but it was a losing battle. The harder she fought not to make a sound, the deeper he'd push the blade in, sending searing pain spiking through her with each cruel flick of his wrist.

Her vision was starting to fade at the edges, the pain mounting to the point where her mind wanted to shut down to protect her. But Lina knew she couldn't afford the luxury of unconsciousness. Nor could she afford to lose any more time. If she did, she may as well thrust the dagger into her heart right now and just get this over with.

It was hard to think past the agony radiating out from Mikel's gruesome design, but a noticeable change took hold of the room, drawing her focus. Lina couldn't tell if it came from her or the robed figures crowding in closer, but the air of anticipation that had swelled along with the ritual's song finally reached its peak.

Energy hung suspended in the warehouse, like a rollercoaster pausing at the highest point of its track right before it hurtled back to the ground.

Whatever Mikel was doing, it had just reached its tipping point.

As the thought crossed her mind, a jarring crash sent everyone's attention to the door. Or what had once been the door. The industrial steel now resembled tin foil as it crumpled and fell to the ground, hitting the concrete with a pathetic wheeze.

Nord stood framed by the doorway, illuminated from behind by a flash of lightning as the storm raged around him, golden strands of hair plastered to his face, his eyes two black pits of fury. Flanking him were Astrid and Finley, weapons in their hands, faces set in expressions that almost matched his in sheer intensity.

Lina's heart lurched at the sight of them. He'd come for her. There wasn't much of a chance to think beyond that because as soon as his gaze found hers, his face twisted in absolute rage, and he let out a roar that shattered the few windows and lightbulbs throughout the room.

Mikel adjusted his hold on the dagger, shifting his stance so he stood directly between Nord and Lina.

"I was wondering when you'd show up."

Nord didn't bother replying to Mikel's taunt. He just shifted to the side so Lina remained in his line of sight. From the look of him, he seemed far beyond something as human as speech. She'd seen the berserker in action many times by now, but this was the first time she understood why the others referred to Nord as the Warrior of Odin. Lightning flickered in the inky depths of his eyes, and he did not look remotely mortal lined up beside the other fighters. He didn't just loom over them; he exuded unholy wrath, as if he'd been sent by the gods themselves to mete out their punishment.

Without hesitation, Nord lunged, going airborne as he leapt for Mikel. With all eyes on them, no one noticed when Lina's shackles dropped away. She recognized the caress of Nord's magic flowing down her arms, as familiar to her as her own. Her body's reaction to being freed was instant, her berserker triggered by her pain and leaving her lightheaded as it swept away all sensation but the need to join the fight.

In a moment of surprising bravery—because who in their right mind would willingly confront a raging berserker—Nico ripped his hood off and stepped forward, using his magic to conjure and throw a three-foot cement block at Nord, knocking him off course. Mikel took advantage of the distraction, picking up the Prism-Codex, shoving it back into Lina's discarded knapsack, and racing toward the back door.

Coward.

Lina debated chasing after him, but her magic had only just started to kick in, healing her wounds, and she didn't want to waste her opportunity to jump in while she was still at such a disadvantage.

Thankfully, dozens of Novasgardians were pouring in through the doors and broken windows. Mikel took one look at them and froze, his face a mask of absolute fury. But whereas Nord's burned white-hot, Mikel's was ice-cold. An odd contradiction, given his mastery of fire.

He took one snarling breath, looking every inch a man whose patience had just snuffed out. As he sucked in air, his body stretched and grew.

Lina blinked, thinking it was blood loss making her see things, but no. The transformation continued. His limbs lengthened and his muscles swelled, the changes punctuated with the snap and crack of breaking bones. Soon he was too large for the spot he'd been standing, and he fell forward onto his hands—claws—raking the sharp points over the floor and leaving thick grooves in their wake.

As his clothes tore away, no longer able to conceal his bulk, Lina noticed his skin was covered in pale green scales the same color as his eyes, and a barbed tail shot out from his back end. His head turned toward her, his nose and mouth extended into a terrifying snout. Puffs of smoke curled from the slits that had once been human nostrils, and his eyes glowed a reptilian shade of amber. But perhaps most shocking of all were the emerald green wings unfurling from either side of the horns protruding along his spine.

Lina's jaw dropped. Her brain took a moment to make sense of the impossibility of what she was seeing. For where Mikel Drake had been a second prior, now stood a living, fire-breathing dragon.

The creature reached out with one dangerous claw, scooping up Lina's bag, which still contained the magical prison. Then it lifted its long neck, fire spewing from its mouth as it burned a dragon-sized hole in the roof.

Shouts rang out as people, Vikings and Animagi alike, dove for cover.

Finley reached her then, his eyes already glowing silver as he set to work, helping speed along her magic's healing process.

"Fin—" she breathed, shock holding her immobile.

"I know, love. I see it too."

Lina shook her head, finally able to open and blink both of her eyes. But the dragon was still there, bracing for flight. She twitched with impatience, and Finley shoved her back down in the chair with a hand to the shoulder.

"Do you know how easily I could fuck this up if you don't remain still?"

"Sorry," she mumbled. But she wasn't. It was killing her to be sidelined while the battle was in full swing around her. Everywhere she looked, Vikings fought with robed figures, weapons and magic colliding as the screams of the dying soon drowned out the wail of the storm.

This was her fight. She should be doing something more impressive than nearly bleeding out.

Worse, Mikel was going to get away.

Not sure what else to do in her current state, Lina did the only thing she could think of. "Nord!"

Nord's head jerked in her direction, the slight distraction providing Nico with an opportunity to fling a blade at his neck.

Instinct, or perhaps his berserker-enhanced senses, helped Nord sidestep the dagger.

Lina pointed to Mikel. Nord's gaze followed her arm, his lips curling up into a snarl as the dragon sprang into the air. He was perhaps fifteen feet away from Nord.

"He's not going to make it."

She hadn't realized she'd spoken out loud until Finley answered. "Yes, he is. Now for the love of God, sit still. I can't focus with you trying to jump up every two seconds."

"Just hurry up," she growled, watching as Nord propelled himself forward, jumping far higher and further than any mortal man should have been able to.

As Mikel began to lift into the sky, Nord latched onto his tail with one arm and drove his blade in between two scales with the other. There was a bellow of outrage as the weapon sank in, and Mikel lashed out with his tail, trying to knock Nord and the weapon free. But Nord held on, letting go of the blade so he could grasp onto Mikel's tail with both hands. A half a second later, his feet hit the floor, and he yanked Mikel back, countering the heavy beat of the dragon's wings and keeping him from fully taking flight.

Lina gaped.

Nord—her husband—was playing tug of war with a dragon. Not only that, he was *winning*.

Mikel's neck twisted back, his eyes narrowing into angry slits. The pale green scales lining his belly glowed as he opened his mouth and let out another jet of liquid flame.

Lina screamed, but this time Nord didn't require her warning. In a brilliant display of magic, Nord vanished the sword jutting out from the tail and transformed it into a shield, which shimmered into being on his forearm not more than a heartbeat before the flame would have engulfed his body. Unfortunately, the defensive maneuver required Nord to drop his hold on the dragon's tail, and Mikel was now in the air and moving fast.

No.

NO!

He couldn't get away. Not this time.

Lina's fury broke free, fueling her with its strength. In the same breath, she drew on her entire reservoir of power, her body sparking with the sudden onslaught of magic. She didn't know, nor did she care, whether she was healed enough to withstand what she was planning, but then, she'd always been a fly-by-the-seat-of-her-pants kind of girl. With no practical understanding of what she was trying to do, she could only look to Mikel's flying form to help shape her will.

"Lina, no," Finley protested, trying to restrain her.

But he was too late. Already headlong into the bloodlust, she felt absolutely no fear about what she was attempting, only pure, boundless rage.

And then she broke free of her mortal body, existing for one blissful moment as nothing more than absolute energy before she reformed into something new.

Something stronger. Faster. Far more powerful than she could ever be in her true form.

With a mighty roar, a dragon the color of ice shot off into the sky in hunt of her prey.

CHAPTER 22
NORD

Nord watched the two dragons take to the sky, torn between the desire to join them and knowing there were more than enough enemies for him to deal with on land. Ultimately, it was an easy choice to make. He dropped his gaze, his eyes zeroing in on Nico. It was only right Lina see to Mikel. She deserved that kill. This one would be his.

The Cuska traitor sneered at Nord from across the room, lifting his hands and conjuring a series of walls and cement blocks in surprising succession. He was nowhere near as powerful as his cousin, but he was fast.

Nord laughed as he realized what Nico was attempting. Did the fool really think an obstacle course would be enough to save him? From a berserker?

He was about to be very disappointed.

Vanishing his shield and feeling his grandmother's sword reform in the harness strapped to his back, Nord started running, easily jumping over, around, and sometimes through Nico's barriers. Nico's eyes widened comically as Nord burst through the last wall, a cloud of dust and debris billowing over them both.

He lifted shaking hands, his voice quavering. "Please. Don't kill me. I can help you. I know where Mikel—"

"Traitors do not deserve mercy." Nord reached for the hilt of his sword and paused. "Nor do they deserve the dignity of being run through by a weapon with a legacy such as this. I will not sully my grandmother's blade with your filthy blood."

Nico's shoulders sagged, the idiot mistakenly believing that meant Nord was going to spare him. But when Nord smiled, he seemed to realize his mistake.

He raised his hands a bit higher, still cringing away as Nord stalked him step for step. "Wait. I'm the only remaining full-blooded Cuska. What's my cousin going to say if you murder her last true family member?"

Grasping Nico on either side of the head, Nord brought their faces together, snarling, "She has a family. *Me.* You, however, are nothing more than unfinished business. You have no place among us. After today, filth, you will be nothing at all. Not even a stain on the floor. She will not mourn you. She will not miss you. She will not think of you at all unless it is to rejoice in your passing."

Nico trembled in Nord's hold, pissing himself in fear.

"Yes. I see you are starting to understand. When you betray a berserker, there is only one means of recourse."

"I'll . . . I'll d-do anything. Whatever the price, I-I'll pay it."

"Yes," Nord agreed. "You will."

Tightening his hold, Nord wrenched his hands upward, snapping Nico's neck and tearing both head and spine free. It was oddly poetic watching the spineless, headless body sag to the floor.

Nord dropped the head, not watching as it bounced and rolled. Instead, he turned and walked away without a backward glance. For it was exactly as he'd promised—as of this moment, Nico Cuska was nothing at all.

Astrid was there to greet him, her face and sword sprayed red with blood. She grinned as Nord unsheathed his blade.

"Shall we finish this, then?" she asked.

Nord dipped his chin in a nod. "Anyone who participated in the ritual is fair game. As for the others, give them a choice to join us. Mikel coerced many. They may not be fighting of their own free will."

"And if they choose not to?"

"Then they will share the same fate as their leader," Finley answered, joining them with his eyes trained on the sky, where two dragons were locked in battle.

The three of them watched for a beat, and then Nord returned his attention to the battle that had spilled outside. Adjusting his grip on his blade, he started moving, calling over his shoulder, "One way or another, the Mobius Council will be purged."

CHAPTER 23
QUINN

Though Quinn hung back while the experts got down to business, that didn't mean she was idle. After ensuring her mother and aunt were safely tucked away, she patrolled the perimeter, on the lookout for traitors attempting to flee the scene of their crime. In the unlikely event anyone got past a Novasgardian, Quinn's job was to issue the command sending them straight back in to face their reckoning.

Nord's order had been very clear. No one escapes. And while not exactly one of his warriors, she had every intention of doing her part to see their mission carried out. Animagi or not, the people in that warehouse had sold their souls to the devil instead of doing what was right. She didn't have it in her heart to forgive them. If she had it her way, she'd watch them all burn.

Her memory was long. Her ability to hold a grudge, eternal.

She'd waited a long time for this day to arrive. Grieved the loss of her father and countless others in silence for decades while secretly working toward this end. Now that the time was finally at hand, she had no intention of failing.

Mikel Drake and every single one of his pathetic sycophants

would die here. Or she'd hunt them down to the very ends of the earth and see to it that they did.

Quinn's lips curled up in a dark smile at the thought. She always accused Lina of being as bloodthirsty as her husband, but she was no better. The berserkers' ruthless version of justice had rubbed off on her, and no lies, she kind of loved it.

She wasn't half the fighter they were, nor would she ever be. But when it came to the people she considered her enemies, she could be every bit as deadly.

You didn't betray a Satori and get away with it. And you certainly didn't fuck with her family and live.

There was a rustle in the trees not too far from her, and Quinn spun, the command already at her lips as her power rushed to the surface.

Kristoff turned to face her, a dagger made of his own bone flying free and straight at her before a single word could leave her lips. Two more followed in quick succession, the Alinari's notorious skill as a sharpshooter evident in not only his ability to conjure the weapons but send them soaring to their target with unfailing precision.

The first landed, sending her gasping to her knees as blood immediately poured from her belly.

"No!"

The roar came from the warehouse beside her. Quinn lifted her head, shock and hope filling her as Finley lifted his own weapon and unloaded it while sprinting in their direction. "You will pay for that with your life, you fucking coward."

Satisfaction twisted through her as each of Finley's spelled bullets landed and Kristoff fell beside her, dead before he hit the ground.

Finley was only a few feet away, his expression thunderous, when two Animagi appeared behind him. One was an Alinari, clearly seeking retribution for Kristoff. The other was a Drake.

"Behind you!"

But her warning came too late.

Finley's eyes bulged as a spear tore through his chest. As he looked down in shock, the Drake called down a bolt of lightning, harvesting it from the storm raging above and channeling it through the metallic tip of the spear. Quinn watched in absolute horror as electricity coursed through Finley's spasming body.

He was still twitching when his body dropped.

She pushed to her feet, struggling to stand and stumbling in her haste to reach him.

"Fin? Fin!"

Quinn pressed a bloody palm to his chest, but he was still. He didn't react to her screaming his name or to her touch. It was hard to think clearly after that. All she knew was that Finley wasn't moving, and it was their fault.

She slowly looked up at the two Animagi closing in on her. A dozen more were right behind them, all of them converging on the one they thought responsible for their patriarch's demise.

Quinn saw nothing but a red haze as she stood on trembling legs, a wail of utter fury tearing out of her throat and stretching on far longer than should have been possible. It was a sound without end, one born of her pain and fueled by her heartbreak. She couldn't have controlled it if she tried. All she knew in that moment was she wanted them dead. It should be them on the floor, not Finley. Never Finley.

It didn't matter which one was responsible; she loathed them equally. They were the reason he was lifeless at her feet. They were the ones responsible for the chasm of utter despair churning inside of her.

She wanted them drowning in her pain.

She wanted them to *suffer*.

The men—those closest to her and all others in hearing range—dropped to their knees, hands crushed to their ears as they tried to block out her scream. But there was no escape because it was no natural wail. Her magic permeated the sound, latching onto each of the men's minds and shattering them completely. Blood dripped from their eyes and poured through their fingers as they fell to the ground. Their cries of agony joining hers until, one by one, they fell still.

Only then did she stop screaming. Only then did she release her hold on their minds.

Quinn's legs gave out, and she crawled back over to Finley. Rain dripped down his face, plastering his hair to his head. She couldn't lay him on his back because of the spear, so instead, she draped her body over his, trying to shield him as best she could from the storm. The world was growing fuzzy, and Quinn distantly realized she was losing a lot of blood, hers pooling with his on the pavement beneath them.

But she didn't care.

The only thing on her mind was the man in her arms.

The one she'd spent so long pretending didn't matter.

The one she knew, without a doubt, absolutely *did*.

She pressed her palm to his cheek, her face hovering over his. "Fin . . . Fin, you need to wake up. Please wake up." Her voice cracked, her tears breaking free as her fear overwhelmed her. Eyes squeezing shut, she pressed her forehead to his, her voice little more than a ragged whisper as she continued to beg. "Come back to me. You have promises to keep. Please, Batman. Don't leave me. Not now. Not . . . not like this. Please, Fin. Please. I love you."

CHAPTER 24
LINA

In the seconds between deciding to chase after Mikel and transforming herself, Lina hadn't had an opportunity to consider what came after. A detail which she quickly came to realize was rather crucial.

There wasn't even time for her to enjoy the sheer majesty of the creature she'd become. Because unlike Mikel, who was a natural shifter containing within him all the innate understanding and instincts of his beast, Lina had none. She was just Lina 'now with a new and improved design.'

Take flying, for example. It was far from a graceful launch. She'd assumed having wings would be the only requirement for flight, but the folds of leathery sinew stretching out behind her were more cumbersome than she'd anticipated. It was like trying to flex a muscle on someone else's body. She had an idea of what she wanted to do, but her brain couldn't seem to isolate the area required to make it happen.

Meaning, to anyone watching, she probably looked like a child learning to ride a bike without training wheels. All jerky steering and wild careening before ultimately leveling out. Thankfully, her wings caught the air and allowed her to glide, which was likely the only reason she hadn't immediately fallen flat on her face.

Now that she was airborne, she was in the midst of a crash course on working her new body. Namely, how slight adjustments vastly affected her direction and speed. Given how complicated mastering this part was, she wasn't looking forward to the landing portion of the course.

Assuming she even lived that long.

Mikel had taken one look at her coming along after him and started sending enormous blasts of fire in her general direction. She'd seriously over-corrected while dodging the first few times, but she figured that was better than the alternative. Luckily, she seemed to have gotten the hang of it and was finally gaining on him.

All right, Lina. You've survived Dragon 101. Now what the hell are you going to do when you catch him?

Fighting in this form felt like it was going to be some advanced-level shit, and she was seriously regretting her impetuous decision. Being a dragon was cool and all, but she probably could have done just as much damage—if not more—as herself.

Well, it's too late now, sugar tits. So you better figure it out fast.

As she was thinking through her options and recalling Nord's advice from when they'd dealt with the wyvern, Lina decided her best bet would be going for the dragon's fleshy underbelly. Though that kind of attack would require close range, and any maneuver that put her in a position to strike with fang and claw would provide Mikel with an opportunity to do the same.

In other words, it really wasn't ideal.

As the novice dragon, she'd be at an extreme disadvantage if they went claw-to-claw. And the last thing she needed right now was another handicap. She'd be better off figuring out a way to fight him from a distance.

Mikel had perhaps a dragon's length on her at most. From her vantage, Lina could see his chest begin to glow with the telltale sign of his next fiery breath.

A lightbulb went off in her mind.

If Mikel could breathe fire, surely her dragon came equipped with that feature as well.

Right? Wasn't fire sort of a default setting for flying lizards?

Granted, she wasn't technically a dragon, nor had she specifically thought to include such an ability when she'd transformed herself. Lina was seriously hoping her magic had been intuitive enough to supply her with a defense system anyway, because she was about to put it to the test.

Now . . . how the hell did she access it?

Having made it this far utilizing her time-honored wing-and-a-prayer technique, Lina decided she may as well keep on with the tradition. Sucking in huge mouthfuls of the stormy air, she filled her lungs near to bursting. Then, right as Mikel released his fire, she expelled the breath from her lungs, praying for a miracle.

And a miracle she got. Or maybe it was just her magic, but it felt pretty miraculous nevertheless.

Instead of fire, however, it came in the form of ice and snow. Momentary shock caused her breath to stutter, and for a second, Mikel's fire broke through her torrent of ice.

Jerking herself away from the fiery gusts, Lina brought herself up so she was soaring behind and above him. Taking aim, she sent her icy breath cascading over his back and wings. Where the ice connected with the drops of rain coating his scales, it froze, covering him in a layer of shimmering frost.

Seeing that, Lina sucked in another huge breath and quickly released it, this time aiming specifically at his membranous wings. As she'd hoped, her frosty breath webbed out, freezing the raindrops stuck to them and locking them in place beneath a thick blanket of ice.

Mikel roared, his body twitching violently as he tried to counteract his sudden inability to use his wings. Lina could hear it crack beneath the strain, but so far, her ice was holding out. Mikel started to lose altitude as he struggled to break free.

Lina whooped with victory, though her cries came out as ground-shaking rumbles. From far below, Novasgardians took up the cheer. Their tiny bodies fanned out as they prepared to take on the falling giant.

That is, all but her mate. Nord was still a ways off, dealing with what looked like an entire contingent of Animagi on his own. She couldn't help her flutter of pride as she witnessed him annihilate his enemies. Even in this form, her bloodlust surged forth, eager to do the same.

Mikel continued to shoot out bursts of flame as he fell, warming the air around him while angling his dragon's massive body toward the warehouse still in possession of its roof.

Lina continued to fly above, circling the air and following him down, ready to hit him with more ice when it looked like his attempts to melt or break the first layer succeeded. She assumed he was going to attempt an emergency landing, though what she really wanted was for him to go crashing straight through and send the whole thing toppling down after him.

No such luck.

The green dragon landed in an annoying display of precision and skill, his claws gripping the warehouse's roof and supporting his weight. Lina was surprised his hold was enough to prevent him from smashing straight through it as she'd hoped.

But Mikel's landing was no reprieve. The Vikings were ready for him. They gathered close, their weapons and spells at the ready the second he came into range.

Arrick, the mage, was the first to strike the snarling beast. He sent bolt after bolt of crackling purple energy at his head, forcing him to duck and bob. Next came Ulf and Søren, who worked together to hurl massive chains around Mikel's body, tethering him to the ground presumably to keep him from taking flight again. Meanwhile, Strega shot bolts from her crossbow, tearing through his wings while Ruhla and Revna launched a seemingly endless number of blades at his face. And those were just the people she recognized. From every direction, dozens more did the same.

The Viking onslaught was overwhelming and furious. Mikel had been caught completely off guard by the sheer magnitude of their assault. Most of their attacks landed and did considerable damage, though sadly, none were enough to fell the dragon. If anything, they only enraged him further.

Mikel lashed out with every weapon in his arsenal. His tail whipped to the side, knocking several Novasgardians over before he flung it back into the air and then slammed it down on some unfortunate soul, crushing them instantly. He roared, sending fire pouring from his mouth and burning a second wave of the fighters, turning them to charred husks in a matter of seconds. It was an absolute slaughter.

At least in the air, Mikel had been too focused on Lina to bother with anyone else. Now that he was on the ground, however, no one was safe.

Horrified, Lina swooped lower, prepared to do her worst. As she got closer, she realized that the Viking Mikel crushed with his tail had been the gentle giant Björn. A fact she only grasped when Astrid began screaming profanities up at the dragon, cursing him for the death of her beloved son as she ran headlong at him with her rune-blade in hand.

Astrid . . . no!

For one beautiful moment, it appeared that the stars had aligned. The runes running down the length of steel glowed with inner fire as she flung it up. Her sword seemed to fly in slow motion as lightning arced in the sky above, illuminating the weapon as it headed straight for the hollow of the dragon's throat.

But the illusion was quickly shattered.

Mikel's head shot forward as fast as a viper strike, despite its massive size. His toothy maw was wide open for less than a second before snapping closed around Astrid and swallowing her whole.

Just like that, she was gone.

Lina screamed, bellowing her rage to the heavens and sending more clouds of frost scattering through the sky.

That's when Mikel's reptilian gaze met hers, taunting her. She would have sworn he smiled. Could practically hear his voice sounding in her mind.

"You'll never beat me, Evalina. All you will find here is death."

Her last coherent thought as she dove toward him with her claws outstretched was, *"The only one of us dying here today, asshole, is you!"*

Before Lina could reach him, one of the assassins—Ruhla—started running, using pieces of fallen roof and other debris to launch herself into the air. Her dagger arced down, aimed straight at one of Mikel's glowing amber eyes.

"Valhalla awaits!" she screamed, her blade inches from his face when the massive head snapped to the side and he bit her in two.

Lina's stomach rolled at the sound of the woman hitting the ground. She'd intended to use her magic to shape her icy breath into something more powerful, like a spear. But after witnessing Mikel's absolute decimation of her friends, Lina acted purely on instinct.

She flew straight into him, her massive body tackling his as she grasped onto him with her claws and flew them both straight up into the storm. She had some sort of half-cocked plan to fly as high as she could and then blast Mikel until he was a block of ice. At that point, she'd drop him, watching his freefall until it culminated in a fatal collision with the ground below.

It might have worked, too.

If not for the Prism.

Mikel fought her grasp with each heavy beat of her wings, but when she'd brought them about a hundred feet in the air, he slashed out with his claw—the one that had somehow managed not to drop her knapsack—and scored deep into her belly. The bag flew open, its contents pressing against her open wound.

Lina hissed at the unexpected pain.

And then, out of nowhere, her wings stopped working.

Wind rushed past her ears as her trajectory changed. Instead of flying up, she was abruptly falling down.

Down.

Down.

As she plummeted, her body twisted and shrank, her dragon form transforming back into her very fragile human one. Lina reached out for her power, trying desperately to create something that would at least slow her fall if not stop it outright. But her magic was sluggish. There, but only just. The faintest whisper of what it should have been. As if this whole time she'd had a leak and never realized it.

As if this whole time, her magic had been slowly siphoned away until there was less than a drop of it left.

That's when she saw her fake Codex falling right alongside her.

A hysterical bubble of laughter burst free. *Well, Lina . . . the good news is your plan to use the Ancient Ones' prison worked. Bad news, it backfired completely and attuned to you before Mikel. So now, right in the middle of your big moment, you're the one without power instead of him, and it's your own damn fault. Congratulations! You might just be the biggest fuck-up in all the realms.*

They'll probably write a song about you. Maybe turn it into a book or miniseries. Really spread the message of your failure far and wide so people can sit on their couches and scream at you for being so stupid. You will literally never live this down, because you're about ten seconds away from dying.

For good this time.

The hysteria-induced hilarity faded as reality seeped in.

This was it. This is how it ended. Not in a blaze of glory, but in spectacular defeat.

And the only person she could blame was herself.

That was when the screaming reached her ears, but whether it was hers or someone else's, she had no idea. As Lina closed her eyes, tears streaming down her face, her only thought was of Nord.

Her mouth tried to form words, but as soon as they left her lips, they were eaten by the storm. She prayed they reached him anyway.

"I'm sorry."

CHAPTER 25
CROMBIE

"Thanks for the invite, boss. Didn't think I'd ever be allowed to set foot in digs this fancy."

Crombie grasped one of the cucumber slices resting over his eyes between his thumb and forefinger, lifting it up so he could peer over at his bodyguard. "Is that your way of telling me my home and club no longer meet your high standards, Linc?"

"It's Zilla now, boss. And you know that's not what I'm sayin'. It's just, places like this, they don't usually cater to clientele such as myself."

"Ah, yes. *Zilla.* Are you ever going to let me in on that little secret of yours, by the by?"

"Does it matter, boss?"

Crombie raised a brow. It was as close to outright defiance as the half-giant had ever gotten. He was surprisingly close-lipped when it came to his sudden name change. Especially given how adamant he was about its usage.

"Not at all," Crombie said, letting the cucumber slice fall back down. "Merely curious."

He reached for the glass of champagne he'd set on the little table beside his lounge chair and carefully navigated it to his mouth, taking an indulgent sip. "Well, enjoy yourself, Zilla. Lady knows you've earned it with those hours you've been working during my little vacation."

Nobody but Lina and her brood knew the truth about where he'd been or why. He intended to keep it that way. No need to have word spreading around that Davis Crombie was not, in fact, the scariest faerie in town.

He took another sip of champagne and set the flute carefully back on the table. "Today's my way of saying thanks. And if you're in the mood for a treat, might I recommend the honey and lavender foot scrub—"

"I ain't letting nobody touch my feet."

Crombie snickered. "Perhaps just the shiatsu massage then."

"The what?"

"It's when they—"

A phantom hook slid through his rib cage and tugged. Hard. Crombie jerked to a sitting position, sending one of his vegetable slices falling to his lap.

"Oh, you've got to be kidding me."

Zilla glanced over at him, looking as fierce as always, even clad in a Turkish cotton robe with matching monogrammed slippers. "Everything all right?"

Crombie sighed as the hook settled in deeper, giving him another yank. "It would appear I'm being summoned to fulfill a vow I made to a lady friend of mine. So much for a day off."

Zilla reached over and grabbed Crombie's champagne.

"What the hell do you think you're doing?"

"Be a right shame to let these posh bubbles go to waste. Not like you can take 'em with you." Zilla lifted the flute in a mocking toast. "Here's to a relaxing day at the spa."

"Oh, piss off—"

This time, when the tug came, Crombie was yanked straight out of his seat and propelled through time and space to the woman he'd bound himself to. Even though he knew only mortal peril could summon him, he wasn't feeling particularly worried. Concerned perhaps, but not worried.

There wasn't a single thing that existed in this realm he feared. No, every creature residing on that particular shit list was safely tucked away in Faerie. And after several weeks of mind-numbing routine and carefully locking away the memories of what he'd endured, he was feeling much more himself. So no matter what awaited him when he arrived at Lina's side, he was confident in his ability to deal with it.

And if there was a slight tremor in his hands belying his bravado, there was no one around to witness it.

Crombie's knees buckled as his feet hit the ground, but he recovered quickly. Straightening, he tightened the belt around his robe as he called out, "Did somebody order a rescue?"

The first thing he noticed was the storm, then the sheer chaos of armor-clad men and women running every which way as they engaged in battle. What he did not see was the woman he was here to save.

There was a roar from above and then Nord's ravaged cry, "Lina!"

Crombie's stomach bottomed out as his gaze slowly lifted.

And there she was. Tumbling from the sky with her limbs flailing and her golden hair billowing around her.

He reacted instinctively, his gift lashing out and holding everything and everyone suspended in time.

His heart continued to clamor in his chest as he rapidly made sense of the scene before him. Lina falling. A dragon chasing her through the air, tendrils of fire snaking free of its mouth. Nord with his face lifted toward her, his body mid-twist as he tried to get to her —not realizing the enemies behind him were using his distraction to punch their blade through his back. Bodies, more dead than alive, were scattered all across the vineyard, which was now on fire despite the pouring rain.

A part of him was almost impressed. This was a far bigger clusterfuck than he'd been anticipating. At least the scale of it was worthy of his aid.

Time to get to work.

Crombie rubbed his hands together, turning to Nord with a heavy sigh. It galled him to admit he needed the whoreson's help, but out of the two of them, the berserker was better equipped to accomplish what Crombie had in mind.

Grasping him by the wrist, Crombie pulled him forward and out of the range of the blade in case he jerked back and accidentally impaled himself. Once that was accomplished, he unfroze him.

Nord staggered forward, his expression twisted in horror before he realized something had changed. He straightened, blinking in confusion as his gaze landed on Crombie.

Crombie lifted his hand in a wave. "No need for thanks. Just keeping my promise."

"I wasn't going to thank you."

Crombie gave a mental shake of his head. Was it any wonder he despised the man when he was so gloriously humble? Oh well, no love lost. He hadn't actually expected thanks anyway. Far scarier for everyone involved if he'd apologized. Such an uncharacteristic display of good manners might just mean the world was, in fact, ending. Good to know things weren't quite that dire.

He pointed at the Animagi still holding their weapons aimed at the place Nord had been standing. "Perhaps you should reconsider."

Nord glowered, not bothering to turn around. "You have something on your face."

Crombie lifted a hand, patting his cheek and finding the second slice of cucumber. "Oh, this." He peeled it free and studied it for a second before popping it in his mouth with a shrug. "I was in the middle of something important when I got the call."

There was no missing the derision as he gave Crombie a slow once-over. "I can see that."

If ever there was a man that could benefit from a little self-care . . . He was so tightly wound, Crombie wouldn't be surprised to learn he shit diamonds. The thought amused him enough he dismissed Nord's implied insult.

"Well," he said, clapping his hands together. "As much as I adore our little chats, we should probably get down to business. Care to explain how all this came about?" he asked as he started walking toward Lina.

"Mikel," Nord snarled by way of answer.

"Yes, that does clarify matters," Crombie said, rolling his eyes. *Gloriously humble and a riveting conversationalist. I'll never understand what Lina sees in him. Muscles alone can't possibly compensate for such obvious character defects.*

Nord pointed to the dragon.

Lady, it's like communicating with a fucking two-year-old. I should have chugged that entire fucking bottle while I had the chance. I deserve a good buzz for putting up with this crap.

Crombie made his eyes wide, his voice dripping with sarcasm. "Oh! You named the dragon. Good for you, not a very inspired choice though, is it?"

"The dragon *is* Mikel Drake."

Crombie glanced back up at the dragon with a new appreciation. He'd heard whispers, of course, but had no proof till now that any member of Mobius was a shifter. He made a mental note.

This could come in handy in the future.

"All right, that tracks. And this?" Crombie asked, summoning his last iota of patience as he gestured to Lina hovering above them.

"I don't know."

Lightning flashed in Nord's eyes, giving Crombie pause. For the first time since arriving, he really studied him. Something was different about the berserker, though he couldn't put his finger on it. Something far more frightening than his usual reticence or blood-lust. Not that Crombie feared him. Still, best to tread carefully. Just in case.

"Well, I'm going to release her, so get ready to put those muscles of yours to use or this will all be for naught."

Nord moved into position.

"Ready?"

He nodded, his eyes trained on the sky.

Crombie gave one last shake of his head. Glad the berserker was about to be Lina's problem again.

He freed her from the web of his magic, and she immediately dropped, her scream intensifying in volume until it abruptly cut off as her freefall drastically slowed. Crombie lifted a brow, nodding in approval when he realized Nord had used his power to counteract the fall.

She floated down to them, her arms outstretched as Nord plucked her from the air and pulled her into him. Her entire body was shaking, blood pouring from a gash across her belly. He pressed a hand to her stomach, healing the wound before hoisting her up higher in his arms.

"I thought I lost you," he whispered roughly.

"Me too. The Prism—"

Nord cut her off with a kiss she eagerly returned.

Crombie cleared his throat, unable to resist a little light ribbing. After all, who really saved the day here?

"Shouldn't I get one of those? I mean, if you're just passing kisses around, I *am* the one ultimately responsible for coming to your rescue."

Lina broke away with a low chuckle. "And here I thought you'd given up your shot at playing the white knight." She gave Nord a soft look as he reluctantly lowered her to the ground. Once she was safely standing once more, she moved over to Crombie and wrapped him in a hug. "I've never been so glad to see you."

Uncomfortably aware of the berserker glaring at him, Crombie patted Lina on the back a few times before stepping away. "Yes, well. I did make a vow. Now what are we going to do about him?"

Lina followed his hand, her eyes narrowing as they landed on the dragon. Then her expression crumpled. "I don't know. My plan—" She shook her head, sending Nord an apologetic glance. "The Prism finished its attunement. That's what caused me to fall. It was siphoning my power . . . there's not much left . . . I don't know if I can stop him."

"Is it a permanent drain?" Crombie asked, not entirely sure what she was referring to but recognizing the defeated slump of her shoulders.

Lina opened her mouth, then closed it again. "I-I don't know."

Nord's gaze was intense as it met hers. "You said you still had some power left."

She nodded.

"Then no," he said, relief heavy in his voice. "The drain is not permanent. Not yet, anyway. The prison would have to siphon your power completely for that to be the case. As long as some remains, it will replenish itself in time."

"But we don't have time. Mikel needs to be dealt with now."

Crombie raised a hand. "As long as I'm here, you have all the time you need. He's not going anywhere until I release him."

"Can you really hold him indefinitely?" Lina asked.

The look she shot him was tinged with hope, like he could just possibly be the white knight she teased him about. Crombie was taken aback by the unfamiliar urge not to disappoint her. He wasn't used to caring about people's opinions of him. He wasn't sure he liked it.

"Indefinitely? Probably not. I've yet to reach my limit, though."

She looked relieved, though her expression soon turned to a frown as her eyes scanned the ground and took in the carnage. "He's too powerful. Especially in this form."

"Powerful, but not undefeatable," Nord said, pulling her back into his arms.

"We should just ask Quinn to have him kill himself and be done with it," Lina muttered. Then she froze. "Where is Quinn?"

"She was patrolling the eastern perimeter. Finley ran off to check on her."

Lina glanced around, her expression worried. "When I was falling, I thought I heard . . ." She started running in the direction Nord had indicated, forcing the others to follow or be left behind.

"Oh, for the love of—" Crombie cinched his robe tighter, grumbling under his breath as he chased after her in his spa-issued slippers. "Would it really be too much to ask for something more appropriate to wear?"

Nord glanced back and smirked, his only warning before a warm tingle of magic rolled over him. Crombie was almost afraid to look down and see what the berserker had selected for him to wear. He was pleasantly surprised to find a pair of black jeans, boots, and a basic T-shirt.

Hmm. Does this mean we're friends now?

He really hoped not. He had entirely too much fun hating the Norseman.

Lina came to a stumbling halt beside two figures huddled together on the ground. She gasped, her hand flying up to her mouth.

"Nord," she pleaded, "do something."

The berserker dropped down beside them, one of his hands resting on each of the bodies. "They're alive."

"Shall I release them?" Crombie asked, surprised by his own relief at the statement. He didn't much care for the Guardian or weaver, but he didn't want them dead either. That was a lot for him. For most people, he wouldn't give their deaths a second thought.

"No. They're in rough shape. It'll be easier for me to heal the both of them this way."

Crombie nodded, even though Nord didn't seem to be looking for any kind of answer since his attention was already trained on the others. Crombie intended on stepping back out of the way when Lina's legs gave out, forcing him into motion. He shot forward, catching her.

She leaned heavily against him. "Jesus. This needs to end. I don't think my heart can take any more near misses. I don't even think I've actually come to terms with the fact that I'm not already dead and just making all of this up."

"Do you really think this is what your version of the afterlife looks like? I have to say, I'm honored to have made the cut."

She glanced up at him. "Good point. You definitely wouldn't be there."

"Hey. Need I remind you I just saved your life?"

She smiled and pressed her lips to his cheek. "Thanks for that. I owe you."

"No. Actually, that's the whole point. You don't. We're even now. This was me repaying you."

"So what does that make us?" she asked, her eyes warily searching his. "Are we enemies again? Begrudging allies?"

Crombie cleared his throat. "Actually, I'd like to try being friends, if you're still amiable."

Her brows lifted. "You want to be my friend?"

Crombie swallowed, feeling unexpectedly vulnerable and more than a little awkward. After everything he'd done, he hardly deserved her friendship. That didn't make his desire for it any less real. There were very few people he'd consider friends, two perhaps, including her. He'd long recognized something kindred in Lina. If anyone could accept the dark, broken pieces of his soul without judgment, he had a feeling it was her. But in the event she was about to tell him to go fuck himself in spectacular fashion, he opted for a far less revealing answer.

"You mentioned it once upon a time. Perhaps I'm merely starting to appreciate the value of such a partnership."

Lina hugged him. "Admit it. You like me."

A tightness in his chest unfurled as he returned her casual embrace. If he happened to be the one leaning a bit more heavily on her this time, she didn't mention it. Though, once again, he soon found himself clumsily patting her back. Straightening, he said, "I wouldn't go that far. But I do find the idea of your death troubling."

"Aw, Crombie. I love you too, buddy."

Nord growled at that.

"Not as much as I love you, husband. Don't worry."

"Husband?"

Lina held up a hand. "We did a thing."

The quiet joy shining from her eyes as she showed him her wedding ring was bittersweet. Crombie didn't resent her happiness, just selfishly wished it for himself.

"So you did. I believe this means felicitations are in order."

She smiled at him. "Felicitations, huh?"

Crombie shrugged. "I seem to be sadly lacking wedding presents at the moment. You'll have to indulge me."

"Saving our lives is more than enough of a present. You don't have to get us anything."

"Good. Because while I'll tolerate your friendship, I'm still on the fence about the Norseman. Giving him a gift would really muddy the waters in a way I'm not sure either of us is prepared for."

She laughed outright, and something in him lifted at the sound. He didn't examine it too closely. These sorts of feelings made him supremely uncomfortable.

Crombie glanced at Nord, who seemed to have repaired the worst of the damage to Quinn and was now focusing on removing the spear from Finley's chest.

"So what was all that about a prison, or did you call it a prism?"

Crombie told himself the question was professional curiosity and nothing more. If there was a new artifact on the market, it behooved him to know about it. Especially if it one day found its way into his hands.

Lina's expression fell. "It's both, actually." She sighed. "I had an idea of how we could win this war without shedding any blood. Needless to say, it failed."

"Exquisitely, it would seem."

She winced. "After everything I've just been through, you won't even pull punches to spare my feelings?"

"That's not my way, sweetheart."

"At least you're consistent in your assholery."

He grinned, their easy banter far more comfortable territory. "I aim to please."

Lina rolled her eyes. "If that's your idea of pleasure, I understand why you're still single."

Crombie opened his mouth to tell her she had absolutely no idea how incredible pleasure at his hand could be, then took one look at her husband and wisely changed the subject. "So this prism stole your magic instead of the dragon's, I take it?"

"Yeah, that about sums it up. I wasn't supposed to be in contact with it long enough for the attunement to finish . . ." Lina trailed off, her eyes taking on a strange cast. "Oh my God . . . Oh my God, that's it!"

"What's it?" Crombie glanced between her and Nord, wondering what mental leap she'd just taken that he clearly missed. Usually when he had women crying out for their savior, he was aware of the reason. Or at least responsible for it.

She grabbed his shirt, her eyes wide with brilliant madness. "The Prism," she breathed, shaking him a little. "I'm attuned. It doesn't matter if I have any magic, because now I can use it instead. Crombie, I can end this!"

CHAPTER 26

LINA

"Are you sure about this?" Crombie asked, looking at Lina like he wasn't certain she was entirely sane.

"Yes. I want that asshole to know he's lost. That I was the one who beat him."

"Just so I'm clear on what you're asking. You want me to release the fire-breathing dragon?"

"That's exactly what I want you to do."

"Forgive me, but wouldn't it be easier if you just dealt with him like this? That way he can't cause any more"—Crombie waved a hand at the massacre around them—"damage?"

"Maybe, but then I won't have the satisfaction of seeing the look in his eye when he realizes I've won."

Crombie's look turned considering. "And that's important to you?"

"After what he's done? You're fucking right it is."

He held up his hands. "Don't get me wrong. I'm not judging you. I understand the need for revenge better than anybody. I'm just surprised you want credit."

"It's not credit I'm after. I don't care if anyone outside of the four of us ever knows what happened here today. But that monster is responsible for the destruction of countless lives, and I want him to know down to the very marrow of his bones that it's over. That he's failed and everything he spent his life masterminding was all for nothing. That in the end, his life was utterly without meaning."

"You want him to suffer," Crombie surmised.

"There's nothing worse for an egotistical megalomaniac like him than to know he came up short. Mikel considers himself a god. It's time for him to learn he's a mere mortal."

"Savage." He grinned. "I approve."

"I wasn't looking for an endorsement, but thanks, I guess."

Crombie shrugged. "You have it regardless. So, shall I free him now?"

"No, not yet. I'll need to borrow Nord's power for what I have in mind."

They looked over to where her husband knelt on the ground, healing the last of Finley's wounds. Lina didn't even want to know how close of a call it had been. Seconds. Minutes. Any possibility was too horrific to contemplate. The simple truth was, if not for Crombie, they probably wouldn't have found them in time. And while there were still so many it was too late to save—her heart gave a little lurch at the memory of Astrid—Lina would be eternally grateful Finley and Quinn were not among the list of people she'd have to say goodbye to once this was over.

"What about the others?" Crombie asked.

Lina chewed on her lip as she contemplated her options. She walked over to one of the Viking-Animagi pairs, disarming the latter. Then she moved to the next group and did the same, slowly working her way around the nearby fighters as she thought it through. When all the Animagi in her vicinity were disarmed, Lina finally said, "I think it's probably best if we leave them for now. Tensions are high. I don't want anybody else to become collateral damage in their attempt to avenge a loved one's honor. Assuming you can handle it, of course."

"My stamina is legendary."

She looked at him over her shoulder. "Sweetie, you don't know the first thing about stamina until you've seen a berserker on their wedding night."

Crombie let out a surprised bark of laughter. "I'm not sure whether that's some kind of dare or invitation. But I must say, I'm intrigued."

"It was neither. She was merely stating a fact. Now I'd suggest you stop looking at my wife like that, or I'll be forced to gouge out your eyes." Nord flashed Crombie a smile that was little more than a baring of teeth as he stood. Then he clapped a hand on the fae's shoulder as he moved to join Lina. "Nothing personal, you understand. We just get a little territorial when it comes to our mates."

"Definitely not friends," Crombie muttered.

Lina snickered as she took in their contrasting expressions, though her smile was quick to fade as her eyes returned to Quinn and Finley. With the way their hands rested between them, it looked as though they were reaching for each other, even in their unconscious state.

"Are they going to be okay?"

Nord nodded, his eyes still more black than blue as he wiped his bloodstained hands on his thighs. "Yes. When they wake, it will be as if the injuries never happened."

"Good. That's good," she said, forcing herself to shove everything but the confrontation at hand from her mind.

His eyes dragged over her face, a small furrow forming between his brows. "I know that look. What are you planning?"

"I'm going to use the Prism."

Lina didn't have to explain what she meant. After all their preparations, Nord was as well-versed in the nuances of the artifact as she was.

Instead of reacting right away, he continued to stare at her. His eyes searched hers. She didn't find any censure there, only a grim sort of acceptance. As if he'd always known it was a possibility.

He reached for her, cupping her cheeks in his palms. "Are you sure you want to risk it? Your power is almost depleted. What if the additional contact drains you completely?"

Lina rested her hand against his chest, right over his heart. "Silly Viking. You should know by now my power means nothing to me. But my future with you? That means absolutely everything. If the price for defeating Mikel is me living the rest of my life without magic, I can live with that. What I can't live without is you."

Nord crushed his mouth to hers, drawing her close and deepening the kiss as he poured his roiling emotions into it. They battered at her, his love and pride and fear. She knew he was still reeling from her fall, focusing on the tasks at hand so he didn't have to deal with the terror that had ripped him apart when he realized he wouldn't get to her in time. He hadn't begun to come to terms with it. Truth be told, neither had she. How could they?

All of that would come later.

They had a dragon to slay first.

Lina pulled back reluctantly, finding Crombie watching them with a bemused grin.

"This must be what mortals refer to as 'The Honeymoon Stage.'"

"This is *so* not my honeymoon," she said.

"Really? Seems like it would be right up your alley."

"You think I find blood and death . . . yeah, okay, I see what you mean," Lina said with a sigh as her eyes shifted to her husband. Berserkers certainly came by their reputations honestly.

Nord winked at her.

Lina shook her head and turned back to the battlefield. Crombie's time-out made it easy to believe things weren't dismal. But, time-freeze or not, until Mikel was good and dead, their predicament remained the same. After her unwilling front-row seat to his ruthless slaughter of their best warriors, Lina knew Mikel didn't need time to make a point, just opportunity.

Which was why there was absolutely zero room for error. Given her track record, she really didn't like her odds. But she was their only hope, and she refused to fail again. Shit odds or not, she was going to do this.

"All right, here's what I need you guys to do. Crombie, see that book? Can you drop it?"

He responded by doing so immediately.

Nord, already aware of what she had in mind, slowed its fall and then reverted it to its original form. She knew he didn't want to take any chances with her power—or anyone else's—when he also conjured its protective case and carefully placed the Prism inside.

"I'd feel more comfortable if you didn't touch it until it was time," he said, handing her the box.

Lina accepted it with a small smile. "Me too."

"Now what?" Nord asked.

"Now I need you to de-dragon Mikel."

"De-dragon? You mean turn him back?"

Lina nodded. "Can you do it?"

Nord ran a hand over his beard. "In theory, yes. But Mikel is still autonomous. I can't control his will, only his physical form. So I can make him into whatever I want, but he'll still have access to his own magic."

"Meaning if he wants to shift back, he can," Lina said.

"Exactly. To keep him in his human form against his wishes for any length of time will likely require me to channel my magic constantly to reinforce the command. It'll work for a while, but I doubt for long. The drain on my reserves will be immediate and intense. We'll only get one shot at this."

"I know. One shot is all I need."

"I assume you won't want him plummeting to his death during this confrontation of yours?" Crombie asked.

"Seeing as how that might make it a bit difficult for him to pay attention to what I'm saying, no. Not really. Can you hold him in place?"

Crombie shook his head. "I only control time. Once I release him, he's out of my hands, if you'll forgive the metaphor."

"I have an idea," Nord said.

"A cage?" Lina asked, since that's the direction her thoughts had taken.

"Of a sort."

They all looked up to where Mikel hovered in the sky. Since he'd tailed her untimely descent, he was only about three, maybe four, stories high. Just far enough up that all they really had to worry about from here was his fire. Ideally, Nord's plan involved a way to keep him there. When he did turn back into a dragon, she didn't want those teeth of his anywhere near her friends.

"Okay . . . on my count then."

Nord gave her a slow nod.

"I'll just go stand over there," Crombie said, pointing vaguely behind him and well out of firing range.

Lina didn't blame him. The temptation to follow was strong.

"One," she said, exhaling heavily. "Two . . . Now!"

Crombie's power kicked in first, meaning for several terrifying heartbeats, a dragon roared in the sky. Its mighty—though slightly damaged—wings flapped, holding the beast suspended in the air. It swerved its long neck, those golden, reptilian eyes swiveling as they searched for their missing prey.

"I'm right here, asshole!"

He shifted, his head snapping in her direction only to be followed a second later by the rest of his body.

Lina swallowed, finding it a lot harder to stand still and play a game of chicken with a dragon when she was trapped in her human form. Her adrenaline surged, the berserker bracing itself for a fight as the dragon came barreling straight at her. Even with a creature born for battle living inside her, the instinct to flee was strong.

Nord's magic took hold, and Lina let out a breath she hadn't realized she'd been holding as Mikel was jerked backward, his body rapidly transforming and drawing in on itself until she was looking at a very different kind of monster.

True to his word, Nord had accounted for keeping Mikel in place.

Instead of a cage, he'd opted for hanging Mikel from a massive oak tree he'd spawned specifically for that purpose. Lina allowed herself one moment of amusement as she watched the bastard writhe and twitch like a worm on a hook.

Gotcha.

Nord grunted beside her, and Lina knew the strain on his magic was even greater than he expected.

Time to finish this.

"Mikel Drake, I hereby sentence you to death for your heinous crimes."

He scoffed, still managing to throw her an antagonistic glare, even red-faced and upside down. "You don't have the authority, let alone power, to enforce such a judgment. You are no one. Nothing. Not even worthy of the air you breathe, let alone the blood running through your veins. The only thing you are, Evalina Cuska, is an embarrassment to your family name." Once he finished speaking, he spat on the ground, as if the additional sign of contempt held any meaning to her.

Lina shifted her weight, overly aware of the box she held cradled in her hands.

"Maybe that's all true. But I find it really hard to give a single fuck about your low opinion of me. In fact," she gave a harsh laugh, "I take it as a compliment. Because you, Mikel, are nothing more than a vile, putrid stain on this earth. You've brought nothing but misery and despair into the lives of those unfortunate enough to cross paths with you. There is not a single honorable thing you've done in your miserable life. You are a terrorist and a traitor, and the world will be a far better place once I rid it of your filth."

Mikel laughed, going so far as to clap. "Is that the best you've got? A few weak insults and even weaker threats? I must say, Evalina, I'm disappointed. Even your uncle put up a better fight than that."

Lina's rage swelled at the mention of Alistair. "The things you've done to our people are more than enough reason to rob you of your life. But after what you did to my uncle? I'm going to watch you burn." She grinned, letting her berserker shine through. "But, please, do keep underestimating me, Mikel. I thrive on it."

For the first time, Mikel seemed to understand the precariousness of his position. His mocking smile fell away, his voice dripping with venom as he said, "What you have never seemed to grasp, little girl, is that it's not life that holds true value, but legacy. And after the things I've set in motion, mine will be eternal. You cannot begin to imagine all the ways I've already started to reshape the face of this world. My death will only solidify them."

"I doubt that."

He sneered at her. "Kill me if you can. It will not change anything. You cannot stop what's coming."

"Lina," Nord warned, not even a second before Mikel's form began to swell once more.

She flicked open the box, reaching inside and grasping the cool white crystal. She'd never dared touch it before this moment, and she wasn't prepared for the current of power that slammed through her. It felt as though a fuse had been lit, and she was the bomb.

Mikel roared, his massive dragon form easily breaking free of his bindings as he shot into the sky.

Power, pure and potent, consumed her. Her body was boiling, burning from the inside out. It was hard to breathe, let alone think through the sheer overwhelm of the magic taking over her. But then Mikel turned his head to Nord, and his chest began to light up with his fire, and it was as if Crombie had activated his gift again.

Time seemed to slow, the moment crystallizing into a single, blinding purpose.

Lina lifted the Prism, holding it up toward Mikel. As Mikel opened his mouth to let out a fresh torrent of molten fire, Lina did the same, though it was not fire but fury that poured out of her. That fury became the catalyst, triggering the crystal in her hand and sending forth a bolt of brilliant, pulsing light. The swirling beam shot up and out until it collided with the beast in the sky, lighting both him and the world around him up as the energy burst through him and exploded outward.

Her potential was limitless, her power surpassing even that of the gods. But in this moment, she didn't want fancy or clever.

She wanted total.

Fucking.

Annihilation.

CHAPTER 27
NORD

In his years with the Brotherhood, Nord had only gotten close to a complete power drain a handful of times. The few occasions one threatened were either because he'd been drawing on his magic for too long without a break or due to dealing with a particularly nasty foe. But even during those admittedly rare cases, he'd never experienced anything close to the strain he felt now.

With his power reserves easily triple what they'd been as a Guardian, it was shocking to find himself nearly tapped out so quickly. Then again, he'd never dealt with anyone as powerful as Mikel Drake. At least not without considerable aid. And he'd already expended a great deal of his power healing Lina, Quinn, and Finley.

Nord gritted his teeth, his muscles shaking under the sheer effort required to maintain his focus. Keeping the shifter in his human form was proving to be far more challenging than he'd ever anticipated. It felt like he'd only just started when Mikel's power struck back, battering at his will and attempting to reassert its autonomy.

He could hear Lina talking beside him, but her words were lost beneath the roar of blood in his ears. His power was slipping. They had seconds, at most, before Mikel would break free. Already he was pushing back, tendrils of his power poking holes through Nord's as it fought against its grasp.

"Lina," he called in warning, needing her to know her deadline was rapidly approaching. Whatever she was hoping to accomplish, she needed to act fast.

As soon as he had the thought, his power's hold was severed. There was a feeling like freefall as the magic he'd grown so accustomed to slipped away, no longer able to answer to his demands.

Nord's hands dropped, his shoulders slumping as he gasped for breath. His body was every bit as drained as his power after channeling so much so quickly. He lifted his eyes to the sky, where Mikel had reverted to the snarling, roaring beast he'd been before. As Nord drew in another ragged breath, he watched Mikel do the same. The pale green scales lining the mighty beast's chest glowing like the brightest embers as he drew in the air required for his deadly flame.

Exhaustion clung to Nord even as the desire to fight pumped through him. He had nothing left save the weapon on his back. So he pulled it free, took aim, and threw it with all the strength and fury at his disposal. He knew it would never reach Mikel in time, not fast enough to prevent what was already happening. But he had to try. It wasn't in him to quit. Not while there was still air in his lungs.

Nord didn't bother watching his sword arc through the sky. Instead, he looked to Lina, fully aware this was her moment. If anyone was going to save them, it had to be her. More than that, if this was how it ended, he wanted the last thing he saw in this world to be her.

He glanced over just as Lina freed the Prism, its protective box falling by the wayside. As her hand closed around the crystal, her body convulsed as if a wave of electricity surged through her. Her expression twisted—not quite in pain, but something closer to rapture.

For a second, it was as if Nord was experiencing the same exquisite rush. An identical burst of adrenaline raced through him, making his skin tingle and blood simmer. It was a heady sensation, one that was damn near impossible to think beyond. Nord forced himself to draw another gasping breath, seeking a reprieve from the unexpected assault on his senses.

As his mind cleared, he became acutely aware of his berserker's need to protect Lina. Of the danger creeping ever closer. While Nord had been seduced by the lure of the Prism's power, his berserker had picked up on the underlying threat. Her body was not made to contain such energy. She needed to redirect it or drop the crystal to cut off the flow. If she didn't, she'd be torn apart by the very weapon she'd sought to control.

He opened his mouth to warn her, but it was obvious she had no awareness of her surroundings. She was lost to the boundless power of the artifact clutched in her fist.

Lina's body began to shine with brilliant, incandescent light as she lifted the hand holding the Prism. She was lit from within, her eyes taking on the same reflective sheen as the crystal. Her hair floated on an invisible breeze, the ends of which crackled with more of the electric light. She was soon blazing so brightly, it felt like he was trying to stare directly into the sun.

Just when he had to squint and shield his eyes, Lina opened her mouth and unleashed the most beautiful battle cry. As she did, the light filling her body changed direction, racing back through her and into the crystal. But it didn't stop there. The energy continued to travel, pouring out of the Prism in a single beam of pure energy. The ray of light blasted through the night sky, heading straight for Mikel.

There was an ear-splitting roar as the dragon screamed, but it was cut short as the light connected with its massive form. Instead of tearing through him, the beam wrapped itself around its body, millions of threads fusing and webbing over him until he was completely bound in ropes of pure energy. Once he was glowing as brightly as Lina had been mere seconds before, the light was absorbed into him, only to explode back out again. It was like watching a firework be lit and detonated all within the same breath.

And when the power came bursting back out, Mikel exploded

with it, the once-mighty dragon reduced to nothing more than bloody bits of gore and ash. Everything happened so fast, it was nearly impossible to make sense of it. But as the light faded and bits of charred dragon flesh rained from the sky, there was no denying the truth.

It was finally over.

They'd won.

Lina's legs gave out, and Nord raced to his wife, sliding to his knees beside her and catching her before she could fully hit the ground. Her eyes rolled back in her head, her body slumping against him. The physical effects on a magic user's body when they'd depleted their power were every bit as real as the flu or a hangover. Lina had been close to empty before what she'd attempted with the Prism, her system already worn way down. It was no surprise to Nord that channeling the Prism's magic had taken such a heavy toll. Even in peak condition, the body was not made to withstand the assault of such power boomeranging through it. It could be days before she made a full recovery. Especially since he was in no state to help her.

Lina still clutched to the Prism in her hand, the once translucent crystal now a foggy gray, with tiny fissures splintering across its surface. Despite the changes in its appearance, Nord knew better than to believe that meant it had been rendered inert. The only way to ensure they'd all be safe was to hide it again as soon as possible. And this time, just to be triply sure Lina couldn't be harmed by it further, Nord would take her place as its jailor, using Alistair's spell to bind the artifact to himself.

He forced her fingers to let go of the crystal, catching it in one hand as it fell free. With the other, he leaned forward and grasped its box. Whether by pure luck or some magical design, the container had not sustained any damage when Lina dropped it. Flicking the lid open with his thumb, Nord shoved the crystal inside and then set the box off to the side beside them. He'd deal with it properly once he was able. For now, knowing it was sealed away would have to do.

"Lina," he whispered, pressing kiss after kiss over her face. "You did it, Kærasta."

She moaned in his arms, her eyelids fluttering as she snuggled deeper into him. "Is it over?"

"Yes, my love. It's over. It's all finally over."

She smiled sweetly up at him, still not quite able to open her eyes. "Good."

Crombie chose that moment to come forward, his hands shoved deep in his pockets, his expression set in its usual bored mask. But Nord was starting to see through it. There was something in his eyes that hadn't been there before his trip to Faerie. An intensity, or perhaps it was vulnerability, he could no longer hide.

"She all right?" he asked.

Nord nodded. "She will be."

"I'll just see to the others then." Crombie started to turn, but Nord called him back.

"Crombie?"

He raised a brow.

"Thanks. I know you were only fulfilling your debt, but none of this would have been possible without you. You saved countless lives today, including my own."

The fae seemed uncomfortable with the praise, shrugging it off. "Don't go getting all sentimental on me, berserker. I'm still pretty sure I hate you."

"The feeling, as always, is mutual."

Crombie smiled at him as he turned away, and Nord had to bite back a laugh at the glittering letters scrawled across the back of his T-shirt proclaiming, *'I don't sweat, I sparkle!'*

"What's so funny?" Lina murmured.

Before he could answer, the world burst back into vibrant life as Animagi and Vikings everywhere resumed their fighting. There was a moment of utter confusion when the former realized weapons they'd just been holding were inexplicably missing.

The rain that had been paused under Crombie's spell began to fall in earnest, only to fizzle out as the storm no longer had anyone to fuel it. The heavy rain quickly became a light drizzle, the thick clouds overhead drifting away to reveal the moon, which bathed the people below in its soft light.

It didn't take long for the Animagi to realize they had lost. Those who didn't willingly surrender died swift deaths at the hands of the Novasgardians. But for once, the berserker had no interest in rejoining the battle. Right now, Nord only had eyes for the woman in his arms.

"We should see to the others," she said. "Fin, Quinn . . . Cora."

"Don't worry about them right now. You've done enough for one night."

She smiled at him, looking exhausted as she leaned against his chest. "You know I won't be able to rest until I'm sure they're okay. So you may as well help me up, Viking."

He couldn't help but grin at her, having expected as much. "All right, wife. We'll see to our friends. But then I'm taking you home and not letting you out of our bed for at least a week."

She smiled at that. The fact that she also blushed at the implication of how he intended to keep her in said bed, especially after all they'd done, warmed him. It reminded Nord that even in times like this, after battles had been waged and won and lives irrevocably changed, some things—the most important things—would always be the same.

CHAPTER 28
FINLEY

He woke with a groan, rain splashing onto his face and his body throbbing with residual pain. His head was foggy, his thoughts fragmented. The last thing he remembered . . .

"Quinn!"

Finley lurched upright, hands pawing at his chest, eyes scanning the horizon for some sign of the raven-haired beauty.

"Fin?" her thready voice came from beside him, sounding every bit as confused as he was.

His heart caved in at the sound of his name. They were alive. *She* was alive.

Thank fuck. He didn't even want to consider the alternative.

"What happened?"

"I don't—"

But then it all came back to him. Blood pouring from between her splayed fingers. The frantic need to reach her and the resulting terror as he realized he never would. Pain stabbing through his heart and then a burning agony unlike anything he'd ever felt. Soft whispers floated through his mind. Words relayed just out of consciousness.

They felt important, like something he wouldn't want to forget, but all he had was the ghost of a conversation and the remembered pain.

He glanced down, half-expecting to see a gaping hole in his chest, but other than a torn and bloody shirt, he was whole.

Finley groaned again. "Jesus, this must be what the DeLorean felt like."

"The what?" Quinn asked.

"Never mind."

Since he'd very obviously been healed, he could only assume she had as well. Still, he needed to see the truth of it with his own eyes. He turned to her, his breath catching in his throat.

Quinn looked back at him with searching, wounded eyes. As if the sight of him alone was too much to bear. Her clothes clung to her body, and she was covered in blood—his blood. Mascara dripped down her face, and her lashes were clumped together from the rain. Or perhaps her tears.

He had the vaguest sense she'd been crying. Deep, heart-wrenching sobs.

For him.

Finley's breath stuttered, and it felt as though a fist had closed around his heart. The sight of her pain cut far deeper than an actual blade. It tore him apart, shredding his insides and leaving him flayed wide open. His soul-deep need to protect her came roaring to life, more than ready to tear the world apart with his bare hands while simultaneously urging him to pick her up and promise her he would never allow anyone to ever hurt her again.

"Quinn—"

And then she was on him. Her hands clawed through his hair as her mouth fused with his. His heart forgot how to beat, seizing beneath his ribs as the woman he wanted beyond all reason willingly threw herself into his arms.

He'd stolen kisses from her before, but this was the first time she'd ever initiated one. He'd never felt more like he'd won something in his life, and he had absolutely no intention of robbing either one of them of the pleasure of such a momentous victory.

Finley grasped her waist, hauling Quinn up and onto his lap to get closer to her. It still wasn't enough. He needed more. Moaning deep in his throat, Finley fisted his hands in her shirt before flattening them again to run down the curve of her spine and mold her body to his.

He was drowning in her. Already drunk on his need, and it had only just begun.

How was it possible for one simple kiss to undo him so completely?

Then again, there was nothing simple about the crush of her mouth against his. Or the fact that he could taste the heartache on her lips along with the truth of what she fought so hard to deny.

No, there was nothing simple about it at all.

"Does this mean you've changed your mind?"

"I don't want to talk about it," she said, capturing his face between her hands and chasing his retreating lips.

Finley pulled back before her mouth could crash into his again. "Oh, we're talking about it."

"Talking requires thinking, and when I let myself think, all I can see is you bleeding out on the ground. So forgive me, Fin, but no. We're not fucking talking right now."

"Quinn? Oh my God, Quinn!" Cora shouted, running toward them from the other side of the lot.

Quinn rested her forehead against his, her eyes fluttering closed as she took a shuddering breath. Finley could already feel her withdrawing, rebuilding that wall of hers and closing herself off from him again.

No. Not this time, damnit.

He grasped her jaw before she could move away, holding her just tightly enough that she had to meet his gaze.

"I want you to listen to me. This isn't finished, Satori. You got it wrong the other day when you said we were over. You and me? We will *never* be over."

Her pupils dilated, and color suffused her cheeks.

"Do you understand me?"

She bit down on her bottom lip and nodded. "Yes."

"To be continued then," he said, releasing her.

"To be continued."

They both shifted, rising to their feet and turning to face Cora just as she reached them.

"Thank God you two are all right. When I didn't see you with the others," Cora pressed a shaking hand to her chest, her eyes lined with tears.

"We're okay, Mama. Just a little banged up, nothing serious."

Cora blanched at the sight of all the blood.

"It's not mine," Quinn assured her.

Cora pulled her daughter into a rough hug, a full-body shudder rolling through her as she held her close. "It's over, mon coeur. The nightmare is finally over."

"Lina and Nord?"

"Both safe. Thanks to your old employer."

"Crombie?" Finley asked. Things must have been far worse than he'd realized if the fae had made an appearance.

Cora nodded.

"And the others? Astrid? Søren?" Quinn asked.

Cora looked away, and Quinn raised a hand to her lips, not needing her mother to elaborate further.

It never got easier, losing a friend in battle. They all knew it was a possibility, but still, the Novasgardians had all seemed larger than life. Losing any of them would leave a hole that would not be easily filled.

"Come on," he said softly. "We should join the others. I'm sure they are eager to return home and see to their dead."

"Of course," Quinn said, weaving her arm through her mother's.

"They probably need your help seeing to a portal or dealing with injuries."

As the three of them rounded the corner, heading back to the area between the vineyard's two warehouses, Lina and Nord came into view.

Lina immediately burst into tears, breaking free of Nord's hold and rushing headlong toward them. She shocked the hell out of Finley by flinging herself at him instead of Quinn. He caught her by pure reflex.

"Hello to you too."

She pulled back, only to slam her fist into his chest. "If you ever go and almost die on me again, I'll kill you myself."

"She means it," Nord said with a small smile.

That's when Finley realized Lina had been the one to find him and Quinn. Affection and wonder ran through him. The reminder that he belonged to a family again, one that genuinely cared about what happened to him, still caught him off guard. Part of him hoped he never got used to it. That way, he'd be sure to never take it for granted.

He pulled her back into his arms, tucking his face down so his words were only for her. "I'm sorry, little sister. You know I'd never willingly leave you. But when it comes down to my life or hers, I'm going to choose hers every time. And you should know by now my choice would be the same if I had to choose between mine or yours."

"I do," she whispered, her voice rough with grief. "I'd expect nothing less from a Guardian. That's why I love you so much. But I'm still mad at you too."

Finley rubbed her back. "I understand. If you want to punch me some more, I think I can handle it."

"No," she said with a watery breath. "I just want to hold you for a minute, if that's all right?"

"That works for me."

She held him tightly for another thirty seconds when Nord finally cleared his throat. "I think you've made your point, Kærasta."

Lina chuckled and stepped back with an embarrassed smile. Then she launched herself at Quinn and Cora, wrapping them both in a hug. The three women talked in animated whispers through their tears as they huddled together. Finley didn't bother trying to make sense of their words, turning his attention instead to Nord, who'd walked over to join him.

"How many casualties?" he asked, pitching his voice low.

"It's too soon to say. None of Mikel's sympathizers were spared. As for our side, Strega and Søren have taken point rounding up those who remain. They've already asked if we'd help them with the return of the bodies."

"Yes, of course. Whatever they need. Now that this is over, will you go back to Novasgard with them?"

Nord's eyes took a far-off cast as he looked at his wife. "Yes, but not right away. There's something we need to see to here first."

"The Council?" Finley guessed. "Or what's left of it?"

Nord nodded. "Yes. But it can all wait. Tonight is for us. We'll deal with the rest of the survivors—and the dead—tomorrow."

CHAPTER 29
LINA

"You do realize that my power was drained, and I didn't contract hypothermia or some other potentially terminal illness, right? Not that I'm complaining, I just don't think I've seen you sit down once since we got here," Lina said, craning her head around to watch as her husband wrapped a fur blanket over her shoulders.

The blanket was in addition to the thick wool socks he'd already insisted on pulling over her feet, the hot toddy she'd already finished, and a bowl of steaming stew he'd placed on the small table between her and the roaring fire.

"I watched you almost die today, so you're going to indulge me without comment while I take care of you."

Lina's heart went squishy and soft. "Okay," she agreed in a quiet, content voice.

Nord pressed a kiss to the top of her head. "Comfortable?"

"Very. It was nice of Cora to lend us her guest house."

"With the penthouse being reduced to a giant pile of rubble, we didn't have many other options."

"We could have gotten a hotel room like Fin."

"We could have," Nord agreed, "but I was under the impression you wanted to be near family tonight."

Lina smiled up at her husband. "You were right, as usual."

He ran a hand down the length of her hair. "I know how it is after days like today. There's comfort in knowing the people you love are within arm's reach."

"Exactly," she said on a heavy exhale. "I wish Fin would have taken Cora up on her offer. I don't like that he's all alone tonight. Quinn's got her mom and aunt, but he almost died today too. Who's pampering him?"

Nord laughed. "Don't worry about Finley. I'm sure he's more than capable of seeing to his own pampering. But if you're really worried, I overheard Cora and Sheridan talking about sending him over something to eat and extending an invitation for breakfast in the morning so we can all head to the Council meeting together."

"Oh, well, that's good."

Lina wrapped the blanket more tightly around her shoulders. Despite her teasing, she did have a chill she couldn't seem to shake. Like her body lost its ability to regulate its own temperature in the absence of her power.

She and Nord hadn't broached the subject of whether hers was gone for good yet. At first, she'd been too exhausted to check. Now, it had more to do with her own trepidation. What she'd told Nord was true; she could live without her magic. Happily. But once she knew one way or the other what its status was, there was no going back. She'd opted for ignorance for the time being, too overwhelmed by the day's events to spare the mental energy on anything else. Some things just weren't worth the stress.

They were alive. Mikel was not. That's what mattered right now. It was worth celebrating the achievement when they'd paid such a high price for it.

"You think you're up for something a little more adventurous than sitting in front of the fire?"

Lina glanced up. "What did you have in mind?"

His grin was slow and sexy and made her insides go fluttery. "Nothing too strenuous. But I did promise to teach you how to make your rings."

She jumped up, the blanket falling in a forgotten heap at her feet. "Yes. One hundred percent yes. And if Crombie shows up and ruins it again this time, I promise to punch him right in the dick."

Nord chuckled. "It seems my little berserker has grown even more bloodthirsty than me. I was going to aim for his throat."

Lina laughed and shrugged. "You may not like the guy, but as a card-carrying member of the tripod club, you tend to avoid hitting below the belt. I, a lifelong member of team vagina, have no such compulsion."

"Tripod club?"

"Uh-huh." She grinned, loving how his eyes lit up when he thought something she said was genuinely funny. He rarely laughed, and she savored each and every time she made it happen.

Nord pressed his fingers to his eyes, shaking his head as his shoulders continued to shake. "I probably shouldn't be surprised by a word that comes out of your mouth anymore, yet here we are." His look was tinged with affection when his eyes returned to hers. "But I'm sure your theory isn't true, Kærasta."

"All right, tough guy. Let's test it. When's the last time you opted for a junk punch, kick, or random maiming?"

"Mataius," he answered without hesitation.

Lina was comfortable enough with her berserker to appreciate the mental image that painted, but also lady enough not to comment on it. "Well . . . consider me proven wrong."

He smirked, seeing right through her. "I love you," he said, hooking an arm around her neck and pulling her in close so he could place a fleeting kiss on her lips.

"I love you too. So, what are we using for our rings?"

"Well, I held onto the Director's dagger. And I found this when we were cleaning up today."

Lina squinted, looking at the white fragments in his palm. "Is that . . . bone?"

Nord shrugged. "Hard to say with the state you left him in. Best guess is dragon bone or part of a horn."

She wrinkled her nose. "Is it weird I don't want part of Mikel touching me? That man was rotten to the core. I bet even his horn fragments have cooties."

"That's what the fire's for. Purification and rebirth. When the items come out, they're something entirely new and contain only the value and meaning we place on them."

"By fire be purged!" Lina said, holding her arms up like she was shouting an actual invocation. Then she realized what she'd just done and slowly lowered her arms. "How much whisky was in that tea?"

Nord smirked at her. "Maybe it would be safer if you let me handle the putting-things-in-fire part."

"Yeah. You're probably right," she said, lowering herself back down on the couch. "I'll just be over here if you need me."

He tipped up her chin, running his thumb over her lips. "I'll always need you."

Her heart swooped, and her core tightened. "Yippee."

Nord huffed out a laugh and set about laying the things they'd need out on the blanket she'd left on the floor.

"Didn't you mention a forge last time?"

"We'll make do with this."

"Will it be hot enough?"

His eyes glittered with the reflection of dancing flames. "When has heat ever been an issue for us, wife?"

She started pulling at the neck of her shirt. He had a point. She'd been chilly before, but she certainly wasn't now. It was practically balmy. Sweltering, even.

Lina watched as he did something to the dagger and broke the blade free of its hilt. Then he melted it down and poured it into a cast so when the metal cooled, it would be a thin rod.

"All right, get over here," he gently ordered.

She obeyed, moving to kneel at his side. "Is it cool already?"

"We're going to work with the bone first."

"Oh. What do we need to do?"

"If the fragments were bigger, we'd use tools to shape them, but since you were very thorough in your obliteration, we're going to cheat a little and use our magic."

"Is that . . ." She bit the inside of her cheek as she searched for the word. "Appropriate? Will they still be special if we deviate from tradition?"

"I don't think anything could be more appropriate. You risked everything to defeat him. Your magic. Your life. If we're being technical about it, magic was the weapon you wielded in the final moment. When making our rings, it's as common to reforge the blade that landed the killing blow as it is to use one stolen from our enemies. So what part of using magic in the creation of the ring doesn't fit our tradition?" Nord raised a brow, his eyes searching hers. As usual, he saw far more than she'd intended. "You haven't checked yet, have you?"

She shook her head.

"Scared?"

"No . . . maybe."

Nord set the fragments down and reached for her. "Well, I'm pretty sure the bond is intact. I can feel you just as clearly as ever right here," he said, taking her hand and resting it directly over his heart. "Can you still feel me?"

Lina nodded. "Yes. And the berserker as well."

"That's a good sign. Do you have a reason for doubting the rest of your magic is still there?"

"Only how weak I still feel," she admitted, hating to have to say it out loud.

"You could never be weak, Kærasta."

"That's not what you said when you first started my training."

"And look at you now."

"Uh-huh, look at you not correcting me."

He smiled. "Reach for your magic, Lina. And when it answers, I want you to shape one of those fragments into your ring."

"When, not if?" Her hand shifted, sliding up so her thumb could run along his jaw. "How is it you never doubt me, even when I doubt myself?"

He leaned forward until the tip of his nose ran along hers. "Easy. I've seen inside your soul. I would have to be a fool of the highest magnitude to doubt a woman filled with as much purpose and potential as you. There is nothing you cannot achieve if your heart is set on it."

"I guess you're right. I made you fall in love with me, after all. It's no small feat to trick a Viking into giving you his heart. They can be a real bunch of stubborn fuckers."

He chuckled, the husky sound rolling through her and wrapping itself around her heart. "You're not wrong, but in this, I was a foregone conclusion. You and I both know the gods put me here to love you. No tricks required."

Lina squirmed, her cheeks blooming with heat as a smile tugged at her lips. "It didn't feel that way in the beginning. I had an entire action plan built around accomplishing the task. Most of which failed, if I recall correctly."

"I remember," he said fondly. "Resisting you was one of the hardest things I've had to do in my entire life."

"And yet you were so good at it."

"Maybe it appeared that way to you, but I was losing my mind with how badly I wanted to give in."

She laughed. "Well, I guess it's good to know my plans when it came to you weren't a total failure. My track record for plans and schemes proves that I fail more often than I succeed."

"But you persevere regardless, for which I am eternally grateful. Otherwise, I might never have gotten to see, what did you call it, Operation Slip and Slide?"

"Let's never mention that again," Lina said with a groan. "But I guess it's safe to say I'm a stubborn fucker too. I took one look at you and knew you had to be mine. That was it for me, no going back."

He lifted a hand to cup her cheek. "You know it was the same for me."

"I do."

"So then you also know you have nothing to fear. Magic or no magic. It changes nothing. I am yours. In this life and every one hereafter."

A weight she hadn't realized she'd been carrying slid away. Lina knew, logically, Nord would never stop loving her over something so superficial. But hearing the affirmation come from his lips soothed the part of her that had been secretly afraid he might not find her worthy of his love if she was little more than mortal.

It was stupid in hindsight.

She was still a berserker, one of two in existence, and the only female one ever. And magic or not, it didn't take away from everything she'd accomplished. Or what they'd been through together.

"Okay," she said, letting out a shaky exhale. "I'm ready."

Nord trailed the tips of his fingers down her spine. "You've got this."

Lina smiled up at him before closing her eyes and tentatively reaching out to the source of her magic. She had to go further than usual until she felt the answering ripple. Her reserves were still very low, barely more than a puddle compared to the ocean she'd become accustomed to, but it was there regardless. Replenishing, just as Nord promised.

She let out a watery chuckle, taking a tendril of her magic and sending it out toward the fragments beside them, holding the picture of what she wanted it to do in her mind before releasing it.

"Beautiful," Nord breathed. "Just like the woman who forged it."

Lina opened her eyes, finding him smiling down at her. "You're biased."

His lips hooked up in a smile. "So you keep telling me."

She tugged him down for a slow, lingering kiss. "Since I passed the test, does this mean I get to play with fire now?"

He chuckled, gently lowering her to the floor as his lips set a blazing trail across her neck. "I think you just started a different kind of fire, Kærasta. We should probably deal with that one first."

"Mmm . . ." Her eyes fluttered closed as his lips drifted lower, her fingers threading through his hair. "And what if I don't want that particular fire to go out?"

He looked up at her with a wicked grin. "Who said anything about putting it out?"

"In that case, burn baby burn."

CHAPTER 30
NORD

As he trailed kisses down her neck and over her collarbone, he splayed his hand between her breasts right above her heart. Lina hadn't caught on yet, but he'd been doing similar things all night. Resting his fingers on the side of her neck or the inside of her wrist. Checking her pulse. Listening for the sound of her inhales or watching for the rise and fall of her chest. Asking her random questions when she'd been silent for too long. Reassuring himself, in every way he could, that she was alive.

He'd never been so scared, not as a child or a man grown. The kind of scared where it felt like you'd been run through and your body ceased to function. A part of him was still trapped in that hellscape. Lost in the moment when he'd felt her fear tear through him. When he'd turned to go to her only to realize he'd never make it in time. That the woman he loved beyond reason was about to be taken from him, and there was not a damn thing he could do to stop it.

That kind of fear changes a person. Leaves an imprint on the soul.

In his darkest hours, Nord would relive that moment constantly.

Not because he wanted to. Gods, if only he could pretend it never happened. But it would haunt him for the rest of their lives because if it happened once, there was always a chance it could happen again.

No amount of vigilance or self-assurance would change the fact that he could lose her.

He was a powerful man, stronger than most. But against death, he would always be powerless. Magic could only do so much. It would heal them from the worst injuries and likely stave off the most debilitating of illnesses, but eventually, death would come for them both.

It was a humbling realization for a man who'd already lived a dozen lifetimes.

The knowledge left him restless, hungry for something he couldn't name.

And then, suddenly, he could.

What he wanted was a way to immortalize the love they had for each other, to know a part of them and their love story would live on indefinitely.

"Hey," Lina said, wriggling her hips. "We were in the middle of something . . . or about to be."

He refocused on her face, his heart starting to race for an entirely new reason. "Let's make a baby."

Her hooded eyes widened, and she sat up on her elbows. "N-now?"

"I don't want to wait. I'm tired of waiting. You told me you wanted a brood of blond Vikings, so let's do it."

She rested a hand against his cheek, chuckling. "I don't think we just get to decide it's going to happen. Biology and Mother Nature are tricky that way."

He gave her a wolfish grin. "You were the one to remind me that we shape reality and manifest our desires. What makes you so sure we can't? If I recall correctly, you were also the one who told me we needed to start believing in ourselves." He crawled up her body until he pushed her back onto the floor, his hands on either side of her head as his hips pressed into hers. "I believe . . . don't you?"

Her breath washed over his face in warm puffs as she laughed, but her laughter faded almost immediately. "You're serious."

"I've never been more serious. You swore we'd start a family when this was all over. Well, it's over. You saw to that. And now I want what you promised me."

Lina swallowed, her pulse fluttering rapidly in her throat. Her eyes searched his, and what he saw there sent his heart soaring.

"Okay," she whispered.

"Okay?"

"Okay," she said again, more enthusiastically and with a nod. "Let's do it. Let's make a baby. Or, you know, try. I'm still not sure we can just will a fetus into my womb, but if anyone has magic sperm, Viking, I'm sure it's you."

He laughed, pressing a finger over his wife's lips. "Let me worry about that."

Her eyes were still warm with laughter as she nipped at his finger. "Now we're getting on to the good stuff."

Nord smirked down at her. "I didn't realize you were so impatient."

"Have you met me? I wanted you inside me twenty minutes ago."

He shifted down, kissing his way down her body as his right hand drew up her shirt. "And now?"

"And now I *need* you inside me."

He chuckled, sliding his hand over the velvety warmth of her skin and up to grasp her breast, feeling her nipple pebble against his palm. "Need? No . . . not yet. But you will."

Nord shifted his weight so he was lying on his side beside her, his hands and lips continuing their lazy exploration as the fire crackled beside them. He used Lina's breathy pleas and the unconscious shifts of her body to guide his movements, letting her indirectly lead him where she wanted. It wasn't long before she was squirming beside him.

He loved how bossy she got when he took her right to the edge and left her there. She really wasn't a patient woman.

"If you're looking to procreate, that's not the body part you should be using."

"I thought you were a fan of my fingers," he teased, curling them forward inside her the way she loved.

Lina's eyes rolled back, and she groaned as her hips rocked into him, matching the slow thrust of his hand. "I do, but . . . ohhh . . ."

He did it again, loving the way her muscles clamped down on his fingers, trying to draw him in deeper. "Are you sure? Because it sounds like you're complaining."

"Not . . . complaining." Her words were labored, her body already chasing the climax he was keeping just out of reach.

He knew her body intimately enough by now to know exactly what would send her flying over the edge. Just how much pressure to use. Where to press and how hard to thrust. But he wanted to draw the moment out. Savor it. When she was like this, desperate, writhing for him, there was no doubt she was alive. Living solely for him and the pleasure he gave her.

Nord took care of the rest of his clothes, chuckling to himself when she wordlessly protested as he pulled away.

"Hush, Kærasta. I'm trying to give you what you want."

"Finally."

He knelt between her legs, lining himself up with her entrance. Her eyes were locked on the place where he held himself. He curled his fingers around his shaft, gliding his hand slowly up and down, knowing how much she loved to watch him pleasure himself. Her breath hitched, and her hips bucked with need as her body sought to replace his hand. He circled her opening, barely sliding in and then pulling back out.

"Nord," she groaned. "Stop teasing me."

"You should know better by now what happens when you use that smart mouth of yours. It only makes your wait longer."

She looked up at him, her face flushed with desire and her

hooded eyes glazed. "You know I'm not responsible for the things that come out of my mouth when your hands are on or in me."

He grinned, slowly sliding back in. "No? What about when my cock's inside you?"

She raked her nails down his back, arching into him. "Definitely not then."

There were no more words after that, not that they were needed. They spoke with their bodies. Each tender caress an affirmation of their devotion to each other.

Every brush of their lips declaring 'I love you.'

Every slide of skin against skin promising 'I will never get enough of you.'

Every drive of his hips into her delicious heat vowing 'I am yours.'

When neither of them could take it anymore, his languid thrusts turned wild. Her cries signaled her approaching climax, and he flung himself off the edge with her, his body shuddering as he emptied himself inside her.

They stayed together there, bodies locked around each other, breaths barely more than ragged pants as they held each other. Suspended in that moment, living in the afterglow born out of the depth of their love for each other. And while any magic may not have been intentional, there was no denying it was there.

CHAPTER 31
LINA

Emotions were nebulous things. Rarely straightforward and often informed by far more than the matter at hand. Lina assumed that was the reason hers were such a colossal mess at the moment. She knew she should feel vindicated now that Mikel was gone, wildly ecstatic even. But standing in the Mobius Council's auditorium, looking out at all that was left of the Animagi, all she felt was . . . empty.

There hadn't been many of them to begin with, a few hundred at most. There were less than a quarter of that now. Mikel's reach had stretched far further than they'd realized. When presented with a choice, most Animagi stayed loyal to him. Quinn said it was guilt and not a real sense of devotion that swayed them. They chose death rather than living with what they'd done.

Maybe she was right. But it was hard to feel good about it when so many had died in the name of his monstrous cause.

"We're ready when you are," Cora murmured softly, giving Lina an encouraging smile before moving away to stand beside her daughter.

Nord took her hand in his, giving it a reassuring squeeze as she rolled her shoulders back and made her way to the center of the stage. The room was quieter than a tomb as her heels clicked across the floor.

Taking a deep breath, Lina lifted her chin, forcing herself to meet the gaze of everyone gathered here today. She'd thought a lot about what she should say to these people. What words might bring solace and hope in the wake of so much destruction. Standing here now, she still wasn't sure what those words should be. All she could offer them were the same ones she'd been telling herself.

"Usually when the bad guy's defeated, it's a time for rejoicing, but it's really hard to celebrate something so tainted with loss. There are a lot of people, good people, who died for a cause they didn't believe in. There are more, arguably not as good people, responsible for those deaths. All of those people were friends. Family. Nothing about standing here today feels good or easy. All I know is that what happened yesterday was necessary to stop the decades of manipulation and blackmail. We had to go to war so the people standing here now can work together to heal and rebuild. Mikel Drake and his supporters had to die so the rest of us could finally live."

Lina took a deep breath, clasping her hands in front of her and feeling the warm surge of Nord's approval and support. She allowed herself a brief moment to lean into the support he provided and re-anchor herself before continuing.

"For centuries, we've hidden behind tradition, telling ourselves we would be safer in the shadows. The truth is, staying in the shadows is how we ended up in the position we did. It's how we found ourselves without allies at a time when we desperately needed them. Never again. As of today, the Mobius Council is disbanded. It's time for the Animagi community to join the rest of the supernatural world and find a new way forward. Hopefully, someone like Mikel never rises to power again, but if the worst were to happen, we won't be without options."

"But Lina, who's going to lead us if we don't have the Council?" a nervous-looking woman from the crowd asked.

She was tempted to tell them it wasn't her problem anymore, that she'd done enough. But she wouldn't. She understood the desire to have someone to look to for guidance, especially during times of transition.

"You'll have to decide that for yourselves."

"What about you?" another man asked. An Alinari, she thought, but not one she recognized.

There were murmurs of assent throughout the room.

Lina bit back a smile, finding it ironic that the same people who watched her get publicly shamed and exiled wanted to elect her now. "I appreciate the offer, but I'm going to have to decline. My home is with my husband"—she looked over to Nord with a smile—"in Novasgard."

Word of the Novasgardians had spread like wildfire after news of the battle reached those who hadn't been directly involved. Lina had heard people whispering about the man with the giant bird and whether they'd get to meet him. She'd have to let Søren know he had a fan club.

Natalia stepped forward. While her expression was somber, she seemed far more relaxed than the last time Lina had seen her.

"Who would you nominate in your stead?"

Lina was surprised by the question, mainly that one of the original Council members would prefer her to nominate a replacement than volunteering themselves. Then again, Natalia surely had her own plans now that she was free from the confines of the Council. Lina wouldn't be surprised to learn she went in search of her daughter directly after this meeting.

"Quinn," Lina answered after a moment's consideration.

"Me?" Quinn asked, her eyes wide. "Why the hell would you go and do something like that?"

"I trust you with my life and know you to be beyond corruption. You've proven it time and again. Even when Mikel threatened you and everybody you love, you were steadfast in your resolve to do what was right, not what was easy. I can think of no one better suited for the role."

Quinn opened and closed her mouth. "Damnit, now I can't say no."

There were chuckles around the room and far more smiling faces than there had been when the meeting first started.

"All in favor?" Natalia asked.

Every single hand in the room went up.

"Well shit," Quinn muttered. "Do you guys even know what you're voting for?"

More laughter.

Quinn shook her head. "All right, fine. I accept. But you should know I don't pull punches. I'm not afraid to tell you if I think you're being an asshole, so don't come to me for advice unless you're prepared to hear the truth. And if you waste my time by asking for my advice and then ignore it, it's your own fault when I don't offer it a second time."

"That sounds like a refreshing change of pace," Natalia said.

"I couldn't agree more," Lina said.

Quinn sighed. "You're both just saying that because you wiggled your way out of being in charge."

"Be faster with the nomination next time, Satori."

"Careful, Cuska. I'm going with you on this little trip of yours. I will have absolutely no problem signing you up to chair every Viking potluck, boat race, and ax-throwing competition I can find. Don't forget who you're messing with."

The atmosphere in the room was noticeably lighter after Quinn's somewhat barbed acceptance speech. Like the Animagi could actually see a future for themselves that didn't involve living in fear.

Lina knew they'd be in good hands. And despite her protests, she also knew Quinn would take her new position seriously. She understood better than almost anyone what they'd suffered at the hands of Mikel, and she'd do everything in her considerable power to ensure that never happened again. Quinn really was the perfect choice for leading the Animagi out of the metaphorical Dark Ages and into the future.

"Well," Lina said, looking back out at the crowd, "that pretty much takes care of everything I planned to address. Is there anything else you guys wanted to say? I know many of us are in mourning and want to get back to our families. I don't want to drag this meeting on longer than necessary."

"Actually," a voice from the back of the room said. "I have something I'd like to add."

Everybody turned to look at the newcomer.

Lina let out a soft gasp as recognition hit her. "Emerson," she whispered.

The lost Alinari heir and Mikel's prisoner.

"In the flesh."

"It's good to see you," Lina said, surprisingly emotional at the sight of her onetime friend and fellow heir.

His lips twitched. "Not as good as it is to see you." He ran a hand along the back of his neck, seeming uncomfortable with the attention. "Anyway, I just wanted to say thanks. There's been a lot of talk about the future and moving forward, but I haven't heard anyone actually stop and express gratitude for all you've done to make it possible. If not for you, none of us would have any futures to speak of. Especially me. So . . . thanks, Evalina, for giving all of us our lives back."

"Oh . . . well . . . um." Lina swallowed, her throat thick with tears.

The room was silent for several heartbeats as Lina fought to stem the wave of emotion Emerson's words brought on, but then the room burst into applause, and Lina lost the battle.

"Why do I always seem to cry at these things?" she asked, turning to Nord, who was already there with his arms open for her.

"Because, my love, you have a warrior's heart. We feel things very deeply. There's no shame in it."

"Says the guy who never goes around crying in public," she muttered, wiping away her tears.

"I cry," he said, brushing his lips to her forehead. "When something really moves me, of course I do."

Lina sniffled, composing herself and awkwardly turning back to the sixty or so smiling faces. "Well . . . now that I've thoroughly embarrassed myself, this meeting is officially at an end. Go. Be with your families. Hug your loved ones. Tell them what they mean to you. If we've learned anything from this, tomorrows are never guaranteed. Make sure to spend the time you do have with the people you love. That's exactly what I'm going to do. Starting right now, in fact." Lina glanced over her shoulder at her husband. "Come on, Strega's waiting for us. It's time for us to say goodbye."

CHAPTER 32
NORD

"Thanks for waiting for us to get here before doing this," Nord said after Strega finished greeting them. Lina and the others went off to the beach to help finalize the funeral preparations, leaving the two of them behind.

"Of course. It was no trouble. There was a lot to coordinate, as I'm sure you can imagine," she said, her lips tipping up in a smile that didn't reach her eyes.

Nord stopped her with a hand on her shoulder. "How are you holding up?"

He knew she'd lost her husband in the battle, along with her mentor. It was a lot for anyone to deal with. Too much.

Strega blew out a breath, her eyes skimming the horizon. "Would you believe me if I told you Björn knew? He had a dream the night before we left. He woke up . . . changed. I can't explain it, except to say he'd made peace with it being his time. He was happy he went out doing what he loved, protecting the people who meant the most to him. For that, I'm thankful. It makes it easier to let him go. Astrid's loss . . ." Strega shook her head. "That one's harder in many ways. She was as much my mother as his. I lost mine when I was very young. I learned so much from her, had so much more to learn. I'll miss her."

"So will I," Nord said, his own feelings surrounding the loss of his cousin giving rise to a fresh wave of sadness.

In so many ways, they'd only just met and hardly knew each other, but Astrid was kin. The final connection to his past. That was a bond he couldn't replace, no matter how much time passed. Astrid's death cut deep, leaving a wound that may never fully heal. Nord was an expert in those kinds of wounds. For as much as they hurt, it was a bittersweet kind of pain, because it meant that you'd had someone in your life important enough to leave it in the first place.

Not everyone did.

He was a lucky man in that regard. Luckier still for having more than one in his life.

The reminder did much to ease the ache.

Strega gave him a considering look. "She loved you, you know, in her own way. Astrid wasn't much for saying the words. She believed actions held far more weight and value. But everyone close to her knew how happy she was to have you in her life."

"It was the same for me."

Strega nodded. "I know. You're very like her in that way. It's why I'm glad she chose you as her replacement."

Nord froze.

"What? She couldn't have been more obvious about her intentions. She declared it in front of everyone."

He shifted uncomfortably, the same anxious energy crawling through him now as it had when Astrid had made her proclamation. "I remember."

Her eyes, though heavy with grief, were shrewd as they assessed him. "You don't want it."

"It's just . . ." Nord searched for a way to explain what he was feeling. When the words didn't immediately come, he settled for, "You're a much better fit."

Instead of demurring, Strega raised a brow. "Are you sure that's what you want? The position is yours by birth and blood."

"If I never returned, wouldn't the position have been passed to you?"

"Yes, but I would have respected her wishes."

Though she didn't say it, and there was no censure in her voice, Nord couldn't help but feel there was an implication that he was not respecting Astrid's dying wish. She'd chosen him. Honored him. And though he loved her for it, he wanted absolutely nothing to do with it.

He sighed heavily as the words he needed finally came to him.

"I am honored, more than I can say, but I have no desire to lead. I'm tired, Strega. So damned tired of fighting and navigating treacherous political games. That's a young person's business, and I'm so very *old*. It's time for me to lay down my sword and find happiness and peace with my wife."

Strega laughed. "What does she have to say about this? Lina doesn't strike me as the idle sort."

"It was her idea."

"Does that mean you'll be keeping the house, then?"

His brows dipped in confusion. "What house?"

Strega gestured to Astrid's home. "She left it to you. Along with several other family heirlooms."

"As jarl, shouldn't the house go to you as well?"

"No. Björn and I have a home. I feel closest to him there, so that's where I will stay. If you do not accept Astrid's bequest, the house will lie empty."

"If you're sure you don't want it, we will take it. I know Lina fell in love with it during our last visit. She already has ideas of how we could add our own personal touches."

Strega raised her brows. "Planning ahead, was she?"

"She loved Astrid's story of how the house had passed through the generations, like a living piece of our family's history. She said she could feel the joy in its walls, and she wanted to fill them with love too."

"Your wife is a romantic."

"That she is."

"Sounds like your retirement will be a busy one, berserker."

"I'm counting on it."

They shared a soft smile, Strega pausing only long enough to add, "Cherish your time with her. You never know when it may be taken from you. One day, the memories may be all you have left."

"If that day comes, I will be right behind her. I have no intention of existing in a world she does not. Where her soul leads, mine follows."

Strega pressed a hand to her heart, her eyes watery.

They didn't speak again after that, joining the group gathered at the water's edge, where boats stretched in both directions. Many of them were filled with pictures and sentimental items for the ones whose bodies were unable to be recovered.

Beside one such boat stood Revna, a small wolf pup whining beside her as it tried to climb into the boat.

"No, Utfall, you cannot go with her," Revna softly chided, pulling the gray pup back.

"Ruhla's sister," Strega reminded him. "The pup belonged to her. Revna isn't sure she's going to stay now that her sister is gone, but she doesn't know what to do with the poor thing."

Nord spoke without thinking, knowing only that it was exactly what Lina would have done. "We'll take her."

Strega blinked. "What?"

"The pup. Lina and I will take her. Anyone with a mother as fierce as hers should be raised by ones who can appreciate such a legacy. We will take her."

"I'll let her know," Strega said with a smile. She pointed to the place where Lina already stood with Cora, Quinn, and Finley. "That's Astrid's. I'll walk with you. Björn is right beside her."

His steps were slow, his heart heavy as he joined his wife and friends. It was never easy saying goodbye. Lina curled her arm around his waist, hugging him when he reached her.

"You ready?" she asked.

"Almost."

Nord stepped forward, an image solidifying first in his mind and then his hand. A photograph of Astrid as he wanted to remember her, his memory of her the day they'd walked in her garden. In it, she was smiling up at him, that mischievous, scheming look in her eye as she'd informed him she'd be organizing his wedding. Her head was tipped back, the sun lighting up her face. It was the happiest he could recall ever seeing her. Usually she'd been much more reserved and cautious about revealing her emotions. He liked that she'd been comfortable enough with him to let her guard down.

While staring at her smiling face, he whispered, "The brave never die. May the halls of Valhalla welcome you home, cousin." Then he laid the picture next to several other items in her boat and stepped back to join the others.

"I've got something in my eye," Lina said, looking away as she wiped her tears away.

Nord wrapped his arm around her and pulled her closer. "Me too."

She chuckled and snuggled into him. "Goodbye, Astrid. You'll be bossing everyone around in no time."

A horn sounded, and one by one, the boats were launched into the sea. From behind them, dozens of archers raised flaming arrows. When the horn sounded a second time, the archers loosed their arrows, and the boats caught fire. With so many boats drifting away, the flames seemed to dance on the sea. It was a beautiful sight. Worthy of the men and women who sacrificed everything so that others could live.

They stood there, watching the boats until many of the other attendees had departed. The sun was less than a glimmer on the horizon when Nord finally turned away to see all of his friends waiting for him.

"Thank you for standing with me. I appreciate all of you."

"We were just lucky to have known her and count her among our friends," Cora said, stepping forward with a small bag.

"Where have you been hiding that?" Lina asked.

Cora shrugged. "I had a feeling you'd be needing them." She winked. "Goodbye for now, you two. Enjoy each other. You've earned it." Then she turned and started walking away.

"What is she talking about?" Lina asked, looking at Quinn.

Quinn shrugged. "Don't ask me. You know how she is." Then she gave them each a hug. "Don't go doing anything I wouldn't do," she said as she pulled away from Lina.

"That doesn't exclude a whole lot."

"I know," she grinned, giving Nord a wink every bit as saucy as her mother's. "You're welcome." Then she followed behind her.

Finley held up his hands before Lina could hound him. "I understand absolutely nothing when it comes to the Satori women. Don't even ask."

Lina snickered. "Maybe you'll finally learn a thing or two now that you won't have all this craziness getting in the way."

His smile stretched. "One can only hope. Though, half the fun is in the learning."

Lina shook her head, lifting on her tiptoes to give him a kiss on the cheek. "Take care of them for me."

"With my life," he promised.

Then he turned to Nord, holding out his hand. Nord pulled him into a hug. "Thank you, brother. For everything."

They held each other for a moment before Finley finally let go and stepped back. "Take care of my sister, all right? I'm pretty fond of her."

Lina sniffled beside him. "Jesus, I'm a one-woman sprinkler today," she muttered.

"I'm pretty fond of her myself," Nord called as Finley turned and walked off in the same direction as the Satori women. "Well, what did Cora think we needed?"

Lina sniffed again and then reached into the gift bag, her expression adorably confused as she pulled out two tiny pieces of cotton. "What—" Then she gasped.

"What is it?"

She lifted up the tiny garments, her hands trembling slightly as she turned them so Nord could just make out the two letters stitched in blue. 'A' and 'T.'

His heart started to race. "Does that mean . . . are you?" He couldn't even get the rest of the question out around the sudden rush of emotion.

"I . . . I think so," she said, blinking up at him. "Nord . . . we're going to be parents. Twins! How the hell did this happen?"

He laughed, his heart full near to bursting as he wrapped his arms around her and spun her around. "Have you already forgotten the other night? Do you need me to jog your memory?"

"I mean, obviously, I know *how* it happened," she sputtered. "I just meant . . . so soon? I honestly thought it would be a while before we . . ." She laughed and shook her head. "Maybe you really do have magic sperm. I should have known better than to doubt you or your virility. Of course you'd knock me up on your first try. Apparently even biology defers to a Viking's will." She threw her arms around his neck, squeezing tight. "We're going to have twins!" Then she leaned back, looking worried. "This is still what you want, right? Are you happy?"

He could feel each rapid-fire shift in her emotions shooting through him, the speed of the transitions giving him whiplash. Even still, none of it could touch the pure joy radiating through him. He took her face in his hands, needing her to feel the truth of his next words deep in her soul.

"Kærasta, I've never been so fucking happy in my entire life."

It barely scratched at the surface of what he was feeling, but it was the best he could manage in the face of his own emotion.

This time, it was Lina who had to wipe away his tears. "Hey, look at that. Vikings do cry. Big salty man tears," she teased, brushing her lips over his.

"I told you I do."

"So you did." She rested her forehead against his, her own eyes damp. "Babies, Nord. Our babies. I guess this means our happily ever after has officially begun."

"I promised you we'd have ours."

"And you always keep your promises. Ever since the night we first met."

"I'd lay the world at your feet if you asked it of me."

"No," she whispered. "I don't need a world. Just you. Just a lifetime of this."

"Then that is what you shall have."

He kissed her then, long and deep.

It's not how he would have expected to find out he was going to be a father. Hell, he'd given up on the dream lifetimes ago. He never dared believe such a thing could be possible for someone like him. And then Lina came barreling into his life with all the finesse of a maelstrom, and suddenly the life he'd always longed for was within reach.

It made a perfect sort of sense, in the most chaotic, wonderful way, to learn they were bringing new life into the world on the same day they celebrated those who'd passed. Like it was kismet somehow. A reminder from the universe that the cycle continues ever onward and how even on the darkest days, there's always a sliver of light.

For him, Lina was that light. And now, their children would be too.

EPILOGUE
FINLEY

inley stepped out of the portal and into Cora's kitchen, where she and her daughter had already started gathering items for dinner.

"Are you sure I can't persuade you into joining us?" Cora asked.

"No, I've intruded on your hospitality more than enough as it is, but thank you."

She made a tutting sound. "You could never intrude. With Lina and Nord gone, the guest house is open. You can use it for as long as you require. No need to waste money on a hotel when we have a private space available for you right here."

The offer was flattering, but Finley wasn't keen on the idea of living within shouting distance of Quinn's mother. Cora was a wonderful woman and all, but there wasn't anything quite like the threat of being overheard by your lover's mum to dampen your ardor. And he had every intention of making Quinn scream his name —loudly and frequently—when they were finally able to pick up where they'd left off the other day.

Finley cleared his throat, not quite able to meet Cora's eyes after the direction his thoughts had taken. "The Brotherhood is already working on setting me up with a new—"

"Actually," said Quinn, reaching into her bag and pulling out a set of keys, "Nord and Lina took care of that for you."

"What's this?" he asked, accepting the ring with its two keys, his heart giving a euphoric lurch in his chest at the slim black rectangle with its beloved red and chrome logo.

Quinn smirked at him. "Don't tell me you don't know what keys are for, Batman."

"Obviously, I know what keys are for, Satori. But seeing as I currently have no earthly possessions, what, pray tell, are these keys for exactly?"

"Your penthouse, of course."

"*My* penthouse? Last I checked, it was a pile of dirt."

Quinn lifted one shoulder in a shrug. "What can I say? I guess it pays to know some people who are excellent renovators."

Cora and Quinn exchanged a glance, telling Finley they'd both been in on the whole thing.

"Oh, and the other key's obviously a, how did Lina put it? A 'long overdue and very well deserved' present."

His hand spasmed around the Bugatti fob. "Present? For me?"

"Yes, Batman. For you. Jesus, I thought you Guardians were supposed to be quicker at putting things together than this. Shall I draw you a picture?"

"Give me a bloody minute here, will you? Thirty seconds ago, I didn't have a place to live or a car. Now you're telling me I have both. Give a guy a chance to wrap his head around the one-eighty, love."

Quinn smiled. "Well, don't you want to go see it?"

Finley already had the portal ready, opting straight for the penthouse's garage level. A house was nice and all, but if the car turned out to be what he thought it was . . . well, he might just be sleeping in it for the foreseeable future.

There was a momentary pang as he stepped through the portal, his once filled garage empty save for a single, perfect automobile.

He almost dropped to his knees and wept at the beauty of it.

The Bugatti La Voiture Noire. His dream car—well, one of them —and the first item he'd highlighted on the list he'd presented to Lina what felt like years ago.

Finley took a step forward, his hands shaking and his heart galloping in his chest. This must be what children felt like when they arrived downstairs on Christmas morning. He couldn't recall ever being so excited about a present in his life.

He circled the car, his hands hovering just above its glossy curves, not wanting to smudge its pristine surface. As he came around to the front, he spied a creamy square of paper tucked between the bonnet and the windshield.

He was smiling so hard at this point, his cheeks ached.

Carefully grabbing an edge of the note, Finley pulled it free and opened it, his smile stretching even wider at the feminine scrawl.

Fin -

I owe you one brand spanking new stable of sexy and ridiculously expensive cars. But since everyone knows any Batman worth his cape has his own Batmobile, I couldn't have anyone questioning your status while we work on rebuilding your collection.

XOXO -

your ~~adopted~~ favorite* sister

P.S: We may not be related by blood, but we've sure as shit spilled enough of it in the name of saving each other. I think that puts us beyond such formalities. You're my family now and forever, Fin. One of the few members I have left.

Take care of Quinn for me while we're gone, and know that if either of you need me, just say the word or throw up the bat signal (Okay, okay, I know I've officially taken the metaphor too far, and that's not even how the bat signal works, but I couldn't resist. Deal with it.) However you send the message, if you need me, I'll always answer.

No matter what.

Love you big brother,

Lina

A tear splashed onto the piece of paper in his hand, and Finley had to push out a breath as he finished reading. It was the kindest, most thoughtful gift anyone had ever given him—her words, not the car, though that was pretty fucking spectacular. He couldn't have been more touched.

Quinn let out a low whistle announcing her presence behind him, and Finley had to clear his throat and give his cheeks a quick wipe before he turned around to face her.

"Beautiful, isn't she?" he asked, his voice hoarse.

Quinn nodded. "That might be the sexiest car I've ever seen, Batman. I'm starting to understand your obsession."

"I'm not obsessed. I'm a connoisseur. There's a difference."

"Is there? You say potato . . ."

Finley rolled his eyes, but she wasn't looking at him. Her gaze was trained on the Bugatti as she moved in close and reached out like she was about to stroke it. Finley caught her wrist.

"Don't you dare. You'll smudge her."

"Her?" Quinn asked, raising a brow. "Since when don't you enjoy getting dirty, Batman?"

"I have no problem getting dirty, Satori. But this piece of mechanical perfection costs almost nineteen million dollars. Forgive me if I don't want to see it scratched in the first fifteen seconds of owning it."

Quinn coughed. "Nineteen million? For something you're going to leave locked up in here? Are you even going to take *her* for a test drive?"

Finley crossed his arms, not about to explain himself to someone who clearly did not appreciate such exquisite craftsmanship.

Quinn's eyes took on a familiar, teasing gleam. "So what you're really telling me, Batman, is that if I asked you to bend me over the hood and fuck me into next week, you'd turn me down. Because you're afraid of a little scratch?"

Finley got lightheaded as all the blood in his body raced straight to his dick. "I . . . uh . . ."

The image of Quinn, her little black skirt pushed up to her waist, baring her creamy skin, her hands splayed on the bonnet as he palmed those perfect breasts and—Finley's phone rang.

"Maybe we could get a blanket," he offered, blinking as he looked from the car to Quinn.

Her lips twitched with laughter. "You going to get that?"

"Get what?"

She rolled her eyes. "Your phone, Batman. It's ringing."

"It is?" He glanced down, pulling his phone from his pocket, the screen reading: Incoming Call, Nate. "Well, would you look at that." There was no hiding the snarl in his voice or Quinn's resulting chime of laughter as he answered. "This better be fucking important. I'm in the middle of something."

"No, you weren't," Quinn singsonged. "But you could have been."

He glared at her, mouthing, "You're going to pay for that."

She raised her hands, pretending to cower. "I'm so scared." Then she laughed and turned away from him as Nate's voice came through the speaker.

"Not anymore, I'm afraid. Vacation's over, brother. We've got a case for you. Oh, and bring the memory weaver . . . you're going to need her."

***

FINLEY AND QUINN'S JOURNEY CONTINUES IN BOUND BY DANGER,
READ ON FOR A SNEAK PEEK...

BOUND BY DANGER
SNEAK PEEK
QUINN

For as long as Quinn Satori could remember, she'd been haunted by memories that were not her own. As an Animagi memory weaver with perfect recall, her mind was a steel trap when it came to retaining information. Which was why silence—blissful, perfect silence—had always been a welcome friend.

Until today.

Never in her long-life had silence been so unsettling.

Even though she was not alone, the oppressive hush in Nathaniel Cohen's office was worse than a tomb. Despite being poshly furnished, the acting Director's designated room lacked warmth. Along with any personal details as to the man it belonged to. It may as well have been empty for all she could glean from it.

Quinn couldn't remember the last time she hadn't been able to sniff out some sort of clue about the person a space belonged to— which meant it had never happened before.

But she knew that had nothing to do with the unease prickling beneath her skin.

They'd been summoned to help the Guardian solve a case. Since the Brotherhood was comprised of highly skilled immortal warriors who were the absolute best of the best, being called in to assist was not a compliment. It was a Hail Mary.

If the Brotherhood had to resort to asking for help, something was very, very wrong. Like 'life as we know could cease to exist' wrong.

In layman's terms, supernatural fuckery was a foot.

Fuckery that had absolutely nothing to do with her.

Quinn shifted in her seat, crossing and uncrossing her legs, adjusting her skirt, sighing heavily. She didn't want to be here. She was done fighting other people's battles. They'd just won a damned war for fuck's sake. Didn't that earn her a vacation?

The way she saw it, she and Finley should be on a beach somewhere, sipping umbrella drinks, wearing little more than sunscreen and their smiles. Or, better yet, they'd be holed up in his newly restored penthouse with him balls deep inside her.

Now *that* would be a real celebration. Because after months of her self-imposed celibacy, she was beyond ready for it to end. She'd made herself a promise: if they defeated Mikel, she would finally admit to her feelings for her British Man of Mystery and let him fuck her stupid. It was a promise she had every intention of keeping, starting—she checked her watch—four hours ago.

Quinn let out a little growl of frustration. Whatever reason Nate had for being late to his own damned meeting better be end of the world level important, because that was about the only justification she'd accept for not being underneath her sexy-as-sin Guardian right now.

At least, she thought he was hers.

Other than a few stolen kisses and impassioned words, they hadn't exactly had a chance to hash out all the details of their relationship. There hadn't been time between nearly dying and dealing with the fallout of a madman's war.

She'd denied herself for months. Years even. Tonight was supposed to be about the two of them finally sealing the deal.

Instead, they were here. Waiting. No closer to falling into bed with each other than they had been before returning from Novasgard.

And it was driving her insane.

Quinn snuck a glance at Finley. He didn't seem to share her impatience. He sat beside her, looking delicious in his tailored gray suit. With his head propped against his fist, hazel eyes with their silver flecks trained on her, and a small knowing smile curving his full lips.

The ass.

He was enjoying this, watching her squirm and likely knowing the exact reason why.

She huffed and looked away, pretending not to hear his low chuckle.

Up until the phone call a few hours ago that had shot her plans for an epic fuck fest straight to hell, Finley had been on administrative leave pending a full investigation for the role he played in ousting the prior Director. The Guardians were notorious for following protocol. They might be leading the game when it came to warfare and strategy, but their stubborn insistence on adhering to centuries-old bureaucracy meant anything requiring paperwork went painfully slow. Whatever happened must have been beyond serious for Nate to reinstate Finley out of the blue.

And that, she realized, was the real reason she couldn't shake the sense of foreboding that had settled deep into her bones.

After everything they'd already sacrificed, danger still lurked in the shadows, hunting them. She almost lost him once. Could still smell the tang of his blood pooling onto the wet asphalt and feel her heart seizing in her chest as she clung to his unmoving body. She'd barely survived losing him once.

She wouldn't be so lucky a second time. Not when she could recount the first with perfect clarity every time she closed her eyes. A woman could only take so much when it came to the man she...

"What's taking him so long?" Quinn snapped, when the silence and her tumultuous emotions became unbearable.

Finley smirked, one dark brow lifting. "In a hurry, Satori?"

Despite the panic clawing at her chest, Quinn adopted her patented breezy tone. "I have places to be...people to do."

His gaze went molten. "By people you better be referring to me, princess. We have an understanding."

"Do we?"

Ah, yes. This was much better. She'd never admit it out loud, but their flirtatious banter had been one of the only things keeping her going during the hell of the last few months. It was her reprieve, her safe place. Okay, fine. *He* was her safe place.

A little sexy small talk was exactly what she needed to stave off the full-blown panic attack threatening to consume her at the mere thought of something else happening to him.

Finley leaned forward, grabbing her chair and slowly pulling it closer until their knees brushed against each other. Forcing her thoughts to scatter and her focus to lock onto him.

Only him.

God, she loved it when he did that. There'd never been anyone else in her entire life who could make her brain shut the fuck up the way he could. The way he *demanded*.

"Just because our business remains unfinished, Satori, doesn't mean you're a free woman. You belong to me, Quinn."

Her heart fluttered at the words, and she barely maintained her aloof tone. "Is that so?"

He reached out, running the tips of his fingers down her cheek and causing her breath to stutter. "Your body betrays you, love. But I'll take the bait." His lips curled in a slow, seductive smile. "Allow me to prove it to you."

"How do you propose to do that?"

He lifted a single shoulder in a shrug. "Just a simple demonstration. A promise of what's to come once we're finished here."

The words confirmed that he had, in fact, known the reason for her restlessness. Or at least part of it. Delivered in his sensual growl, they had the added effect of sending a bolt of lust slamming into her.

A dull throb pulsed between her legs, the echo of her racing heart. She swallowed.

"A demonstration? Here?"

He gripped her chin lightly, leaning close until she was consumed by the mint and clove scent of him. His words were playful, but his gaze was anything but. The intensity she found there seared her, sending arousal zinging through her body.

"Wherever I say, whenever I say. That's how this is going to work, princess." He shifted, his mouth all but touching hers. "Now... take off your knickers."

Her body's reaction was instant. Her nipples pebbled beneath the silk of her camisole, her core tightened, and that dull throb transformed into a full body tingle. For a second her mind went utterly and blissfully blank. Then her brain caught up with her. She wanted to obey, to give in to his every demand, but curiosity had always been her downfall. She couldn't resist the temptation to push back, to find out how he'd respond to her small act of defiance.

She dropped her voice, matching his low, seductive tone. "What makes you think I'm wearing any?"

His lips quirked up in a knowing smirk. "Prove it."

God. The things that did to her. She wanted to crawl into his lap then and there. Quinn only just managed to check the impulse, enjoying their game too much to give it up that easily. Especially when it gave her something else to focus on.

"You want me to *prove* I'm not wearing any underwear?"

"That's right, love. Lift up that skirt of yours, spread your legs, and show me."

Her breath hitched. Fuck this was hot. And besides the fingers holding her chin, he wasn't even touching her. If it was this good already, she knew she'd probably combust when she got all of him. She couldn't help but wonder just how far he intended to take this.

"Now, princess."

Heart racing, Quinn sat back in her chair, a pang of disappointment at losing his touch underscoring her rampant lust. She slid up the sides of her skirt, just enough that she'd be able to follow his next order, aware with every wild beat of her heart that the door could open at any moment and Nate could walk in.

As she parted her knees, Finley's gaze traveled down her body, a muscle in his jaw ticking when he noticed her nipples straining against her shirt. And then lower, his head tipping slowly down so he could see what she had on beneath her skirt.

She could feel his gaze moving over her like a physical caress. Her body was hot, achy. She'd never been this turned on by something as simple as a few filthy words and some heated looks. But then...she'd never had Fin. Not like this. Not completely. And he was power and dominance and sex all wrapped up in one delicious package.

Better still, he was hers...or he was about to be. Just as soon as they finished up this fucking meeting.

"Naughty, minx. You lied."

Quinn's laugh was just this side of breathless. "Oops."

"Take them off, Satori. They belong to me."

She cast a furtive look at the door.

"Don't worry about him. It's my job to worry. It's yours to obey. Now, take them off, or I'll bend you over my knee and do it for you."

Quinn almost whimpered. The thought alone was enough to make her hesitate. She liked option two. A whole fucking lot. Clearing her throat slightly, she forced herself out of her chair, hooking her fingers beneath the scraps of lace and silk and tugged it down, aware with each inch of the brush of her skirt over her bare skin and the cool air over her desire-heated flesh. She was so turned on it was boarding on painful. Her skin was hot, each scrape of the fabric a reminder that it wasn't the touch she craved. She wanted more. *Needed* more.

Once she'd tugged the lingerie to her knees, she was leaning forward enough that her shirt gaped and Finley made no efforts to hide the fact he was blatantly staring.

What's good for the goose... Quinn let her eyes drop to his lap, a soft gasp escaping at the thick bulge in his pants.

Jesus. It was hot, so hot, seeing how turned on he was by the simple act of her undressing. No. That wasn't it. He was turned on by her obedience. Fuck, so was she. She was practically high with it. There was something incredibly freeing in doing what she'd been told. In allowing her mind to empty of everything except for him.

For a second, she wondered if he knew that taking charge of her this way was akin to him coming to her rescue. Of saving her from the nightmares haunting her every waking thought. But then she caught that heated look in his eyes again and hastened to obey. What did it matter if he knew, so long as it was true?

She pulled her panties down the rest of the way, hooking one finger through the scrap of fabric and offering it to him as she straightened.

Finley reached for to claim the damp piece of lace, but she tugged her hand back.

"I want those back when you're done with whatever game you're playing."

"Never gonna happen," he said, snatching them from her. Then he sat back in his chair, his eyes never leaving hers.

"What now?" she asked, her voice betraying her need.

He raised his brow, held her panties up to his nose and inhaled. His eyes closed and he let out a deep, pleasure-filled rumble. "Delicious."

Quinn had to clench her thighs together to prevent the proof of her arousal from dripping down her legs.

After a second he pinned her with his hazel gaze. "Now, princess, you're going to sit down and suffer through this meeting with me."

"What?" she snapped, the sudden shift feeling like ice water dumped straight over her head. "Th-that's it? You're just going to leave me like this?"

He smiled and it was so filled with carnal promise that she whimpered. He leaned forward, his eyes pinned on hers, his voice barely above a whisper. "I want you to sit there, aware of your dripping cunt and how badly it aches for me. I want you desperate and needy and ready for everything I have planned for you once we get home."

Quinn forgot how to breathe, her next words sounding thin even to her own ears. "Why wait?"

His grin stretched. "We have a meeting to attend."

"You sonofabitch."

"Bastard is more appropriate. But be a good girl, princess, and I'll give you everything you could ever want."

Her eyes dropped meaningfully to his lap. "Right now there's only one thing I want."

Finley chuckled. She never knew a man's laugh could sound so fucking sexy, but that husky rasp was just as potent as his gaze. Her body responding as if he'd touched her.

"Consider my cock your reward," he said, sitting back and propping his ankle on his knee. "If I recall correctly, I believe that's what you refer to as motivation."

"I—"

The door clicked open. Quinn's eyes flew wide, and she sat down gracelessly giving the sides of her skirt a tug in a desperate attempt to pull the fabric down to a more appropriate length. Her heart lurched in relief when she spotted Finley tucking her pilfered panties into his suit jacket.

His eyes twinkled and he winked at her, a small smirk playing about his lips. "To be continued," he mouthed as Nate strolled into the room.

BOUND BY DANGER IS OUT NOW!

GLOSSARY &
PRONUNCIATION GUIDE

AUTHOR'S NOTE: These are the notes I send to my audio narrators. I am no pronunciation expert, as you'll see, so when I go for phonetic spellings, I base it off what makes most sense in my mind (which you should all know by now is a scary, scary place. Ha!) In some case, pronunciation can vary depending on region, and while I generally default to the Old Norse and Norwegian versions of words, sometimes a matter of personal preference may sway me to something else. All of this is to say, while I do my research, I am far from an expert and this is all just how I hear things in my head while writing. You may keep or disregard these as you will.

Animagi (plural): Ani (as in animation) Maji (hard J)

Animagus (singular): Ani (as in animation) Mag (as in magazine) Us

Ástvinur: Oust-vin-er, *literal translation "love friend", means darling/beloved*

Dragestil: drog-eh-steel, *Dragon Style*

Elskan mín: El-skon (like the british pronunciation of scone) min (as in minute), *My Love*

Ektemann: Ek-te-mon, *Husband*

Eiginkona: E-in-ko-na, *Wife (kona for short)*

Faering: Faer-ing, *Small, canoe-like boat with oars*

Gunnar: Goo (like goose) na (like nah) r (soft – a British v. American r) *Gunnar is a male first name of Nordic origin (Gunnarr in Old Norse). The name Gunnar means fighter, soldier, and attacker, but mostly is referred to by the Viking saying which means Brave and Bold warrior (gunnr "war" and arr "warrior").*

Häxa: Hex-a (long a at end), *a witch (woman who knows or uses magic) Though it is not used like this in the book, it can also be used in a derogatory way to mean an ugly or unpleasant woman.*

Jarl: Yaa-rl, *a Norse or Danish chief.*

Kærasta: Ki (like in Kite) ra (like radish) stuh *Nord uses it as a term of endearment, like sweetheart, though a more direct translation would be girlfriend.*

Knörr: Nor, *A large merchant ship used in mediaeval Scandinavia.*

Móðir: (Old Norse) Mow-Dear (o sound slightly extended) *Mother*

Mon coeur: (French) mon kurr *My heart*

Novasgard: Nov (as in nova) – as – guard

<u>Sanguinina</u>: Sanguine (just like usual) + ee-na (like Lina), *a lily-like flower that only grows where Fae blood was violently spilled*

<u>Novasgardians</u>:

- Arrick: Eric
- Björn: Bee - Yorn – (like horn)
- Brynhild: Brin-hild (with r slightly rolled)
- Huginn: Hoo-gin
- Revna: Rev (as in revolution) - nuh
- Ruhla: Roo-la
- Søren: Sore – en
- Sten: just like it's spelt (as in stencil)
- Strega: Stray – ga
- Ulf: Oo (like boo) – lf (like wolf)

A NOTE FROM MEG

I can't believe its the end (at least for our berserkers)...what a bittersweet ride this book was for me. I cried more than I expected to, though I've been told I wasn't alone in that regard. I've finished series before, but I haven't had to say goodbye like this to one of my couples. At least not after spending almost two years exclusively in their world. It wasn't prepared for how hard it would be. Thankfully, I have #Quinley to look forward to.

If you read the sneak peek then you already know their story is going to be a spicy one. And they've certainly earned it after five books worth of edging, I mean build up. I hope you are as excited about it as I am!

One of my favorite thing about this series is the role that family plays. It wasn't even something I was aware of at the time, but came into clear focus for me over the last two books. Namely the way that all of these characters are searching for family, either to replace people they've lost, or to stand in for the ones they do not have. I've been blessed to have not only a wonderfully supportive family I was born into, but also one that I've built over the years. I would not be the woman or writer that I am without them. I guess, in my own way, I wanted my characters to get to experience that as well. Specifically, the power that comes from being chosen as a person who is worthy of love by someone we look up to, and the way it changes our view of ourselves.

It is my wish for all of you, that you experience this kind of love at least once in your life. And if you haven't been fortunate yet, remember this: Family is not determined by blood, it is determined by love and loyalty. Choose wisely.

Until next time, stay safe and happy reading!

XOXO,

♡ Meg Anne

I

ALSO BY MEG ANNE

THE CHOSEN UNIVERSE

THE CHOSEN

A FATED MATES HIGH FANTASY ROMANCE

MOTHER OF SHADOWS

REIGN OF ASH

CROWN OF EMBERS

QUEEN OF LIGHT

THE CHOSEN BOXSET #1

THE CHOSEN BOXSET #2

THE KEEPERS

A GUARDIAN/WARD HIGH FANTASY ROMANCE

THE DREAMER (A KEEPER'S PREQUEL)

THE KEEPERS LEGACY

THE KEEPERS RETRIBUTION

THE KEEPERS VOW

THE KEEPERS BOXSET

THE FORSAKEN

A REJECTED MATES/ENEMIES-TO-LOVERS ROMANTASY

PRISONER OF STEEL & SHADOW

QUEEN OF WHISPERS & MIST

COURT OF DEATH & DREAMS

ABOUT MEG ANNE

USA Today and international bestselling paranormal and fantasy romance author Meg Anne has always had stories running on a loop in her head. They started off as daydreams about how the evil queen (aka Mom) had her slaving away doing chores, and more recently shifted into creating backgrounds about the people stuck beside her during rush hour. The stories have always been there; they were just waiting for her to tell them.

Like any true SoCal native, Meg enjoys staying inside curled up with a good book and her fur babies . . . or maybe that's just her. You can convince Meg to buy just about anything if it's covered in glitter or rhinestones, or make her laugh by sharing your favorite bad joke. She also accepts bribes in the form of baked goods and Mexican food.

Meg is best known for her leading men #MenbyMeg, her inevitable cliffhangers, and making her readers laugh out loud, all of which started with the bestselling Chosen series.